John Belushi...Dan Aykroyd.
America's comic assassins! They made it big on NBC's controversial variety show *Saturday Night Live*. Their Blues Brothers record album has sold in the millions!

Now the dynamic duo hits the big screen in *The Blues Brothers*—the uproarious story of "Joliet" Jake and Elwood Blues who are trying to reunite the members of the funkiest band in town!

JOHN BELUSHI DAN AYKROYD
THE BLUES BROTHERS

with
JAMES BROWN, CAB CALLOWAY, RAY CHARLES, CARRIE FISHER, ARETHA FRANKLIN, HENRY GIBSON

Written by
DAN AYKROYD and JOHN LANDIS

Executive Producer
BERNIE BRILLSTEIN

Produced by
ROBERT K. WEISS

Directed by
JOHN LANDIS

A UNIVERSAL PICTURE

THE BLUES BROTHERS

**A NOVEL BY MIAMI MITCH
BASED ON A SCREENPLAY BY
DAN AYKROYD AND JOHN LANDIS**

A JOVE BOOK

Copyright © 1980 by MCA Publishing, a Division of MCA, Inc. All rights reserved.

All rights reserved. No part of this publication
may be reproduced or transmitted in any form or
by any means, electronic or mechanical, including
photocopy, recording, or any information storage
and retrieval system, without permission in
writing from the publisher.

"Gimme Some Lovin'" words and music by Steve Winwood, Muff Winwood and Spencer Davis. Copyright 1967 by Island Music Ltd. All rights for US and Canada controlled by Island Music (BMI). All rights reserved. Reprint by permission.

"Rawhide" excerpts appear courtesy of Mrs. Dmitri Tiomkin.

First Jove edition published June 1980

10 9 8 7 6 5 4 3 2 1

Printed in the United States of America

Jove books are published by Jove Publications, Inc.,
200 Madison Avenue, New York, NY 10016

THE BLUES BROTHERS

chapter one

Artesia Papageorge tasted her own blood. It trickled into her mouth, salty and warm as tears. She ignored it, biting down even harder on the towel clamped between her jaws. Artesia lay back exhausted on her cot. Within seconds the next hit of pain arched her high in the air. A local nurse and Cissy, a trustee, shredded clothes and bound her to the metal frame. Now her struggles caused the entire cot to scrape across the concrete floor.

Artesia's pretty face was drained to a sickly paraffin color. Her brown eyes were locked open and unfocused—a cave fish lost in the dark prison cell.

Shapes and faces drifted in the gray: the ancient judge who sentenced her for a murder she swore she couldn't remember (and didn't commit), a handsome man she might have loved. Some images were comforting, almost familiar, and some, strange and ugly, swooped at her from the blackness. Artesia kept silent through the fear, concentrating on the vision of a little boy—all curly dark hair and brown eyes. Wide-eyed, she studied this unborn son floating innocently above her.

The odds in the Dwight Illinois Women's Correctional Institute ran ten to one that Artesia wouldn't live the night. They also ran nine to five that the baby would die inside her.

Cissy Wright lay a cool rag across Artesia's forehead. She gently brushed back the damp hair from Artesia's face.

There wasn't much more to do. Cissy's wrinkled black hands caressed her friend's pale cheek.

"Don't worry, chile," she murmured. "It's almost over. Everything be okay by mornin'. You trust Cissy." The dying eyes knew better.

"How the hell did she get knocked up in here?" The gray nurse barked, washing her hands in the sink.

Cissy shook her head. "Nobody knows fo' sure. Maybe she came in that way. Maybe . . . you know . . . it just happened. This is one special lady. Some say magic-like." Cissy looked down at Artesia's face, shiny with sweat, almost glowing in the half-light. "There's somethin' kinda . . . holy about her."

The nurse threw a bloody towel into the trash and positioned herself between Artesia's legs. "Well, whatever, it sure as hell isn't helpin' her now. It'll be a miracle if we can even save her kid, weak as she is."

Suddenly Artesia gripped Cissy's hand, squeezing it tight. Her eyes seemed to focus, looking up at the black woman. Cissy took the towel from Artesia's mouth and leaned closer. In a whisper, almost a sigh, Artesia Papageorge spoke a name: "Jake."

Cissy's tears fell on the small white hand.

"Cissy. Please. You call him Jake."

"It's showtime," the nurse screamed. "Here comes the kid. Keep her awake, we almost got 'im."

Cissy desperately shook her friend. "Push, honey . . . help!"

Artesia's grip relaxed, and for the first time that endless day, her eyes closed. She opened her mouth as if to speak, but instead a soft final moan rose from her. One long, sad note. At that very moment the baby cried to life, letting loose a fierce wail. Their two voices met in soulful harmony. On key—and as sweet as Marvin and Tami, Otis and Carla—their voices sailed by the restless inmates, through the steel bars and out into the chilly Illinois night.

Sister Mary Stigmata cradled the silent baby close to her. Funny, the poor little thing hadn't cried all night. In fact he hadn't made any noise at all since Officer Delaney brought him by after dinner. The sister shook her head sadly. Delaney said some salesman had pulled up to a newsstand and tossed a dime for the *Gazette*. Instead of the newspaper, somebody had dropped this sleeping baby through the open window of the car, into the salesman's lap. Sister Mary had named him Elwood because he was the fifth child left at the Saint Helen of the Blessed Shroud Orphanage that week, and *E* was the fifth letter of the alphabet. (It was a pet system of hers.)

Someone coughed at one end of the huge room, and Sister Mary gazed down the long row of sleeping boys. Bits of dreams and muttered nightmares escaped into the dorm. The place was deep with sleep. The orphans insisted that the room, with its high dim ceilings, hid scary shadows. But it was more a barracks than a haunted house; even fear was too romantic for this building. It was functional, and the sister and her fellow nuns were caring, if impersonal. Still, it was the only house and family these kids had. And right now the home was jammed; not a free bed in sight. Well, the sister couldn't stand there and hold Elwood forever. He'd just have to double up with somebody.

Suddenly Sister Mary knew she was being watched! She whirled around, and staring straight at her—that amazing hustler's spark in his two-and-a-half-year-old face—was little Jake Papageorge. Wide awake and calm as an undertaker, he checked out the nun and the child in her arms.

"All right, Mr. Papageorge," the sister said, somehow knowing he could understand her, "it looks as though you have a new friend." She placed Elwood in bed with Jake.

3

"I'm *sure* you two will get along famously." Jake made room for the infant as if he'd slept there forever. As if they were brothers.

The husky man fixed the thin black tie around his neck, tightening it with a grimace. He put on the baggy black suit jacket (matching his baggy black suit pants) and set the narrow-brimmed black porkpie on his head. He scowled into the dressing room mirror, smacking a fist into his opposite palm for effect. His eyes glinted even through his black Ray-Ban 50-22 G15 shades.

Suddenly Otis Redding's "I Can't Turn You Loose" rattled the dressing room door, mean brassy horns battling a thunderous rhythm section for soul supremacy. The big man smiled into the mirror. Sitting on a couch, a taller, thinner, but identically dressed man attached one loop of a pair of handcuffs to a black briefcase. There was a knock on the door.

"You're on, boys. Jesus, they're going nuts out there."

The thinner man slapped the other end of the handcuffs around his wrist. "You ready?" he asked. His voice sounded like a cop's. The big man put a stick of Wrigley's into his mouth and picked up a long gold chain with a key on the end of it. He twirled it in a smooth, flashing circle.

From outside, the announcer's excited baritone rose above the charging band. "Good evening, ladies and gentlemen." The crowd screamed as one voice.

"Thank you. Thank you. Now please join me in a warm Rose Room welcome for the band of Joliet Jake and Elwood Blues—the Blues Brothers."

The roar rattled a water glass in their dressing room. Jake Blues smiled his hustler's smile. "C'mon, Elwood." One eyebrow arched above his midnight shades as he hissed the strangely familiar words, "It's showtime."

A white spot hit the two bluesmen as they reached the raised parquet stage, Jake casually whipping his gold key chain, Elwood dead serious, the sinister briefcase locked to his wrist. Two thousand people rushed the stage. Jake calmly took the key and unfastened the cuff on his brother's wrist. Elwood, in turn, unlocked his case, reached in and pulled out a microphone and a gleaming Special 20 Blues Harp. He held it before the crowd like a splinter from the Cross as the band kicked into "Hey, Bartender."

The audience knows them by heart; grown women squeal and men bellow as each one's favorite band member takes a turn at a solo: Donald "Duck" Dunn, orange halo of hair and curved pipe glowing above his bass; Willie "Too Big" Hall riding the back beat; Steve "The Colonel" Cropper, slick as a Saturday night, bending those Memphis riffs till his Strat smoked; Matt "Guitar" Murphy, angelic smile and muscular blues; Murphy "Murph" Dunne, keyboard man of a thousand fingers; and Lou "Blue Lou" Marini, Tom "Bones" Malone, and Alan "Mr. Fabulous" Rubin, the blues horns, firing like a finely tuned soul engine.

This was a band to testify to, a band to pray for. In an age when music, raw and alive, had been eaten by machines, when computers duplicated any sound an engineer could conceive, these boys were the last hope. They had crawled out of their day jobs clutching their axes and following the dream Jake held before them—that the people still wanted real music.

The Blues Brothers Band wasn't just in it for the gold. *Nobody* drives all day, plays all night, and hits the highway again at dawn for thirty-seven dollars and change. They had chugged enough beef grease and bad fries to wear out new assholes. They'd slept under bridges, in the Bluesmobile, and ten in a single bed. And even though they would surely deny it, they did it for the *music*.

For two years now they had toured nonstop, crisscrossing

the Steel Belt like funk evangelists, playing everything from pool halls to gay bars—anyplace and anybody who would listen. Those boys stormed onstage until even the cold Midwestern skies thundered back. Joliet Jake, the true believer, and silent Elwood spoke through their music, and finally the people followed.

Tonight was the first taste of payoff. Even if it was only the Falls Hotel in Falls End, Wisconsin, it was still a big room with *spotlights*. The end zone was really in sight, and after the gig the band partied like winners.

"Hey, son, you gonna drink that shit or piss in it?" Duck yelled across the suite to Murph Dunne. Murph, unfortunately, couldn't answer. Slumped against the bathroom door, a bottle of Johnny Walker Red dangling dangerously from his hand, his beautiful paisley vest odorous and stained beyond reclaiming, he was lucky he could breathe. The bathroom door opened and abruptly hurled Murph face-forward onto a sleeping blond room-service waitress. The Colonel looked at his handiwork and smiled. "Nine ball in the side pocket," he drawled. The Colonel grabbed the bottle of Johnny Walker and picked his way toward Duck. Even though dawn lit the room with its ugly gray light, he still stepped on fellow bluesmen, the floor being thickly carpeted with bodies and bottles.

"You are a true saint, Steve," Duck said as the two friends sat down to breakfast.

"You seen Jake or Elwood?" Steve asked, taking a hit. "I wanna congratulate them on this weekend. It felt real nice."

Duck reached for the bottle, nodding. "Last I saw of Elwood, he was riding up and down the elevator, singin' 'Got My Mojo Workin'.'"

Steve nodded along, unsurprised.

"An' ol' Jake, that boy was floatin' around the heated pool with his clothes on. He had these two fine cheerleaders from Falls End High holdin' 'im up. They was making bubbles with their mouths."

Steve smiled. "As long as they're okay."

The door suddenly swung open and Willie Hall, an enormous blonde Midwestern Viking woman under each arm, screamed into the alcohol haze, "Boys an' girls, now ain't 'Too Big' too much?"

It had to be the Penguin. Only Sister Mary Stigmata could hit so hard, so fast. Elwood curled into a protective fetal ball, but still the kicks came, shuddering painfully through his whole hung-over body. He tried to open his eyes... really tried, but there was a faulty transistor blocking his brain's command. Elwood felt two hands shaking him violently. Thank God for that, because it shook open his eyes. His pupils recoiled from the harsh fluorescent light as he focused on the outraged, hulking shape of Bill Halvorsen, general manager of the Falls Hotel.

Elwood's right hand hurt like hell. He looked up and noticed it dangling above him—handcuffed to the railing. "Jesus," he marveled aloud. "I'm handcuffed to the fucking elevator railing."

Halvorsen smiled like he had a mouthful of bile. "Nice guess, Mr. Wizard. Now where the hell's your big brother? Do you know that your band ran up a *three-thousand-dollar* room service bill this weekend? Shit, someone with a Southern accent drank five hundred dollars worth of my Napoleon brandy alone!"

Elwood drew himself up with all the dignity available to a man handcuffed to an elevator, and said, "Sir, we have several band members with Southern accents—Bones, Duck—"

"I'm not finished, El-wood," Halvorsen interrupted. "I haven't gotten to the two thousand dollars in fire and water damage. That's right, Mr. Blues, your boys wrote their names in various liquors and colognes in my third-floor hallway and then lit them. I'm sure it made a pretty fire—" Halvorsen's face was dangerously red, the veins in his neck bulging like hydraulic cables— "but it also destroyed my carpets and set off the sprinkler system, which flooded the entire floor."

"Sir," Elwood said, standing up shakily as the elevator hit the second floor. "Sir, my brother and I will be glad to pay—"

"I'm not finished, *Blues*." Halvorsen took a menacing step closer, and Elwood felt like a monarch butterfly pinned to velvet. "My night man said he saw my . . . my daughters swimming *nude* with that pig brother of yours! They are *sixteen years old* . . . do you know what that means?"

"We've reached my floor," Elwood said as the doors opened. He leapt for them, only to come flying back in a handcuffed heap. Halvorsen put his swollen face inches from Elwood's and shrieked, *"You are dead men!"*

Jake washed his face with his sunglasses on. "How did I know they were his daughters? They didn't look anything like the swine. And besides, they told me—"

"Sure, fine, Jake. I don't care. But what about the nine grand?" Elwood pleaded. "That's all the money we made this weekend. We promised the band we'd cover their expenses *and* pay them."

Jake took handfuls of paper towels from the dispenser and dried himself. "Jesus, those boys don't know the meaning of the word moderation. But hell, I promised, I gave my word, and this band is built on trust and loyalty." Jake threw the soggy towels into the sink. "Besides, if I don't pay 'em, they'll leave."

"Exactly." Elwood nodded, proud of his brother's moral compass.

"So, Mr. Dick Tracy Junior, where are we gonna find five thousand dollars?"

"How 'bout we enter the Colonel in a big-stakes pool game?"

"On what? Put up your year's supply of white bread as collateral?"

"Christ," Elwood spat, hurt. "I was just thinkin' out loud."

"I know, I'm sorry, pal," Jake consoled. "It's just I'm under a lotta pressure here."

A horn honked from outside.

"Shit. That'll be them," Jake said, quickly polishing his shades. "Just be cool an' dummy up. I'll think of somethin'."

The two brothers walked out into the gray Illinois sunset. The lights at the Clark gas station were just going on. The station, right off the highway, was jammed with cars; the pump jockeys scurried hysterically, sorcerer's apprentices trying to service the mob. Off to one side, a battered blue '58 Cadillac with manta-ray fins idled noisily.

"Well, well, if it's not the two hottest bandleaders since Sonny and Cher." Alan "Mr. Fabulous" Rubin applauded from the Caddy's front seat. The rest of the band joined him. After the cheers died, Alan jumped out and opened the door. "So, my captain, where do we dine in Chicago? I believe a celebration is in order. Many cases of fine champagne . . . If you will allow me to suggest—"

"Sure, sure," Jake chuckled. "Soooo, you boys are pretty happy, huh?"

A shower of beer cans answered him.

Unfazed, he continued, "Thank you, thank you *very* much, gentlemen. Now, Elwood's gonna drop you off at the Stake Pit, a mother beautiful beef joint a few minutes away, and we'll both meet you there within the hour. Hey, all the brew you can drink!"

The band grew silent, wary. Willie Hall tilted up his

visor and nailed Jake with a cold eye. "You fuckin' around wit' us again, Jake?"

Jake backed away, waves of shock and hurt crossing his face.

"Willie, I can't believe my ears... No, I don't want to... We're *brothers*. How could I... Have I ever lied to you?" Quickly he added, "Elwood and I have a meeting with a major promoter that I'd like to wrap up before we hit Chi town."

Elwood nodded in agreement, falling completely for Jake's line of bullshit.

"Now, off you go and don't drink too much before I get there, ha ha."

Elwood walked over to Jake as the band settled back in the car, properly chastised.

"So, Jake, when did you set up this meeting?"

"You frighten me, man. There's no fucking meeting," Jake whispered. "Be back here soon. I wanna hit this station before it closes at six."

"Hit the station? Jake, are you sure? *That's armed robbery*. You'll get a nickel, *at least*."

Jake stared deeply into his brother's Ray-Bans. "I promised the band, Elwood."

"Where you gonna get a gun at this hour?"

"We'll use that toll gun you got, the one that fires quarters into the toll booth. Shit, it looks like a real gun to me. That way no one'll get hurt. Don't worry, baby brother, I got it locked. You just hustle back."

Elwood walked to the Caddy, shaking his head and muttering unintelligibly. Jake headed back to the bathroom to take a major tension dump.

Traffic was as heavy as ever. The station sat blazing with neon and headlights.

THE BLUES BROTHERS

"Jake, it's almost seven. The band's been drinkin' beer for two hours," Elwood whispered from their hiding place behind the men's room. "Christ, we'll have to rob a bank to buy the Stake Pit."

"I don't know what's wrong. They should have closed by now." Jake cocked the toll gun and pulled his hat lower over his shades. "I'm goin' in. You wait in the Bluesmobile an' keep the fucker idling."

The two brothers looked at each other, hesitating, on the edge.

Jake slapped his brother on the shoulder.

"See ya in a few minutes. Be cool."

Elwood watched his brother's solid body swagger to the brightly lit, glass-walled Clark's station. "Jake can handle himself," he thought. "He always handled himself."

Elwood ran to the Cadillac and turned on the ignition. Slumped in the front seat, he watched the robbery as if it were a drive-in movie.

The bulky man in the black suit and shades pulled the strange-looking gun on the old man next to the cash register. The old man sat frozen. The robber waved the gun around violently. The old man opened the register, grabbing handfuls of cash and sliding it across the counter.

"Good, good. Jake, you're beautiful. Now go!"

But the big man pointed the gun to a case of Valvoline stacked in the corner.

Elwood screamed, "Nooooo! Jake, we don't use Valvoline!"

And then, as if in a dream, the Illinois state trooper cruised almost silently into the picture. Even Elwood didn't see him until it was too late. The trooper pulled his revolver, curiously watching the bizarre tableau as Jake, cash falling out of his pockets, balanced the heavy case of oil.

Suddenly Elwood saw—and leaned hard on the horn. Jake jerked a look over, catching the cop as he ducked behind his patrol car and assumed a two-handed firing position.

Jake dropped the oil. Thinking quickly, he handed the gun to the palsied station owner and threw up his arms as if *he* were being held up.

The trooper laughed out loud as a stream of quarters bounced off the big man's white shirt.

Elwood, tears streaming from beneath his sunglasses, hit the slab at sixty and headed for Chicago.

The dream was over.

chapter two

The time passed slowly.

For Jake it was three years of agony, waiting for letters that never came, listening to music that existed only in his own mind, a long nightmare of imagining what it would be like to be on the outside again, whether it would ever end. He became a robot, doing so little that he gained weight on the stringy kale and rancid pepper steak that passed for food in the prison system.

For the band, the end of Jake's involvement was also the end of them as a group. Something was missing. They tried to hold it together, for their own sake as well as his, but they managed to catch fire with less and less frequency. Elwood did his best. Others tried to fill the inspirational void. Inevitably, all failed. Jake's leadership was sorely missed, so sorely that within six months the Blues Brothers band, once a group as mean and righteous as a fist, had ceased to exist.

Elwood attempted to keep tabs on where each of them was, but it was like spearing waterbugs. Only a half-step ahead of the Traffic Division cops himself, Elwood changed addresses regularly, sold the blue Cadillac, and even temporarily retired from the entertainment business. In desperate need of money, he took a job with a manufacturer whose specialty was putting various products in aerosol spray cans—Propellants Packaging Corporation. His analytical mind helped him learn the business in a hurry, so that before long he was an assembly-line troubleshooter. He also learned how to make a very handy bomb with materials on hand at the factory, a skill he was sure would be useful some day. Somehow the days and weeks passed, but it just wasn't the same without Jake.

On several occasions he dropped by St. Helen of the Blessed Shroud Orphanage, where he and Jake had been raised, partly because it reminded him of their times together and partly because he had promised himself to keep an eye on Sister Mary Stigmata, Jake and Elwood's favorite nun. The ancient building was, after all, the only home they knew, and despite the disciplinarian upbringing to which they had been subjected, both he and Jake had a fondness for the place.

About a month before Jake was scheduled to be released on parole, Elwood visited the orphanage and was surprised to see that he was not alone. As he entered the main hall, a group of about a half-dozen young men were standing at the far end, gesturing animatedly to the ceiling and walls, which were held together by a tenuous network of wooden braces and beams.

"It's just like it!" one of them shouted excitedly. "I have a replica of it in my Christmas garden, and this is the same."

Elwood started to walk away, satisfied that Sister Mary Stigmata was not in the main hall.

"Achtung!" he heard someone call after him. "Oh, you, sir! You with the glasses."

Elwood glanced back over his shoulder. Several of the men were moving quickly toward him. They had short haircuts and looked like Shriners or Kiwanis members.

"Are you from the tax assessor's office?" the first man asked.

Elwood shook his head.

"Do you work here?"

Another headshake.

"You're not a deaf-mute, are you?" the man said, smiling at his companions. "Because if you are, we have ways of helping people like you."

The others laughed, jabbing each other with their elbows.

"This place is a perfect double for the München beer hall. It even has the little stage at the end and everything," the man explained, waving his arms about. "We could restage the *putsch* every year at one of our monthly meetings. Of course, we have to buy this place first, but that shouldn't be too hard. We hear they can't make the payments. So we can probably get it for *eine lied*."

He laughed and the others followed suit. Then, clicking his heels ceremoniously, he gave Elwood a little salute and offered his hand. "*Gruppenführer* Dietrich Albrecht at your service," he said. "Illinois National Socialist Party."

Elwood declined the handshake. "Nazis," he said.

"I'm glad to hear you don't work here at this papist hideout for blacks and other inferior types," Albrecht said. "Because when we take over the facilities, we'll probably fire everyone just on principle. Spies are everywhere, you know."

"Spies and creeps," Elwood said, nodding.

It went over the man's head. "*Ja*, you're right," he said. "That's the only reason they won the war, you know. Because they were better at being sneaky. They hired Jews for that, you know. Like the Rosenbergs. I wonder how our Jew-loving Americans explained the Rosenbergs, eh?"

"Look, I've got a date with some poison ivy," Elwood said, moving toward the door.

"If you see the papist Mother Superior, tell her we're going to buy this place and make her earn an honest living."

As Elwood turned the corner, he could hear the brittle laughter of the Nazis echoing through the hall.

"Tell her *der Tag* is coming," Albrecht shouted after him. "*Der Tag!*"

15

The day. It had finally arrived.

Jake stood at the front of his cell, his hands gripping the pea-green bars, listening to the early-morning sounds of prison. Far away, an electric door buzzed and clanged shut, punctuating the low thunder of men snoring in restless sleep. Footsteps echoed hollowly on the concrete floor. The predominating smells were stale food and disinfectant. But now that was about to end. He had paid his debt to society, as they say over and over in old prison movies, a sentiment that Jake no longer found vaguely amusing.

Shortly before seven o'clock, Jake had a long moment of panic, the terrifying thought entering his mind that something would happen to keep him in confinement another day, a week, or perhaps—through some unthinkable administrative error—indefinitely. The guards arrived on time, however, indicating with the barest movements of their heads that he was to follow. Jake got the distinct impression that they did not relish opening the steel doors nearly as much as they enjoyed slamming them.

He passed down the long upper tier onto the "birdcage," the huge square center hallway of steel bars into which funneled the four wings of the prison. Passing through three sets of double doors, they moved into the corridor leading to the release center, where Jake was shown into a small cubicle for out-processing.

After a brief lecture dealing with the system of parole and probation, he was led to a supply cage and handed a box with his personal belongings. As the clerk removed each item, he checked it against a list made up when Jake had first been incarcerated. Rather like a tired auctioneer, the clerk also recited a brief description of the belongings:

"One soiled man's hair comb, one inexpensive Timex digital watch, one unused prophylactic, two gold- or brass-plated finger rings, one black suit jacket, one pair black suit pants, one yellow . . . er . . . white Arrow shirt, one old-fashioned thin black necktie, one pair dark sunglasses.

Seven dollars and twenty-three cents. Sign the receipt, please."

He handed a ballpoint pen to Jake, who made an X at the bottom of the form.

Ten minutes later, a box of assorted belongings under each arm, Jake passed through the main sallyport to the front gate. He had changed from his prison clothes to the dark suit and dark glasses, a transformation that affected him mentally as much as it did physically.

Now his walk was more confident, his expression almost arrogant as he glanced up at the guard in the main tower. "I told you this joint would never hold me," he said.

A battered black and white 1974 Plymouth Fury four-door sedan, with some sort of state seal half sanded off, wheeled up as Jake passed through the final gate. Elwood got out, wearing the same type of outfit as Jake, and walked toward the newly freed man. Taking one of the boxes, he threw it into the back seat and opened the door. Jake got in, and Elwood threw the car into drive and burned rubber out of the prison drive onto the main highway.

"So how was it?" Elwood said, a quarter-mile down the road.

"Boring. How was it for you?"

"Boring."

"So where's the band?" Jake asked, releasing the question that had haunted him for three years. "Where's Matt, where's the Colonel, where's Duck? When do we start rehearsing? Where are we rehearsing? When's our first gig? Where are we playing? Where are your harps? Are we playing tonight?"

The questions came in a rapid stream, as if by delivering them so quickly he would leave no time for answers he did not want to hear. During his time in prison, Jake had received only a few letters, most of which talked of trivia rather than bad news, but he was constantly afraid that the band had disintegrated. While in prison, he had forced himself not to think about it too much. Only now could he ask.

Elwood's reply was not encouraging. "Come on, man, get serious," he said defensively.

Jake refused to accept the words as an answer to his questions. "Well, if not tonight, when?" he persisted. "Man! Where's Blue Lou? Murph? Bones? Willie? Mr. Fabulous? Where are they—in the trunk? What songs are we gonna do? How about, 'I Got Everything I Need . . . Almost'? Where's the band?"

"What do you mean, where's the band?"

"I mean what I said—where?"

"Split. Everywhere, man! Gone."

Jake shook his head angrily. "Elwood, it was your responsibility to keep it together," he said. "I was inside. You promised me you'd keep it together."

Elwood stared at the road ahead. "Well, I got a few leads . . . I got some telephone numbers," he said weakly. "I mean, it wasn't easy keeping track of those guys. How many of them wrote or visited you, huh?"

Jake refused to buy it. "They ain't the kind of guys who write letters," he shot back. "You were outside. You promised you'd keep in touch with them."

"Well, I got a few leads. We'll find them again."

"A few leads! I want to know! When are we gonna play again?"

Elwood sighed helplessly. "Hey, man, you knew how things would be when you went inside," he said. "You knew everything would fall apart. Without you there were no gigs. It wasn't the Blues Brothers anymore. I mean, I couldn't go out myself and just sing 'Rrrrubber Biscuit.' There were no gigs, no money, so what was to keep everybody there? That's why they split."

"But I kept asking you about them," Jake murmured, shaking his head sadly. "I asked if we were going to play again and you didn't say no."

"So what was I supposed to do?" Elwood replied. "Take away your hope? Take away the only thing that kept you going? I bullshit you."

They drove in silence for several minutes. The sun of freedom, which had felt so good against Jake's skin on leaving the prison, now seemed to have turned cold. "You don't know where they are?" he said finally.

"No. They split. Took straight jobs, man. It'll take some time to find them again."

Jake fished in his pocket, took out a bent cigarette, and pushed the lighter on the dashboard. It refused to stay in.

"And what's this?" he demanded angrily. "This stupid car. Where's the Cadillac?"

"I traded it in."

Jake threw the recalcitrant lighter to the floor. "You traded the Bluesmobile for this hunk of shit?"

"No," Elwood replied evenly. "I traded it for a microphone."

"I can dig that, but what the hell is this shitbox?"

"Look, man," Elwood said testily. "The Cadillac was finished, burnt out. And on every cop list in five states. I needed a car, so I bought this."

"You were robbed."

"The hell I was. This was a steal, a bargain. I picked it up at the Indiana State Police auction last spring. It's an old police car."

"Thanks a lot, pal," Jake muttered. "The day I get out of prison, and my own brother picks me up in a police car."

"You don't like it?"

"No, I don't like it."

They were on a long straight section of two-lane highway, behind a line of traffic waiting at a barrier to a split-swing bridge. Hitting the accelerator, Elwood swerved around the cars and raced toward the bridge, which was just in the process of rising. Jake glanced at the speedometer, saw the needle jump from thirty-five to sixty-five, then noticed a swirling sea of panicked faces in cars to his right, a blurred form of a barge disappearing beneath the bridge. The air rushed past and his stomach turned just as it used to when he was a kid and the roller coaster hit the first plunge, except that now they were heading vertically upward instead of downward, the tires of the new Bluesmobile squealing as they tore into the concrete roadway that seemed to end in the sky. For a long moment they hung in the air before plunging sharply downward onto the other side of the swing bridge, landing with a force that nearly carried both men into the windshield. Swerving to the right, Elwood avoided the first cars waiting on the other side and slowed to a modest fifty.

"Car's got a lot of pickup," Jake said finally, straightening his tie.

"Yeah." Elwood smiled, obviously feeling vindicated. "I can see why you didn't like it, though. It looks like it's got nothing, but it's got a cop motor, a 440-cubic-inch plant. They don't make them like this anymore. This was a model made before catalytic converters, so it can run good on any kind of gas."

Jake nodded. "Okay, I'm sold."

"Is it the new Bluesmobile, then?"

"Not until you fix the cigarette lighter."

Ten minutes later they were in Calumet City, a decaying industrial section on the Illinois-Indiana line. Looming ahead of them was a factory with a gritty sign above it, reading ILLINOIS DRAG LINE COMPANY; to the right was a similarly depressing plant labeled CHICAGO PRESSED HEADS METAL MILLING. Between the two gray structures was a narrow, red-brick, three-story building with a curved roof. A modest sign above the center window, between the second and third floors, read: SAINT HELEN OF THE BLESSED SHROUD ORPHANAGE—1923.

"Why are we coming here?" Jake asked, as Elwood

stopped in front of the middle building.

"You promised you'd visit the Penguin the day you got out."

"I didn't!"

"Yes, you did," Elwood persisted. "Anyway, *I* promised her."

They got out. Looking up at the old building's familiar facade, Jake was suddenly impressed by how narrow and decayed it appeared. Spray-paint slogans covered nearly every inch of concrete along the structure's side.

"What a shame, huh?" Jake said.

"Yeah," Elwood said, nodding. "It used to be such a palace."

"Somebody ought to give it a new coat of graffiti," Jake said.

They entered the building and moved through dark corridors with peeling paint until both, as if on cue, stopped at the doorway to a long chamber housing rows of small iron-frame cots with a sink, a table, and a chair next to each one. The windows were covered with wire-mesh grating. Together the men walked silently into the room, almost as if they were entering church.

"Look, our old beds," Elwood said.

Jake nodded. "Yeah, with chairs. Boy, these kids really got it plush."

Continuing down the line of beds, they were soon at the base of a narrow set of stairs leading into an artificially lit crevice above. Halfway up the staircase, they suddenly heard a gravelly woman's voice shouting, "Shut the door! There's a draft!"

Closing the door behind them, they clambered up the dark steps until they could see a bulky silhouette ahead of them.

"Who is it?" a woman's voice demanded.

"Jake and Elwood," Jake replied.

"Get up here!"

Seconds later, they were in the austere garret office of Sister Mary Stigmata. It was a peculiarly shaped room with a sloping ceiling, exposed beams and a smell of exposed insulation. Behind a heavy oak desk littered with files and papers sat Sister Mary Stigmata, wearing the traditional nun's habit, complete with cowl, black robe, white bib, and thick, square, wire-rimmed glasses. She was no longer young, perhaps well into her seventies, but the slate-blue eyes that sparkled at the young men contained no hint of advancing age. "Hello, boys," she said in a cavernous voice. "Nice to see you. Take a seat."

Jake and Elwood looked around the room. The only chairs were a pair of one-piece, grade-school writing desks against the wall. When the men hesitated, Sister Mary Stigmata repeated her offer in a way that made them instantly squeeze into the tiny seats.

"Bring your desks over here so I can see you," she said.

Elwood slid out of the seat and moved it over next to Sister Mary Stigmata's desk. Jake, unable to extricate himself, walked crablike, the chair clinging to his posterior and scraping its legs on the floor as he proceeded. With a sigh, he relaxed next to Elwood.

"So, Jake," Sister Mary said. "Was it worth it?"

"What?"

"Was the money you stole worth the penalty you paid for threatening the life of a fellow man?"

"No, I guess not," Jake replied. "But I didn't really threaten anybody."

"Where were you when your brother was stealing?" Sister Mary asked, fixing Elwood with a baleful glare.

"I was in the car waiting for him."

"Therefore you were an accessory to the crime, as they say."

Elwood nodded.

"More than that," Jake said. "He was an absolute necessity."

THE BLUES BROTHERS

"How come you were caught and he wasn't?"

"The cops couldn't catch him. He was in the Bluesmobile."

"Actually, it was pretty close," Elwood said, "until I got in the funeral procession. It took me out of my way, but it was worth it."

"Neither of you sounds contrite," Sister Mary said accusingly. "Not in the slightest."

"We didn't have any choice," Jake replied. "We needed the money fast. There wasn't any other way out."

"There's always another way out. A Christian way out. God doesn't encourage people to be thieves. You just didn't look hard enough."

"I did, I did," Jake protested. "Honest, Penguin . . . I mean, Sister Mary. We even used the Yellow Pages."

"Don't be a wiseacre. You know what I mean about looking. You didn't ask the Lord for a better way out. Chances are, if you'd done that, He would have shown you the light."

"It was getting awfully late to go around looking for the light. We didn't have time."

"There's always time. Sometimes you see the light in a split second. God works in strange ways. He'd have given you the answer if you'd given Him half a chance."

Jake shrugged, indicating resignation if not defeat.

"Anyway, you don't realize how lucky you've been," Sister Mary continued. "A lot worse things could have happened to you than being raised here. Church money raised and fed you. You could at least have thought of the Church once during your time of need. It makes me think you learned nothing during all your years here."

"That's not true," Jake objected, smiling. "We learned to duck."

"Ingrates," Sister Mary chided them, but her tone was no longer angry.

"How's the orphanage doing?" Elwood asked, anxious

to change the subject from their character—or lack of character—to something else. In addition, he was genuinely concerned about the old building.

Sister Mary Stigmata sighed. "These days, education is a tough business. We have a class here in supplemental mathematics for gifted children, and as long as we run these classes the Board of Education gives us money. Of course, the money's not enough. The upkeep on this old building is terrific. Every month we fall a little bit further behind." Suddenly angry at the situation, she slapped the top of her desk with a ruler, a gesture left over from her teaching days. Jake and Elwood responded to the old stimulus by nearly jumping out of their seats; they were prevented only by being tightly wedged into them.

"What's the matter?" Jake asked.

"It just makes me angry," Sister Mary said. "The county did a tax assessment on this property last month. If we don't make a payment in the next ten days, they're going to put the place up for auction."

"How much is the payment?" Elwood asked.

"Five thousand dollars is the amount we'll have to pay to keep them from offering it for sale."

"Doesn't the Church have that much?" Elwood responded. "Seems to me they could pay that easy."

"They could, if they were interested in keeping this place," Sister Mary murmured. "But they aren't. I don't guess you can blame them. It's dilapidated and not much to look at. But it serves a good purpose."

"Kind of like you," Jake said, the warmth in his eyes belying the flippancy of his remark.

Sister Mary looked darts at him, then laughed. "Well, that's exactly it, you know," she said. "We take kids here that can't go anyplace else, and do a pretty good job of raising them. If St. Helen goes, I don't know what might happen to some of these children."

"What'll they do with the building?" Elwood asked, suddenly recalling the Nazis who wanted it just because it resembled Hitler's Munich beer hall.

"They'll sell it to somebody who has some other use for it," Sister Mary replied. "Either that or tear it down."

"And what'll happen to you?"

"Oh, I don't know. I'll be sent to the missions . . . Africa, Latin America, Mexico . . ."

Jake shook his head. "Forget it," he said emphatically. "That would be a waste. You belong with these kids here."

"Thank you, Jacob," Sister Mary smiled. "Actually, I agree with you. This is the thing I've worked at for forty years, and it's the best thing I do. But we have to do what the Church orders . . ."

"You're gonna stay right here," Jake said. "Five grand is no problem. We'll have that for you in no time. Matter of fact, we'll get it by tomorrow morning." He shifted his rear end quickly back and forth, pulling himself laboriously to his feet. "Come on, Elwood, let's go."

Sister Mary slammed the ruler against the desk again.

"No!" she said sharply. "No! I will not touch your filthy money!"

"What filthy money?"

"The filthy money you're planning to steal. No! I simply won't accept it."

Jake looked at her for a long moment, then lit a cigarette. He felt as if she had just thrown cold water in his face. Only hours out of prison, and he had offered to risk going back for her, an offer she hurled back at him. He tried to calm himself, but heard the words come from his throat. "Then I guess you're really up shit creek," he said.

"I beg your pardon," Sister Mary replied, her eyes narrowing. "What did you say?"

"I offered to help you. You said you wouldn't take our filthy money, and I said I guess you're really up shit creek," Jake repeated methodically.

She was still quick as a cat, leaping to her feet and

backhanding Jake across the shoulder and lower jaw with the ruler. He recoiled, threw up his hand, and received another crack on the knuckles.

Elwood got between the two of them, only to be rewarded for his peace-keeping activity with a swat to the back of the head.

"Hey, you fat penguin!" he yelled. "Take it easy!"

The epithet served to infuriate the bulky nun even more. Swinging effortlessly, like a kendo master from *Seven Samurai,* she landed a series of blows first on Elwood, then on Jake, who quickly retreated to the door, sliding a chair between his body and Sister Mary. Slipping and falling as the result of his hasty retreat from the onslaught, Elwood found himself wedged into a corner by the nun, who quickly capitalized on the development to rain new blows on his hands, which had risen to protect his scalp. Half-sliding, half-running, Elwood somehow managed to make his way to the door, following Jake's tangled body down the stairway to safety. At the bottom of the steps, they lay in a heap, looking up at Sister Mary, who regarded them from a religious height.

"You really are a disappointing pair," she called down to them, scarcely out of breath despite the exertion. "I prayed so much for you. It saddens and hurts me that two young men whom I raised to believe in the Ten Commandments should return to me as two thieves with filthy mouths and bad attitudes. Now get out and don't come back until you've redeemed yourselves."

She slammed the door.

"Boys, you gotta learn not to talk to nuns that way."

Jake and Elwood turned in the direction of the familiar voice. It was Curtis, the old black man who had first taught them about the blues many years before. Now his short hair was mostly gone, leaving only wiry white curls around the edge of his thin face, which seemed little more than a thin layer of smooth wax poured over a well-shaped skull. Although he had always been lean, a hint of frailness now revealed itself in his gait. But the wide smile and crinkling eyes were the same as in the old days. Bounding quickly to their feet, the two young men pumped both of his hands vigorously.

"Curtis!" Jake said. "It's good to see you."

"You look fine, man," Elwood said, beaming.

"Thanks, boys," Curtis said. "Say, if you'd like to step down in the boiler room, I'll buy you both a drink."

A few minutes later, the three had made themselves comfortable in the low-ceilinged maintenance-boiler room which served as Curtis's living quarters. The constant light hiss of steam leaking from an overhead pipe provided an accompaniment to their conversation. To Jake and Elwood, who had not visited the hot and oppressive room since their teens, the walls seemed to have pressed inward like the movable walls of B-movie torture chambers.

Producing a bottle of Wild Turkey from behind a six-inch pipe, Curtis poured the boys a drink and indicated that they should sit on his bed while he took the straight-backed cane chair. As they all raised their glasses in mute toasts and sampled the whiskey, Jake noted that two of Curtis's weathered-looking guitars still hung against the wall.

"Looks the same as always," he said.

"Yeah," Curtis replied, "but it may not be that way for long."

"What do you mean? Is the old place really that close to being sold?"

"It sure is. Next to no time, I may be on the street."

Elwood frowned. "They wouldn't turn you out, would they?"

"Shit," Curtis said. "What's one more old nigger to the Board of Education if they buy this place? And if those others buy it, I'll be lucky if they don't put a brand on my ass."

"The Nazis," Elwood said. Then, when Curtis nodded,

he added, "Is it really possible those creeps could get this place?"

"If they got the money, anybody can have this place."

"But what about the orphans?" Jake asked.

"That's the sad part," Curtis said. "The kids come in this place and I get to talk with them and they get to talk to me... orphan boys... I never had no children, and you boys and all the others are like my sons. That's what's really gonna hurt me—they're gonna take all my sons and put them in state institutions."

Jake took a long swallow of his drink, then wiped his mouth. "Don't you worry, Curtis," he said. "We'll get the money. Elwood and I will get the five thousand bucks."

Curtis shook his head wearily. "Boys," he said, "that money's gotta be in the Cook County Assessor's office Tuesday a week. That means you got ten days. How you gonna get five thousand bucks in that short a time without ripping somebody off?"

Jake sighed. "What you're saying is, you don't want us stealing, either, just like Sister Mary."

"I guess I'm saying that," Curtis said. "Even though I know the boys here deserve something better than state institutions, I just ain't sure stealing's the answer. Now, that might make me old-fashioned or something. Maybe I just got so old somewhere along the line that I started to believe that two wrongs don't make a right."

"What you're saying is, stealing don't sit well with Christ," Elwood said.

"I guess so. Why, He didn't even steal from Caesar, you know. Caesar with all that money from the Roman Empire. Why, Jesus, He could have said, 'Take that man's money and give it to the poor.' But He really thought that kinda thinking would lead to bad things. So even while He told the rich to sell everything and give it to the poor, He was against stealing. No two ways about it."

Jake finished his drink, exhaled wearily, and leaned back

against the sweating pipes. "Then how the fuck are we gonna get five thousand dollars in ten days?" he asked.

"You heard the Penguin," Elwood said. "We got to get redeemed, see the light."

Jake stood up. "I just can't buy that!" he exclaimed. "Wait around for Jesus to show me the light? That's plain dumb. Jesus never done me any favors in the past, so why should He now?"

Curtis smiled. "Maybe He's been saving up for the right time. I mean, how many miracles you think you got coming, Jake Blues? Could be Sister Mary's right. You boys could use some churching up. Maybe if you go where God is, He'll be more likely to show you something, like if you'd slide by the Triple Rock and catch the Reverend Cleophus. You boys listen to what he has to say and something might happen."

"Curtis, I don't want to listen to no jive-ass preacher," Jake muttered. "It was bad enough in the joint, when I had to listen to them on radio or TV."

"Jake, you get wise and get to church," Curtis said. "Soon's you leave, I'm gonna start praying for you to do that."

"And maybe I'll do that," Jake answered, "just to make your prayers come true. But that ain't no guarantee God's gonna say one single word to me."

"I'm sure all He wants is a chance," Curtis said.

It was, finally, the day. The alarm went off shortly after dawn, jangling noisily less than a foot away from where the beautiful blonde's head lay on the pillow. Her eyes opened quickly as one hand silenced the alarm. Then, contrary to what might be expected, the lids did not close again to allow the sleeper another twenty winks. Shifting her feet out from beneath the covers, the young woman put them on the floor, rubbed her eyes one time, then dropped down on the pile carpet to do fifty pushups.

The two minutes of rapid exercise served as a tonic. The woman sprang to her feet and strode to the closet, where she drew out a pair of jeans, a sweat shirt, knee-high woolen stockings, and jogging shoes. A minute later she emerged from the bathroom, looking as if she had spent an hour with a Hollywood makeup expert. In the kitchen of her modest apartment, she drained a six-ounce glass of unsweetened grapefruit juice, downed a half-dozen vitamin C tablets, and was out the door.

A ten-minute drive brought her to an abandoned sanitary landfill between Marquette Park and Ogden Dunes, Indiana, a flat section of land broken only by irregular piles of unburned detritus missed by the bulldozers. Otherwise the area resembled the stunted remains of a bombed-out city that had been buried by its own former inhabitants out of sheer embarrassment. Because it was still quite early, long before the wind would blow in off the lake, a heavy fog clung to the ground, transforming the godforsaken territory into an eerie moor.

The woman parked her car near one of the mounds and went around to the trunk, from which she withdrew a long object wrapped in a blanket. Sticking the blanket and the object under one arm, she picked up a sheet of heavy cardboard lying on the floor of the trunk, leaned it against the fender, and closed the trunk. She then picked up the cardboard and walked several hundred feet to the nearest pile of unburned garbage, against which she leaned the cardboard, arranging several large stones so that it would not slide or fall down.

Satisfied that the cardboard was just right, she moved a hundred yards away, paused, frowned, then continued walking until she was perhaps three hundred yards from the pile against which the object rested.

After a lengthy examination of the stunted landscape to make certain no one was watching her, the blonde dropped the blanket onto the ground, baring a heavy metal-and-wood object that veterans of World War Two would have recognized immediately as a Browning Automatic Rifle. Jamming a clip of ammunition into the piece and sliding the bolt to pump a round into the chamber, she dropped to her stomach and allowed the weapon to rest on the bipod support at the end of the barrel. She then took a deep breath and fired two rounds singly, followed immediately by a rapid emptying of the entire clip. As soon as the piece was empty, she reached for a second clip, inserted it, and squeezed the trigger until the sudden silence and array of shell casings to her right told her she had expended the ammunition.

With another glance around the landscape, she wrapped the BAR in the blanket and retraced her steps to the garbage pile and the cardboard target. Surveying the results of her quick fusillade, she smiled, noting that no less than ten shots had struck the area roughly corresponding to the shape of a man.

Even better, four of the irregularly shaped holes were within the boundaries of the victim's head, which just happened to be a life-size glossy picture of Jake Blues.

"I'd rather die," Jake declared.

"Don't be ridiculous," Elwood murmured, turning into the parking lot of the large white clapboard church, above which was a neon sign reading, TRIPLE ROCK BAPTIST CHURCH. Locating a space, he edged the Bluesmobile into it and cut the engine.

"But why now?" Jake demanded. "I just got out of prison and already you're taking me to church."

"We don't have any time to waste," Elwood said. "If we're gonna make that move toward redemption, we better get to church right away. It won't help if we wait a week or so, what with our having only ten days to get the money."

"I still think we ought to steal it," Jake muttered.

The service had already started by the time Jake and Elwood entered the structure. An organ played softly as a choir filed onto a raised platform behind an ornate pulpit with a gooseneck microphone. Immediately behind the pulpit was a bandstand supporting four black musicians in dark blue jackets. The congregation was made up primarily of black men, women, and children, although a few young whites could be seen here and there. The men were bearded, Jake noted, thinking negatively that they were probably liberal college types who wanted to display their feelings of brotherhood in a way that everyone would be sure to notice.

The organist ended her interlude as the Reverend Cleophus James, elegantly clad in a royal blue robe with gold trim, stepped into the pulpit, rested his hands on the speaker stand, and looked dramatically around the hall. Only when the church was completely silent did he speak.

"Now, people," he said in a powerful, chanting voice, "when I awoke this morning, I heard a disturbing sound. I heard this sound in my car and in the streets and it shook me up, people."

Jake noticed that a subtle orchestration was at work already in the church. Instead of remaining silent during the sermon, the organist had started playing a low, plaintive melody, against which some members of the congregation were humming and moaning in harmony.

The Reverend Cleophus continued, "What I heard was the jingle-jangle of a thousand lost souls. I'm talking about the souls of mortal men and women who departed from this life and were not received into the Kingdom of Heaven."

Taking their cues, the organist's melody became rather

more threatening, the voices of the congregation dropped into a lower mournful pitch. Jake noticed that Elwood's head was bowed, his eyes closed.

"Yes, my friends," Reverend Cleophus intoned, "I heard these lost souls roaming unseen over the earth, beyond any hope of salvation, seeking a Divine Light they'll never find, because it's too late for them to ever see again the Good Light they once chose not to follow."

As he spoke, his hands closed tightly around the top edges of the pulpit and he leaned toward the congregation like a plant bending in the direction of the sun.

"And, people, every time one of these poor lost souls meets another one, there is a jingle-jangle as they pass each other in their tormented wanderings. And this day I have heard a thousand and one jingle-jangles. So wake up, people. Don't be lost when your time comes. Get yourselves ready, 'for the day of the Lord cometh as a thief in the night.' Amen."

As soon as the word "Amen" was heard, the organ and choir broke into a rousing gospel song, the words of which everyone apparently knew without the help of a hymn book. To Jake, raised in staid Catholic ritual, the spontaneous outburst was surprising and exhilarating. True, he knew such things existed, had seen them on TV, but standing in the middle of it was another thing. He could feel an almost physical power emanating from those around him. The music, meanwhile, grew more intense, the tempo faster and faster until it seemed nearly out of control. Hands beat together in furious clapping, feet stomped, here and there a person leaping high above his neighbors could be seen. Then they were in the aisles, the most demonstrative half-dozen members of the congregation, unable to contain themselves within the narrow confines of the pews. Past Jake they flashed, doing cartwheels and flips and splits, their eyes wide with excitement, mouths moving rapidly as they sang and shouted words of praise.

"Show us the Light, Lord!" they shouted. "Show us the Light!"

Suddenly Jake was blinded.

It was not an emotional thing, but a physical one. Clutching at his eyes, he buried his face in his hands and looked down at the floor, only daring to open his eyes gingerly after half a minute. He could still see, he was relieved to discover, but the image was still there, as if burned into his vision.

He had been watching one of the people in the aisle when he turned to say something to Elwood. As he swung his head around, the beam of light struck him with what seemed laser force, a searing blast of blue and red causing him intense pain. Now, having recovered from the initial shock, he slowly moved his eyes toward the light, which was still there close to his face, hot and intimidating, so powerful that Jake did not yet dare look directly at it.

"Jake," he heard Elwood say. "What the hell's the matter? You look funny."

"What do you mean?"

"Your face—"

Elwood continued speaking, but Jake did not hear the rest of his brother's words. Despite the pain, he had moved his eyes closer and closer to the ray of light which seemed to have singled him out from everyone else in the church. A skeptic would have said that it was nothing more than a freak reflection of the sun, perhaps glancing off a mirror, through the small stained-glass window, past the guitar player, and into Jake's eyes. But to Jake, it was his vision, incredibly beautiful, the intense colors surrounding the silhouette of a man playing the guitar, the whole picture so powerfully limned that it was impossible to discern objects or persons beyond its borders.

To Jake it was a parable, the answer! As Sister Mary Stigmata had said with perfect truth, sometimes the word of God comes in a split second.

"What is it, Jake?" Elwood asked, his voice sounding very hollow and far away.

"It's . . . it's the Light," Jake heard himself reply. It was strange; he was surprised by the sound of his own voice. He had intended to say something reassuring but vague, instead of the comment about "the Light." Once he had articulated them, however, he realized that the words were exactly right. That was what he had seen. Now, in a flash, he knew what had to be done.

"The band . . ." he whispered.

"Jake, are you all right?" Elwood asked.

He watched, fascinated, as Jake suddenly moved several steps to his right, then leaped—was almost pulled—into the aisle with the other testifying congregation members. His presence was noticed immediately by the Reverend Cleophus, who pointed from the pulpit and shouted, "Have you come to join our flock, my little lost white lamb?"

The singling-out did not seem to embarrass Jake. If anything, he lost some of his hesitancy, his feet beginning to move up and down in time to the music as he said, "The band . . . the band . . ."

"Have you got the spirit, brother?" Reverend Cleophus shouted. "Have you got the spirit?"

"The band," Jake repeated, softly at first, then with rising spirit. "The band . . . Jesus H. Christ . . . the Band!"

"Do you see the Light?" Cleophus demanded.

"Yes, yes!" Jake shouted back. "Jesus H. Tap-Dancing Christ! I have seen the Light!"

Elwood, having followed Jake gingerly into the aisleway, looked around cautiously. "What light?" he muttered.

"Praise God!" Cleophus shouted. "Our white friend has seen the Light!"

A chorus of singsong voices joined in shouting praise of the great event. Faces, illuminated with happy smiles, were turned toward Jake; hands reached out to touch him, pat him on the back, embrace him. His feet, meanwhile, continued to move faster and faster, a soul machine with wheels of fire. Then, with startling suddenness, he did take off, flipping himself into the air and turning a somersault, followed by another and another, until he was halfway down the aisle. The Reverend Cleophus threw his head back and laughed with joy.

Thinking his brother was having a seizure of some kind, Elwood bounded down the aisle after him, grabbed him finally by the shoulders and held him in place. "What is it, Jake?" he asked.

"The band! Don't you see the light, Elwood? The band!"

Elwood wanted to understand. In fact, he felt, amid all the noise and wonderful confusion, that he was on the verge of understanding, that all he needed was one final clue. As the hysteria continued to mount, however, he felt the need for a clue begin to dissipate; looking at Jake's wild and happy eyes, Elwood himself began to believe. The band. Yes, the band! Of course. That was the answer! Why hadn't he seen that before? It was so obvious!

"The band!" Elwood heard himself shouting. "The band! Yeah!"

He and Jake began to dance together, throwing each other over their backs like 1940s jitterbuggers.

"Praise God!" the Reverend Cleophus shouted from the pulpit.

"And God bless the United States of America!" Elwood shouted back.

An hour later, they drove along the Adlai Stevenson Expressway, the cassette player blaring "Hold On, I'm Comin'."

"So you saw the light? which is to get the band together and make the money for Sister Mary?"

"It was there in living color," Jake said. "A blinding light playing around that guitar, aimed for me and me alone. What else could it mean? Hell, Elwood, what's the matter? You were the one who said we oughta go to church and be redeemed."

"I know, but I didn't think it would happen."

"Well, it happened," Jake said with conviction. "Now we're on a real mission. A mission from God. Doesn't that make you feel a hell of a lot better?"

Elwood nodded. "Sure, but getting the band together won't be easy, Jake. I don't even know where to start."

"Don't worry. We'll figure out something. You said you wrote down some phone numbers, didn't you?"

"Yeah, if I can remember where," Elwood said glumly.

They rode in silence for a while, enjoying the music, until Jake suddenly became aware of bridge lights on the Chicago Sanitary and Ship Canal flashing by. "Hey, where are we headed?" he asked.

"Home," Elwood said.

"I thought you said you were living at the Bond Hotel."

"I am."

"Well, what are you getting on 55 for? The Bond is back at Lake and Wacker."

"I know," Elwood replied. "I'm taking the long way. You see, I put most of the money from my day job into this car, and I can't sleep unless I get out on the slab once a night and open her up."

"Sure," Jake said, nodding. "Maybe one of these nights you'll even get around to putting in a decent cigarette lighter."

Elwood smiled slightly but did not answer. Instead he booted the Bluesmobile. With a noticeable change in the pitch of the muffler's rumble, accompanied by a hiss from the exhaust pipe, the car blasted from its right-lane position across four streams of traffic into the hammer lane, drawing angry honks from several nearly missed cars. Once freed of the traffic, Elwood pitched along at a steady one hundred, reading the other drivers' rhythms so well that he was able to weave in and out of cars for about five minutes without varying his speed by more than a mile or two per hour. Jake, impressed by Elwood's skill but having been through it before many times, relaxed by turning up the volume of the *Best of Sam and Dave* cassette to thunderous volume. As an encore, Elwood blasted along at 125 for perhaps a mile before veering off an exit ramp, the Bluesmobile backfiring in a contented way, rather like a racehorse following a strong run. At the bottom of the ramp, Elwood turned right into a two-lane divided thoroughfare, proceeded through an amber light at the first intersection, and headed home.

He was just past the gas station on the corner when he spotted the white police car rolling from behind the pumps, turning on its lights as it did so.

"Shit," Elwood muttered.

"What is it?" Jake asked sleepily, still caught up in the spirit of "Soothe Me," from the tape player.

"Rollers."

"No."

"Yeah."

"Where are we?" Jake asked.

"South Park Ridge."

"What the hell are we doing way up here?"

"Does it matter where you are when you got cops behind you?"

"Maybe they're after somebody else," Jake said, just as the lights of the police car cast a brightly ominous glow in the rearview mirror. Elwood hesitated just a moment, then pulled obediently to the curb.

The police car parked behind them and a young, clean-cut officer with a mustache reaching just to the top of the upper lip walked to Elwood's side of the car.

"What?" Elwood said. "What did I do?" Jake thought

to himself that Elwood's voice was literally dripping with innocence.

"Fail to stop on a red light," the officer said evenly.

"The light was yellow . . . sir," Elwood corrected the officer politely.

"May I see your driver's license, please?"

Elwood reached above the sun visor and pulled down a laminated card, which he handed to the cop. With a nod, the officer walked back to the police car.

The brothers sat for a moment in morose silence. Then Jake said, "Jesus, why didn't you just go home?"

"I wasn't ready to, man," Elwood replied. "I think when I'm driving. Your getting out of prison today changes my life a lot, you know? Having to look for the band and everything, think about finding a place for you to stay. I had a lot to think about."

"You make it sound like it was my fault," Jake muttered. "Why don't you just tell him *I* went through the damn light?"

Elwood shrugged. "Anyway, it shouldn't have happened. He snuck up on me. Usually I don't let them near me. Damn. I haven't been pulled over in six months."

"South Park Ridge. You ought to know how straight it is out here," Jake chided.

"I do know. And I know something even worse. Out here they got Scmods."

"Scmods?"

"State-County Municipal Offender Data System."

Jake shook his head. "I don't know exactly what that is, but if I ever knew a State-County Municipal Offender, it's you."

Immediately to their rear, the police officer opened the door of his vehicle and sat down sidesaddle fashion, keeping the door partway open. Across and under the dashboard, straddling the transmission hump, was a computer system consisting of video display console, keyboard and telephone receiver. Clamped in a vertical position on the dashboard next to the video display was a shotgun. After another quick glance at the car ahead, the officer slipped Elwood's driver's license into a slot on the keyboard, switched on the video console, and waited for the license number to appear.

"So what do we have here?" his partner asked as they waited for the computer to feed them information.

"I don't know. They look like they might be from Cicero, with those dark glasses and funeral-director suits."

The computer began lining out information on the video display, green letters against a dark gray background:
ILL. B. 9653-217——BLUES——ELWOOD J.—— LICENSE STATUS——CURRENTLY UNDER SUSPENSION——WARRANTS OUTSTANDING—— STATEWIDE——TRAFFIC——MOVING VIOLATIONS——56——

"Jesus Christ!" the officers said in unison.

——WARRANTS——PARKING——COOK CO—— 117——ARREST DRIVER——IMPOUND VEHICLE.

"A hundred seventeen parking tickets," the driver said, noting that the computer was flashing the last two lines in highly excited fashion. "You can bet your ass we'll arrest that dude."

He got out, walked briskly to the Bluesmobile and leaned down next to Elwood. A comparatively new man on the force, he still recalled the advice given at the training academy: be polite. As he spoke, he therefore even managed a slight smile, which disarmed Elwood to the point where he thought he might get off with a warning.

"Mr. Blues," the officer said, quickly dispelling Elwood's mood of optimism, "we show your license currently under suspension. Step out of the car, please."

Elwood and Jake exchanged quick glances, reading each other perfectly. Ramming the gear shift into drive, Elwood roared away from the curb, spinning the officer like a top as he first tried to grab the vehicle and then did his best to let go.

THE BLUES BROTHERS

A half-minute later, Elwood burned around the corner to the right, hoping to find some traffic in which to get lost. But the street was residential, with only a few cars in sight. The flashing red and blue light of the police car was right on their tail.

"Shit," Elwood muttered, making a U-turn across a grass plot and heading up a side street.

"They'd better not catch us, brother," Jake warned. "I don't want to go back to prison. That kale and pepper steak they serve is for shit."

"They're not gonna catch us," Elwood promised.

Flying through a red light, he swerved past a group of panicked motorists who had just barely managed to skid to a halt, and raced a quarter-mile up the left side of the boulevard until he saw that the right lane was crowded, and turned the wrong way into a one-way street.

Behind them, as quickly as possible without endangering pedestrians or other motorists, the officers pursued, one white-knuckled at the steering wheel, the other white-knuckled at the radio. "Park Ridge 12 in high-speed pursuit southbound on Route six-two," the officer at the radio said in a voice that was unusually high-pitched. "Black 1974 Plymouth sedan with Illinois plates. Request assistance."

A static-fogged voice promised the same.

A few minutes later, traveling down a four-lane road on the edge of a posh suburb, Elwood saw flashing lights ahead of them at the next intersection.

"Looks like they called up reinforcements," he said.

"Yeah, they usually do."

A quarter-mile ahead of them, the lights took the shape of two police cars blocking the intersection, ahead of which stood a single officer waving a flashlight. Behind them were two other sets of flashers; the divider between north- and southbound traffic was a curved section of concrete approximately three feet high. "What do you think?" Elwood asked in a conversational tone.

"About what?"

"That divider strip. Looks like pretty cheap stuff to me." They were roaring toward the blockade at better than eighty, but Elwood's voice continued, matter-of-factly, "Tensile strength of that type divider stinks. The contractors charged the city top dollar, but it's mostly sand and crusher in those things."

"Maybe you should write a book about it," Jake said.

They were nearly on top of the police cars. The officer continued to wave the flashlight, but something in the bend of his knees indicated that he was ready to break and run at any moment.

"Guess it's about time," Elwood said.

Slamming on the brakes, he brought the car to a screeching halt for barely a second, then cranked the steering wheel to the left and hit the accelerator full force. The Bluesmobile literally leaped to its left, the front wheels far enough off the ground to clear the divider wall, which shattered into fragments as the rear wheels took the brunt of the collision.

Swerving to avoid oncoming traffic, Elwood roared up the road's shoulder to the next intersection, hung a right and darted down a smaller side street.

"I've never seen a U-turn quite like that," Jake said.

"Goddamn," Elwood rasped.

"What happened, did we lose a wheel or something?"

"No, dammit, they're still behind us. They must have called up the whole state police."

Jake turned, and noted the flashing lights to their rear. "Damn it, Elwood," he said, "you promised we wouldn't get caught."

"We'll be all right if we can just get back on the expressway," Elwood said.

"Fat chance. It's the other way, ain't it?"

"No. It's just ahead."

As the speedometer edged toward ninety, the Bluesmobile approached a bright expanse of lights that indicated the presence of a huge shopping center.

"This don't look like no expressway to me," Jake rasped, suddenly angry.

"Well, you don't have to yell at me."

"What the hell do you want me to do, motorhead?"

"Try not to be so negative all the time," Elwood said. "Why don't you offer some constructive criticism?"

"It ain't easy to be constructive when you got cops all over your ass," Jake shot back. "First you trade the Cadillac for a microphone, then you lie to me about the band, and now you're gonna put me right back in the joint."

"They're not going to catch us," Elwood soothed. "We're on a mission from God."

They were rapidly approaching the main entrance to the shopping center, a maze of molded concrete slabs punctuated by speed bumps. Behind them, the police car gained rapidly even as another set of lights appeared to their front and off to the left.

"What are you thinking?" Jake asked, his gaze shifting between Elwood and the rear window.

"I'm thinking we should do some shopping."

Giving the steering wheel a sharp turn to the right, he roared into the EXIT ONLY lane, fishtailing wildly as he swerved to avoid a line of cars on their way out. The resultant chaos caused Elwood to smile and hit the accelerator harder, leaving the cruiser to their rear hopelessly snarled in a mass of confused and angry motorists. "Got to find me a mall," he said, the words coming out in singsong fashion, "Got to find me a mall. The cops just don't like driving in malls."

"Try that," Jake suggested, pointing off to the right, where a break in the line of shops and increased pedestrian traffic indicated that a mall was at hand. Elwood nodded, barely slowing the Bluesmobile to fifty as he jumped the curb and raced between boutiques down a lane so narrow that the car nearly scraped the storefronts. Quick-witted shoppers ducked into entranceways; the less fortunate threw

THE BLUES BROTHERS

their packages in the air and ran, barely making it around the corner before the car completed its course.

"Good work," Jake said as the last of the packages which had fallen on the windshield fell away. "You didn't hurt a soul."

"Let's hope the cops are as responsible as I am," Elwood said, noting the flashers slowly following them, siren blaring.

Veering left, the boys both spotted the wide stairway at the same time, exchanged a quick glance, and headed for it.

Bounded on either side by escalators, the long series of steps was about ten feet wide, a piece of cake for Elwood to negotiate. Leaning on the horn, he bumped the Bluesmobile down the stairway, pinning shoppers to the sides as the car bounced by in a cloud of exhaust smoke. Making a 180 as soon as he hit the bottom of the stairs, Elwood tore through the underground parking lot, then up an entrance ramp, and gained the main thoroughfare at top speed. Jake turned to look through the back window, and was happy to note that there was not a police cruiser in sight.

"Maybe we'd better pull into a side street and lay low," he suggested.

"You mean let them turn us into low-life cowards," Elwood said. "Never."

"Then for Christ's sake, at least slow down."

With a nod, Elwood dropped the Bluesmobile to within twenty miles of the speed limit. After driving six blocks more, they entered an area of heavy traffic and were able to mingle with it for several miles on a road that ran against the grain of the former chase route. They saw two police cars, but since they were headed in the opposite direction, Elwood maintained an even, painfully slow speed until they were safely past.

"Well," he said finally, a quarter-hour after the shopping center, "I kept my promise, didn't I?"

Jake nodded, grunted. "You did fine, Elwood."

They were back in downtown Chicago soon, the Bluesmobile rumbling slowly down State Street past the usual lineup of hookers, pimps and street people hanging out in front of the all-night movie theaters. Then, as they moved deeper into the seamy section, they passed beneath the elevated railway tracks and down a long, narrow road lined with freight bays and old warehouses—tired buildings which had never been beautiful and now were made even uglier by the inevitable bars and gratings thrown up across entrances and windows. Twisting down one side street and up another, Elwood brought the Bluesmobile to a halt almost directly under the El, threw the car into reverse and trained the lights on a small garage with a modern steel door. A plaque bolted to the door read: CTA E-TRAIN POWER TRANSFORMER—HIGH VOLTAGE—DANGER.

Getting out as he pulled a ring of keys from his pocket, Elwood unlocked a heavy brass padlock on the door and flipped the latch. As the door came open, Jake noticed that it led not only to the interior of the garage, but to a seven-foot-wide blind crevice between the garage and the adjoining building.

Returning to the car, Elwood smiled. "Batman had the Batcave," he said with a wink. "This is the Bluescave. Get out for a minute, will you?"

Jake hopped out and Elwood eased the car into the crevice, the slightly wider back bumper scraping both sides of the opening. On the driver's side of the car, the wall was absolutely straight, but on the right, just above door level, the line of cinder blocks fell away approximately a foot. After turning off the motor and lights, Elwood slid over to the passenger's side, crawled out the window and onto the roof of the Bluesmobile, then slid back to the ground. A few seconds later the steel door was locked once again.

"It's not exactly convenient," Elwood said, "but you sure can't beat the rental fee."

They walked under the El tracks toward the Bond Hotel,

a weathered old building crammed next to the railway in the manner of a drunk leaning against a doorway. A garish neon sign, on the verge of blinking its last, gave the name of the hotel along with the rather pathetic invitation, TRANSIENTS WELCOME. Even at a considerable distance it was possible to see that the front door was covered with a thick wire mesh, although one might have wondered what was inside that was worth stealing. The buildings on both sides of the hotel were boarded up with thick plywood, on which was printed: PROPERTY OF CHICAGO HOUSING AUTHORITY. NO TRESPASSING.

"Nice neighborhood," Jake said.

"But the people are friendly," Elwood replied.

The words were barely out of his mouth when suddenly the sound of machine-gun fire shattered the comparative quiet of the evening. Elwood felt the rush of wind past his head and just to his rear, exactly where Jake was, then heard the splintering of wood even as he saw sparks and dust fly from the front of the abandoned building. The burst continued for a few seconds, sending a shower of debris raining onto Elwood's hat and covering his glasses with soot and concrete powder. By the time he ducked, the gunfire had stopped and been replaced by the sound of a car roaring away.

Jake was lying facedown on the sidewalk. Elwood rushed to him just as his brother rolled over.

"Are you all right?" Elwood asked.

"Yeah. Slipped on some dogshit just a second before that car backfired. Dammit."

"What do you mean, dammit?" Elwood said. "That wasn't a car backfiring. That dogshit probably saved your life."

He pointed to the neat circle of bullet holes decorating the part of the building where Jake's body might have been, had he not slipped to the sidewalk.

Jake shrugged. "You were saying the neighbors were pretty friendly."

"Yeah. I don't know how to explain that, man. It was a machine gun, too. World War Two. Thirty caliber. They're pretty rare in this neighborhood. The folks here are down-to-earth. Shivs and cheap Italian specials, you know. Nothing fancy."

Jake finished cleaning the bottom of his shoe against the curb. "Okay, let's go," he said.

The interior of the Bond Hotel perfectly augmented the outside, consisting of a floor and walls made up of black and white mosaic tiles, badly chipped and stained with urine. Two bare radiators and three ancient armchairs were the sole contents of the foyer, not counting a pair of square pillars. Against the far wall was a floor-to-ceiling cage of inch-thick Plexiglas armor with a small porthole in the center. Inside the transparent cage, an old man sat watching wrestling on television.

"Hey, Lloyd," Elwood said. "Anybody call me on the phone?"

The old man shook his head. "No calls," he said, his voice raw and hoarse. "Some guy left his card, though. A cop. Said he'd be back."

He slipped a card through the hole in the armor. Elwood took it, passed it to Jake.

It read: ILLINOIS STATE DEPT OF CORRECTIONS—BURTON MERCER, OFFICER—PH (514) 232-4777.

Jake moaned.

"Something the matter?" Lloyd asked, turning his attention from the television, real-life misery apparently interesting him more than the wrestling variety.

"This here is my brother Jake," Elwood explained. "He just got out of the joint and he'll be staying with me for a few weeks. I guess he didn't expect the cops to try getting in touch with him so soon."

Jake nodded and sighed. "Nice to meet you, Lloyd," he said, extending four fingers through the small opening for the old man to shake.

THE BLUES BROTHERS

"Glad to have you, son. This may not look like much, but it's a nice quiet place."

The words were barely out of his mouth when an El train thundered by, sending a fine spray of plaster down from the ceiling.

"Except for that, of course," Lloyd amended.

The three of them became aware of another's presence at the same time, their eyes turning toward a tall, wide, square-looking man in his fifties with close-cropped gray hair, wearing a light brown polyester leisure suit. As the man drew near, he reached into his pocket and pulled out a badge case containing a Department of Corrections shield.

"I'm looking for Jake Blues," he said.

"Here," Jake said, holding up his hand.

"I'm Burton Mercer, of the Department of Corrections. It's Saturday night, you know. You're supposed to be at Viking House."

"Viking House?" Jake muttered. "What happens there? It sounds like a place where they push Swedish furniture."

"The conditions of your parole state that you have to spend weekends—that's Friday, Saturday and Sunday nights—at a halfway house," Mercer explained. "That's Viking House. It also means inside at ten o'clock, which means you're in violation of parole right now."

"So?"

"So you can go back to prison tonight."

Jake blinked. "Oh, come on, man," he said. "This is my first night out."

"But it's a weekend, man," Mercer said, his mannerisms and speech lightly satirizing Jake's. "It's Saturday night. You violated parole, so let's go."

Jake wasn't sure whether he was serious or not, but decided to take no chances. "Aw, gimme a break, will you?" he pleaded. "It's my first night out. I forgot about this weekend thing. I came to see my brother. It's been three years."

"We even went to church," Elwood added. "That's what helped make us late."

"I swear I'll check into the halfway house tomorrow," Jake said. "Just let me stay with my long-lost brother tonight—okay?"

"Jake, for a big man, you beg pretty good," Mercer smiled. "Okay. Since it's your first night out, I'll be a softy. You just make sure you call me Monday, because after this I'm not giving you any slack."

"I understand," Jake said. "House of Danish tomorrow, and you first thing Monday."

"Viking House," Mercer corrected, taking a card from his wallet with the establishment's address and handing it to Jake. He smiled quickly, nodded, turned and left.

"Close call," Jake said, crumpling the card and tossing it into a corner.

They lurched up three flights to Elwood's room and got inside just as another El train ripped past, causing the mirror to shimmer weirdly in the garish light of the naked bulb swinging from the ceiling. Outside one window was a track-level view of the El; outside another was a huge yellow Illinois highway sign reading: NO PASSING THIS LANE. Only if one stood against the windows and looked directly upward was it possible to see real sky.

"Well, it ain't much, but it's home," Elwood said.

Jake sat on the edge of the only bed, looking very depressed. "How often does the train go by?" he asked.

"So often you don't even notice it after a while," Elwood replied.

Jake leaned back against the pillow, causing several aerosol spray cans to roll out from under the bed.

"What's that?" he asked.

"Just some junk I been stealing from work."

"Maybe I should just let them take me back to prison," Jake said suddenly.

"What's the matter? Why do you say that?"

"I'm depressed."

"Why? It's a great day. You got out of prison. You're free. It's the start of a new life."

"A real great life. One day out of the joint, and already I've been chased by the cops, fired at by a machine-gunner, rousted by a parole officer, and sentenced to life imprisonment in the House of Danish."

"But you saw the Light, too," Elwood added, trying to pump some life into his brother's spirits. "And tomorrow we'll start looking for the guys in the band. That'll make you feel better."

"It makes me feel worse," Jake murmured. "That screw said I have to be in a halfway house weekends. But if we get the band together, I'll be working weekends. On the road. It'll be my job. That's the way I'll be able to rehabilitate myself, not by going in some halfway house. But they'll expect me to take some day job. I can't hack that. So what am I gonna do?"

"We'll work something out," Elwood promised.

"And you," Jake sighed, stretching out his feet and folding his hands across his stomach. "What are you gonna do, Mr. Leadfoot? Mr. Hot-rodder? Mr. Motorhead? Those cops took your driver's license away. They got your name, your address..."

"No, they didn't get my address," Elwood replied with a grin. "I falsified my renewal."

"Mmmm," Jake mumbled.

"I put down 8383 North Clark," Elwood continued. Then, when Jake did not respond, he said, "Get it—8383 North Clark. That's Wrigley Field."

But Jake did not appreciate his brother's cleverness. Already snoring loudly, he was fast asleep.

chapter three

Sunday morning they were in the Bluesmobile and on the road early, more than an hour before noon, the night's rest having strengthened their determination to have the band operable before the tax assessor's deadline. After a quick stop at the local greasy spoon, where Jake downed a double order of pancakes while Elwood ate his usual white toast, they cruised along Wacker for several minutes, collecting their thoughts and belching loudly at passersby.

Finally Jake got down to business. "Okay," he said, "where's all these leads you have on the boys?"

"In there," Elwood said, pointing to the glove compartment.

Jake punched the button, immediately activating a torrent from the orifice—beer cans, gasoline receipts, scraps of paper, wire, matchbooks, a coat hanger, damaged cassettes spilling entrails of mutilated tape, and bits of unidentifiable metal. Some of the debris dropped to the floor; most landed in Jake's lap.

"Look for a torn-up Marlboro package," Elwood said.

With a disgusted look, Jake sorted through the mess until he finally located a red and white pack, the seams of which had been flattened and torn in order to make writing easier. It was covered with crude scrawlings that looked like a foreign language.

"What is this shit?" Jake asked.

"That's it," Elwood nodded. "It's the last known addresses and phone contacts of the band."

As they slowly cruised along Maxwell Street, gently

parting hordes of flea-market customers, Elwood leaned across to get a better look at the package.

"Nobody can read that shit," Jake challenged.

Elwood cleared his throat, then read with authority: "Steve 'The Colonel' Cropper. Last known address, the Lucky State Pool Room, 2990 South Indiana..." He paused to make a left turn, then returned his attention to the package. "Willie Hall, apartment number 282, block 19E, Section Q, Southway Projects... Bones Malone and Blue Lou Marini, Taranto Boarding House, 3636 Trieste, Cicero..."

"Okay, let's check that one out first," Jake said. "Maybe we can get two at once."

A quarter-hour later, they pulled onto a quiet old residential street populated by families in their Sunday church clothes: teenage boys in three-piece suits, looking proud of themselves but vaguely uncomfortable; children skipping; older couples walking along the tree-shaded sidewalks. Rumbling to a halt in front of a pink triplex dating from the late 1960s, Jake and Elwood strode briskly up the front walk.

"Let me ask the questions," Elwood said in a staccato tone. "I'm better at getting the facts."

He rapped on the door, an aluminum storm door graced with painted bullrushes. After a few seconds, a dark-haired woman in her late fifties opened the inner door.

"Mrs. Taranto?" Elwood said.

"Tarantino," the woman corrected.

"Sorry, ma'am. My name's Elwood Blues and this is my partner, Jake Blues. May we come in, please?"

The woman stood aside. "Yes, of course," she said.

They walked into the cool foyer, and looked around briefly. Then Elwood continued, still in his clipped detective manner, "Sorry to bother you, Mrs. Tarantula..."

"Tarantino."

"Tarantino, but we'd like to know if you have a Thomas

Malone or Lou Marini living here."

"No," she replied. "They moved out a long time ago. I don't take any more boarders. Not for a long time."

"Did they leave a forwarding address or telephone number?"

"No."

"How about their personal habits? Did they live quietly?"

"Well, they were nice boys, but they did make a lot of racket, especially at night. They didn't tell me where they were going, I guess, because they owed me a week's rent."

"Just like those two," Elwood said.

"Maybe if you find them, you can get my money for me," the woman said. "You are police officers, aren't you?"

"No, ma'am," Jake said. "We're musicians."

Their next stop was South Indiana Street, a montage of grimy storefronts.

"Hold it," Jake said. "That's the place."

They parked the car and went into the Lucky State Pool Room, a shadowy room composed of ten brightly illuminated rectangular islands of green, around which moved seemingly headless figures whose faces appeared only when they bent low to make their shots. For a minute, the two brothers merely stood and studied bodies and faces, hoping against hope that the pool shark-guitarist named Steve Cropper would be among the players. Before they arrived at a decision, a wide black man stepped out of the gloom toward them.

"Sorry," he said in a tone not exactly dripping with sorrow. "No tables for three days. We got a worldwide championship tournament going on."

"Oh yeah?" said Elwood, with a Sergeant Friday smile. "Who's playing?"

"We got New York Ray and New York Ray up against each other for a one-hundred-snooker game trial tonight, and the winner will play thirty games of American pool tomorrow with Wisconsin Slim and Yellow Charlie."

"We're looking for Tennessee Steve the preacher," Jake said.

"The Colonel, you mean," said the proprietor.

"That's what some call him," Elwood said.

"The Memphis Moneymaker, too. Yeah, Colonel Steve's bad news around here. Some people think he's a witch. Either that or a cheating man."

"And what do you think?"

"I think people get hurt by the Colonel because he plays a better game of pool. I think the man is just very skilled at billiards, that's my opinion."

"Yessir. When did he last come in?" Jake asked.

"Last year, once."

"Did he ever leave a phone number or an address where he could be reached?"

"Fat chance."

"No way you can think of that we might be able to get in touch with him?"

"I hear he left the state."

"No idea where he headed?"

"Nope. What did he do?"

"Nothing. We're just looking for him so we can talk to him."

"Sure, I'll bet. You guys are cops, ain't you?"

"No sir," Jake said solemnly. "We're musicians."

On the road once again a few minutes later, they played back their day's work so far and were less than delighted.

"Three up and three down," Jake sighed. "At this rate they'll be running up a Nazi flag over St. Helen's any day now." He slammed his fist against the dashboard, causing the nonfunctioning cigarette lighter to fall on the floor and rattle under the seat. "Damn," he said.

"Take it easy," Elwood said evenly. "Nobody said this job was going to be easy."

"Yeah, but we're getting nowhere," Jake fumed. "Tell me we ain't going nowhere."

"That depends," Elwood replied. "Sometimes if you go nowhere often enough, you end up somewhere."

Jake sighed, exhausted already, but he could not keep hope from bubbling to the surface as his brother nosed the Bluesmobile onto the freeway. Victoria Spivey and Lonnie Johnson teamed on "Let's Ride Tonight," filling the car with cool sounds; Elwood drove with determination, passing trucks on the right, occasionally adding a burst of speed that carried them across three or four lanes of traffic. Soon it was difficult not to feel that theirs was, after all, a mission for God. Surely, in His wisdom and mercy, He would protect them from despair, physical danger and, perhaps most miraculous of all, arrest for moving traffic violations.

It was only late afternoon, but the attractive blonde decided it might be best to get herself into position before the lack of light made footing precarious. Locking her car, she picked her way across the street in front of the Bond Hotel, carefully avoiding the larger glass fragments littering the concrete from curb to center line. As the El train thundered overhead, she instinctively ducked and looked up, but no missiles appeared. Taking it as a good sign, she smiled tightly and walked briskly in the direction of the row of condemned houses in the triangle facing Lake and Wacker. Under her arm was a large briefcase, not the sort of thing that would attract attention, although a single woman walking by herself might bring out the creeps.

Pausing on the northwest corner to glance around, she flicked a wanton curl off her eyelid with a toss of her head. Let them try something, she thought, just let them try. Tucked up against her left armpit, the shoulder holster, with its .380 Beretta, gave her a genuinely warm feeling of comfort. Recalling the look on the face of the overweight clown who had accosted her last week, only to find himself staring into the muzzle of her quickly drawn weapon, she almost wanted to see another lecher appear from around the corner of a building.

She quickly dismissed such fantasies, however, realizing that an encounter of that sort might frustrate her mission. She had already met with failure once, and though it was largely a result of bad luck rather than poor planning or execution—she smiled ironically at the word—on her part, she was distinctly unhappy at the need to repeat the whole business.

On the other hand, there was a certain bizarre and decidedly mordant pleasure in setting up her task, seeing the pieces fall into place, feeling the tension grow as the moment of expectation neared. Even now, she experienced an almost sexual joy as the plywood barrier to the back door of the house gave way to the pressure of the crowbar she had removed from her briefcase. With barely a squeak of resistance, the section of rotting wood fell away a good six inches, more than enough for her to reach inside and use the weight of her upper body to force an even larger opening.

After giving her eyes a minute to adjust themselves to the darkness of the boarded-up house, she stepped inside and pulled the barrier closed. She then picked her way through the debris to the stairs. Being careful to keep to the wall side of the steps, where she was less likely to fall through, she climbed up two flights to what had once been the back bedroom. The floor was littered with old newspapers, rags, empty beer cans, several spent .30-caliber cartridges, ripped-up linoleum and assorted mounds of excrement, both human and animal. Treading softly, the woman walked to the window and looked out.

It was exactly as she had hoped. Immediately below were the tracks of the elevated railway, to the right and below was a section of freeway, and directly opposite was a double window looking into the apartment occupied by Elwood and Jake Blues. It was empty now, but the woman could make out the cot to the far right and the stove to the left. The double window was covered only with the remains of a cheap curtain, so torn and rotten that it provided next to no privacy.

Opening the briefcase, the woman replaced the crowbar and withdrew three sections of olive-drab pipe, each about three inches in diameter and eighteen inches long. Deftly, she screwed the sections together so that, together with a hand grip, they formed an obsolete but decidedly lethal World War Two–style bazooka. Bracing it against the window frame, the young woman sighted into the Blues Brothers' apartment, estimating the range at no more than a hundred yards. For the exploding power of the projectile in her briefcase, that was point-blank distance, the type of situation that eliminated the necessity for a direct hit. She smiled, recalling what had happened to the target earlier at the sanitary landfill. Then, leaning the bazooka against the wall, she looked for a reasonably sanitary place to sit while awaiting the arrival of her prey.

After a minute of careful study, she finally decided to stand.

"Willie 'Too Big' Hall," Jake said, holding the ruptured Marlboro package at an angle so as to capture the last bits of sunlight. "Apartment Number 282, Block 19E, Southway Projects."

"Block 19E," Elwood repeated, cutting quickly over to the left lane. "That sounds like prison."

"It *is* prison. It's the ghetto."

"Not a public housing project?"

"Okay, so it's a government-sponsored ghetto." Jake shrugged. "We'll be lucky if we get out of there alive. Do you think it's worth it?"

"Just because this is a mission for God doesn't mean every address has to be in Palm Beach," Elwood said sagely. "Anyway, that ought to be a good one. Willie gave me that address himself. I met him in Ray's Pawn Shop just a couple months ago."

"Yeah, and what was our little drummer boy up to?"

"He pawned his cymbals to buy a pump-action shotgun," Elwood replied matter-of-factly.

"Goddamn," Jake sighed. "If Willie needs a shotgun..."

"Jesus saves," Elwood said. "Or at least deflects."

It was nearly dark by the time the Bluesmobile passed through the old ghetto, marked by large, once-middle-class homes on spacious lots; through the intermediate ghetto, marked by blocks of two-story projects, each with a tiny plot of what used to be grass but was now dirt; and into the new, government-sponsored ghetto, marked by vast, forbidding high-rise apartments with no yards other than concrete-and-anchor-fence aerial walkways. Between the huge monoliths was mostly macadam roadway and pebble gardens, although here and there a twisted stump showed where a tree had tried to survive and failed. Aside from the gray of the buildings, the prevailing color of the area was green, a sickly glow emanating from vapor lights placed so high they were out of stone-throwing distance.

"Here it is," Jake said, not bothering to fight the depression he felt at the sight. "Southway Projects."

The project's entrance was through a pair of graffiti-marked concrete blocks, to each of which was affixed what remained of two lines of large metal letters. On the right, the sign read:

S TH Y BL C HO   ING AS ISTAN PROJ S
 U SD T F HEA   D CA ION AND ELF   E

The left-hand sign read:

SO HWAY P BLI H USIN SSIS ANC RO ECTS
S DEP OF H ALTH   EDUC   ND ELFARE

Elwood whistled softly. "You must be pretty good at puzzles, Jake, to have figured that out so fast."

"It was just a case of putting the two together and having them spell mother," Jake said modestly.

As they edged into the project, a volley of stones, sticks, soda bottles and beer cans bounced off the hood and windshield. The throwers were not visible.

"Whew," Elwood said, wincing, "this is gonna be tougher than I thought. I wonder where's a safe place to park the car?"

"I don't know," Jake said, recoiling from a shower of pellets striking the side window. "How far is Salt Lake City?"

Getting up speed, Elwood was able to free them of the invisible attackers, but any sense of relief was tempered by their striking regular speed bumps at fifty. Finally, spotting a narrow roadway leading to a series of one-story, bunkerlike row houses, Elwood slowed to a respectable speed, and even smiled as he caught sight of a spotlight bolted above one building's main entrance.

"There's a heat station," he said. "We'll leave the car here."

Pulling in next to an abused-looking four-wheel-drive GMC Blazer and several plain vehicles marked HOUSING POLICE, Elwood and Jake got out, locked the Bluesmobile and walked up to the spotlit building, on the front of which was the Chicago City Police emblem and the legend:

S THWA   HO SI G   POLI E

"They must have taken a long lunch hour one day," Elwood said, noting the missing letters.

Inside, they located a surly matron and two officers—both glancing nervously out the window—who answered their query concerning Block 19E by showing them to a large wall map, bolted to the wall and covered by Plexiglas. "Please hurry up, though," the woman said. "It's past the time when we're supposed to be here."

"Darker than hell out there now," one of the officers said. "I'd better call my wife."

"Apartment block 19E appears to be here in Grid 30," Elwood said, locating the spot with his finger. "Looks to be about a half-mile from here."

They exchanged glances, looked at the three housing officials, all of whom quickly became preoccupied with something else.

"Let's go," Jake said.

Outside in the gathering gloom, they stood for one long moment before plunging in the direction of Block 19E. "Maybe we can do without a drummer," Elwood said.

"It would be nice if we could," Jake replied. Then, straightening his shoulders, he said, "This is a mission for God, remember. Into the valley of the shadows . . ."

"Yeah, man," Elwood sighed.

They were barely a rock's throw from the housing police office when the sounds began, a high-pitched chatter of obscene abuse pouring out of the darkness from a dozen mocking silhouettes. Like wolves tracking a wounded moose, the forms followed, most at a respectful distance, although occasionally one or two would dash across the path of the two men in order to hold up a finger or yell an incestuous remark. Jake and Elwood were gratified to note that their tormentors seemed to be pre-adolescents.

"They look pretty young to me," Elwood said, attempting to bolster his and Jake's confidence.

"They're probably the oldest ones here," Jake muttered. "The rest have been killed off already."

As the gang continued to grow, a disturbing thought crossed Jake's mind. "Are we cops or musicians?" he asked, looking at Elwood apprehensively.

"Let's hope it doesn't come up," Elwood replied.

A minute later, they were relieved to see the large sign reading 19E on the building directly ahead of them. Jake shortened his stride, took out a cigarette and casually lit it. The sudden change of attitude seemed to disconcert the gang leaders, who stopped in their tracks, regarding the two whites now with more suspicion than scorn. Jake looked the tallest of them straight in the eye and said, "Shouldn't you guys be inside doing your homework?"

The young blacks exchanged surprised looks until one of them, unable to control his sense of the ridiculous, suddenly snorted and began laughing. Soon the entire group joined in, screaming among themselves.

"Any of you guys know Willie 'Too Big' Hall?" Jake asked, deciding it was the right time to try getting the gang on his side.

"Never heard of him," one of them said.

"Good," Jake replied, flicking his cigarette away. "That means he lives in this building."

He walked up the steps and held the door for Elwood. The hallway was predictably grim-looking and might have contained the world's longest unbroken graffiti—a purple swirl from an aerosol paint can that ran the entire length of the building and disappeared around the corner. As they walked and looked for apartment 282, Jake tried to plan their strategy. "What do you think we should do if he's working for somebody else and making good money?" he asked.

Elwood frowned. "That's just what I was thinking about. I know one thing, man. We just can't go in there and say, 'Hey, Willie, we're getting the band back together. You want to play with us again?' That's too direct. He'll laugh in our faces if he knows we want him and we need him. You know him, he'll hold out forever. We gotta approach him in the right way."

"Here it is," Jake said, stopping in front of 282.

"Don't worry," Elwood said in response to Jake's unasked question. "We'll think of something once the conversation gets rolling."

He reached up to knock, then quickly withdrew his hand as the door suddenly opened and three lanky black men in broad Stetsons and sharp three-piece suits came out. Moving aside hastily, Jake and Elwood watched them move quickly down the hallway. Only the last man out of the apartment acknowledged their presence, with a slight curl of his upper lip. A teenaged black girl, obviously very stoned, appeared at the door, stared curiously at Jake and Elwood for a moment, then stood aside to let them come in.

Hearing music and drumming, the two men exchanged hopeful glances.

The apartment's decor was basically Chrome Modern, one entire wall covered with a display of fluorescent paintings on black velvet of naked black women and men in copulatory poses, several of them so complex they seemed almost like puzzles.

Another wall was nearly hidden behind a huge stack of precariously piled expensive stereo equipment, including an amplifier, preamp, tape deck, speakers, turntable, cassette deck, and noise suppressors. At the bottom of the heap rested a big color television with several clock radios on it. The effect was of a musical appliance shop whose inventory had been tossed on the sidewalk.

Against the wall directly opposite was a deep modular couch, a chrome-and-glass coffee table, and an oversized Naugahyde ottoman. The couch was occupied by a lean young black man and another stoned woman. The man, who was indeed Willie Hall, wore a set of expensive headphones connected to the tape console. Eyes closed and head moving rhythmically, Willie busily tapped out a beat on a rubber percussionist's practice pad with a set of aluminum drumsticks. He did not notice Jake and Elwood until the teenager who had let them in kicked him gently but firmly on the elbow.

It took a few seconds for Willie to place the faces, but once the recognition was made, he came alive. Taking off the headset, he leaped to his feet and offered the open palms of his hands to the boys. Jake and Elwood slapped them courteously.

"Well hey, what's happening?" Willie smiled. "You looking good, *both* of you."

The Blues Brothers nodded in tandem. Sensing that they wanted to discuss something with him, Willie turned to the woman slumped on the couch. "Hey, baby, take your sister to the bedroom and watch some TV, okay?" he said.

The woman rose slowly to her feet, rather like a cobra swaying to a fakir's flute, and, trailed by the younger woman, disappeared around the corner.

"So what's happening with you guys?" Willie asked as soon as they were alone. "It's great to see you. Jake, aren't you out early? I thought they gave you three to five or something like that—"

"Good behavior," Jake replied. "I guess I was inspired by all the nice letters and cards I got from my friends. The gifts were really nice, too, and so were the visits."

"Hey, man," Willie said, looking at Jake askance. "I can't handle hospitals and jails. You understand, man."

Jake was unrelenting. "I guess you're afraid to lick a stamp," he said, then put his hands on his hips and made a rapid visual survey of the apartment. "So this is what became of Willie 'Too Big' Hall," he said sardonically. "The great drummer, the backbeat of the Blues Brothers. This is the way he has chosen to spend his retiring days... with disco music, pot parties, pretty girls, the lucre of crime..." Then, twisting the knife even deeper, he picked up the drumsticks and examined them like infected limbs. "And what are these? *Metal* drumsticks? Why not *plastic*? And this," he added, turning his attention to the murals. "Sexy department store art? The great performer has turned into a spectator, a peeping tom who uses metal drumsticks?" Then, noticing some white powder on the arm of the couch: "And what's all this? Heroin?"

"Come on, man, you know that's not my thing," Willie protested, looking to Elwood for help but finding none.

"And what *is* your thing?" Jake shot back. "Man, it sure isn't the development of your talent as a player, Mr. Metal Drumsticks!"

"Lots of cats use aluminum drumsticks," Willie said, but there was a decidedly defensive tone to his voice.

Continuing to attack, Jake returned his attention to the powder. "And do 'lots of cats' push speed?" he demanded.

"That's not speed," Willie replied quickly. "I'm not into speed. And anyway, just because I worked for you once doesn't give you the right to enter my home and aggravate me like this. Look what I have to show after two years away from you . . . I got more money than you ever paid me, man. And I got power in my own right. I *run* this grid . . ."

"The kids outside never even heard of you," Elwood interrupted.

"Aw, shit, you know they never admit to anything," Willie said. "It's the law of the jungle. Anyway, I'm telling you, I run this grid and soon all the top people in the project will come to me because they know that I can get whatever they need. And what do you have to show for *your* last two years? The same suit you been wearing since the last time I saw you."

Jake didn't back down. "Yeah, yeah," he said. "Well, listen, Mr. Junior Crime Czar, you just go ahead and push your angel dust to high school kids—"

"That's not angel dust! I don't mess with that shit, man."

Jake continued as if he had not heard him. "You just go ahead and push your stuff, Mr. Junior Superfly. Go ahead, Mr. Pusher. Keep on wallowing in this filth and lucre with your pretty girls and pot parties. Keep hammering away with your tin drumsticks, and keep wearing your Stevie Wonder glasses and tank tops and keep listening to disco music and maybe your brain will rot out at the same time as your body." He looked at Willie with unfeigned disgust. "I guess the time is long gone," he added wearily.

"What time?" Willie asked timidly.

"The time when you were the nerve center, the pulse, the backbone, the guts of a great blues band—that's the time that's gone, Willie. I mean, you don't even have a drum kit. Maybe that's because you're not the hot raw talent you used to be. Hell, back then you could set a better beat with your elbows than most good drummers... Now, well..."

"Why not? Who says I can't?"

"Why not, Willie? Maybe because your brain and soul have been softened and eaten away by disco, pot parties and small-time crime—"

"Listen to who's talking about small-time crime!" Willie yelled in retaliation.

"Come on, Elwood," Jake said, gesturing toward the door. "Let's get out of here. It's kind of sad being around a has-been."

"Hey, don't you call me that, man," Willie rasped, clutching at Jake's sleeve. "I can still play. I still have my drums."

"Then where are they?"

Willie's eyes avoided Jake's stare. "At the moment, they're involved in a little exchange program I got going—"

"With Ray's pawn shop," Jake added scornfully. "The great big grid king has to pawn his drums!"

"Hey, I can get them back. I didn't do it for money. The guy wanted to try them out. I can get them back now. *Right now.*"

"Are you sure, Willie?" Jake asked, his tone softening. "Because if you can—"

"Yeah?"

"Aw, what's the use? I don't even know if you can play."

"Why? What's happening?" Willie demanded.

"There's a big, big gig coming up. A *recording* gig. Elwood and me, Matt, the Duck, Murph Dunne, Blue Lou..."

"No shit? The Duck? Blue Lou?" Willie's eyes were wide and alive with interest. "When did you see them guys?"

"Soon," Jake said, then quickly corrected himself. "I mean, we'll be seeing them again soon. I been out a month, setting it up, plus they all visited me in the joint, every day."

He paused, holding his eyes on Willie until the black looked away in shame.

"Anyway," he continued then, "we're all gonna do it this Friday night."

"Where?" Willie asked eagerly.

"I'm sorry, Willie," Jake said with a pained smile. "I can't give that information to anybody who's not a member of the band."

"Hey, come on, man," Willie moaned, pressing his hands against his forehead.

"Well, you know how it is," Jake said. "There's so many people out there who want to see us back again for the first time that we're having trouble keeping it quiet. I mean, who wants a riot when a couple hundred folks can't get in, right?" Without waiting for a comment from Willie, he continued, "Another thing is the competition. If too many jealous cats know where we're gonna be, they might take steps to stop us, dig? Because they know that once we're back, they're gonna start looking real bad."

"Who you got?" Willie challenged. "I don't think you got anybody."

"We got everybody but you, Willie."

"Bullshit. You got *no*body. If you had all those guys, you'd tell me where it was."

Jake shrugged. "Okay. It's at the Jovial Club in Calumet City. How's that?"

"That's one of the best places around," Willie muttered. "Are you sure you—"

Jake smiled, starting for the door. "Stop by and see us, Willie. The guys'll be glad to see you, especially if I don't tell them how you're screwing up high school kids."

"Wait a second," Willie said. "Who you got on drums?"

"Guy named Cheat O'Toole."

"Never heard of him."

"Probably because he's white."

Willie sneered. "Are you shitting me? A white cat?"

"Ain't you ever heard of equal opportunity, Willie?"

Willie stood in front of the door, one hand at his side balled into a fist, the other pointed directly at Jake's forehead. "Now you hold it right there, mister," he ordered. "You ain't putting no *white* drummer in *that* blues band! I can't see that. You always said I was the pulse, the backbone of the band . . . well, if you told the truth, you'd want me playing behind you. And if you were lying, you're dead!"

"Come on, Elwood," Jake said.

"Wait a second," his brother replied. "Maybe it would be nice if every member was there. Cheat's got promise, but he's not one of the original Blues Brothers . . ."

"That's right!" Willie exclaimed, nodding his head furiously. "The Jovial Club, Calumet City, this Friday night. I'll be there with my drum kit!"

"And aluminum sticks?" Jake asked derisively.

"No, sucker."

Jake shrugged. "Okay," he replied meekly. "I guess we can't keep you out."

Jake and Elwood nodded and left then, neither trusting himself to speak until they were outside the building. Then they broke into a barrage of self-congratulatory laughter that continued until they were better than halfway to their car. Then, as the darkness suddenly closed in around them, both became aware of their situation. "Damn," Elwood said, looking around the depressing man-made landscape of concrete blocks and eerie green lights. "We should have asked Willie to come with us."

"Well, it's too late now," Jake murmured "We're closer to the car than to him."

"If the car's still there, you mean."

As they neared the darkened Housing Police building, which they noticed was now protected by a full-length steel grating, they were able to see the Bluesmobile sitting by itself on the parking lot. Elwood sighed with relief. "Looks like those cops pulled out and left us all alone," he said, "but at least—"

He paused.

"Yeah," Jake said. "I see it, too."

The Bluesmobile now rested royally on four concrete blocks, its tires and rims neatly stripped away.

Jake looked around a full circle. He thought he saw some movement near the closest building, some heads ducking back accompanied by barely suppressed laughter. It figured, of course, that the thieves would want to catch the boys' reaction as icing on the cake.

"Don't worry about it," Elwood said, sensing Jake's anger. "They were old tires anyway. The cord was showing on two of them. It's a good thing they were stolen or I might not have gotten around to putting on better rubber."

"That's great to know," Jake muttered. "The cord was showing on two of them and you were hopping bridges."

"Yeah, I see what you mean," Elwood said. "But you can relax. We're covered."

He went to the trunk and unlocked it, revealing four good but deflated tires lying on the floor.

"You always carry extra tires around?" Jake asked.

"Ever since I had to walk home from Geneva one night. Anyway, you've been all safe and cozy for two years in prison. The city's changed a lot in that time. That's why if you want to keep rolling in this town, you've got to be ready."

He tossed the first of the tires out, and reached for the second.

"How do we blow them up?" Jake asked. "With a bicycle pump?"

Elwood shook his head, threw the other tires out, and rooted around in the trunk until he found a large metal can. "Here, this will fill them," he said, handing the can to Jake.

"What'll I do?"

"Just uncap the valve on the tire, fix that can on there, and the tire fills up."

Jake did as instructed. To his amazement, the soft tire grew to rock-hardness in less than thirty seconds.

"What is this shit?" Jake asked.

"I don't know. Air, I guess. I got lots of it. It's from the stuff I stole at work."

He already had the jack under the rear bumper. Jake started to roll the tire over. "Shit," he said suddenly, letting the tire fall to the ground. "I just thought of something else."

"Yeah, I know, but it's okay," Elwood said. "When they steal your tires, the bastards are never kind enough to leave the bolts behind. So I carry an extra set."

He located a large brown envelope in the trunk, rolled the tire onto the rim, and was soon busily screwing the bolts in place. Fifteen minutes later, the Bluesmobile was ready to move. "Now let's haul ass," Elwood said, "before they decide to charge us."

"For what?" Jake asked.

It was after ten o'clock, and she had just started to think they were going to stay out all night, when the distinctive rumble of the Bluesmobile brought a smile to the blonde's lips. She stretched her arms, arched her back, and jiggled her fingers in the style of an athlete warming up, conquering the nervous tension accompanying an important contest.

The clear and familiar sights of the afternoon had now blended together into nearly indistinguishable masses of dark gray and black, with here and there an outline of light, a flickering television, ribbons of headlights, and the inevitable stroboscopic effect of the El trains as they thundered by at regular intervals on the tracks below. But neither the lack of light nor sudden flashes of it in the evening distracted her from her target across the way. The double window of Elwood's apartment still beckoned, a black-on-black outline that the blonde could see even when she closed her eyes.

She sat on the windowsill, smiling as she spotted the two familiar figures walking slowly across the street toward the front of the Bond Hotel. Once or twice a word or phrase of conversation drifted up to her hiding place; otherwise the endless drone of night traffic was relieved only by the sound of feet crunching against broken glass. After Jake and Elwood disappeared around the corner of the building, the blonde followed their progress in her mind's eye, through the grungy lobby, slowly up the stairs to the door of the equally grungy room. With surprising accuracy she saw a sliver of light break across the wall of the room just as she imagined them unlocking the door. A moment later, the entire apartment was illuminated by the overhead bulb.

Jake and Elwood stepped inside, both obviously weary. Elwood threw himself across the cot, and put both hands over his eyes. Jake flopped in a chair opposite, and began looking through a pile of record albums.

It was, she decided, perfect. Hoisting the bazooka to her shoulder, she inserted the round of ammunition, attached the static line to it and peered through the sighting mechanism. As she did so, her right index finger moved deliberately toward the trigger, its slender gentleness belying the deadly mission it was readying itself to carry out.

Jake stood up and began to walk slowly toward the window and stove. Even better, she thought, tracking him smoothly, amazing herself at how little anxiety she felt at this moment.

In the apartment, Jake was experiencing second thoughts about getting himself something to eat. He was tired, and the only food Elwood had, besides plain white bread, was a can of soup. Ever since childhood, Jake had disliked soup; but when his stomach started rumbling again he decided to fill it with something. Taking the can of soup from the shelf above the stove, he looked around for a can opener as he reached out to turn the stove on.

Jake's hand was on the knob when he heard Elwood yell, "No!" At the same time, from the corner of his eye, he caught sight of a sudden movement to his left, as of his brother leaping off the cot in his direction.

"No!" he heard Elwood scream again.

But the moment refused to stay frozen. Slowly, as in a super-slow-motion film, Jake saw his hand turn the burner knob, and a split second later saw and felt the orange-and-blue flame leap from the burner toward his face.

In the back room of the boarded-up house, the blonde, her finger on the firing device of the bazooka, also saw the surge of flame from the stove. What had happened? Had the weapon she now held on her shoulder somehow delivered its projectile in total dreamlike silence? She was simultaneously mesmerized and shocked by the sequence and, in the manner of one who dreams of stepping off a high curb in the early stages of sleep, her entire body gave one mighty twitch. The left arm supporting the bazooka dropped even as the finger on the trigger activated the weapon. With a mighty *whoosh!* the round was fired. The blonde felt herself slammed backwards against the windowsill.

A moment later her vision cleared, and she was able to see the damage caused by the projectile's blast. Despite the late hour, a surprisingly large crowd milled about the first car of the elevated train. Smoke emanated from a large hole in its side. The Bond Hotel, meanwhile, still stood serene and undamaged.

"Shit!" the blonde hissed, looking about for her briefcase and another round of ammunition.

But from the chaos below, a single voice reached her ears.

"Up there!" someone yelled. "There! Up at that window!"

The blonde stopped in her tracks, the bazooka poised for reloading. Flame was pouring from the El car, people were being assisted from its torn side, and general confusion reigned. In the midst of that panic, however, she could make out a half-dozen figures staring in her direction, their arms pointing toward her or waving about, signaling to others. A couple of the figures moved along the edge of the El platform toward the window where she now crouched, until others indicated that the only way to reach the mysterious attacker was by going down the stairs and across the road to the boarded-up structure.

"Shit," the woman said again, noting that a small posse of men was now moving in that direction. If she was quick, she would have barely enough time to get away.

Throwing down the bazooka and grabbing her briefcase, she raced for the rotten stairs and safety.

In the hotel room, Jake heard the explosion and subsequent shouts from the crowd as he slowly removed his hands from his face. With a sigh of relief, he realized he could still see and seemed to have most of his eyebrows left.

Elwood was at his side. "Goddamn, I'm sorry, Jake," he said. "I should have warned you about that stove. It does that all the time. There really isn't much danger, but it scares the shit out of you if you're not expecting it."

"Yeah," Jake said softly. "You really oughta get that fixed, Elwood."

"I complained to the landlord once, but he just asked for the rent."

Both became aware of the fire and shouting on the El platform. "What the hell's going on?" Elwood said, looking out.

Jake shrugged.

"Looks like a fire of some kind," Elwood murmured. For a long moment he considered the possibility—a bizarre one, he had to admit—that there might be some connection between the minor conflagration in their apartment and the major one just fifty yards away. But try as he might, he could see no logical cause-and-effect relationship. With a little laugh, he turned to Jake, or where Jake had been standing just a few seconds before.

"You know what?" he began. "I was—"

Jake was not there. Elwood looked around quickly and made a rapid, futile movement toward the apartment's only bed. Too late. Jake was on it, eyes closed, light snoring sounds emanating from his contentedly quivering nostrils.

"Shit," Elwood muttered. For the second night in a row, he made preparations to sleep on the floor.

"Shit," said the blonde woman, regarding the scene from a niche of safety a block away. Hidden in the space between two buildings, she could see the smoke from the El station, the window at which she had so recently waited, and, infuriatingly, the serene double window of the Blues Brothers' apartment, as undisturbed by violence as when she had first glimpsed it earlier in the day.

chapter four

"Which reminds me," Elwood murmured, downing the last piece of white bread and licking his lips with satisfaction, "didn't you say something about checking in at that Viking House last night?"

It was just after eight o'clock on Monday morning, and Jake was still comatose. Having slept fitfully on the floor, Elwood had risen early, repaired the gas line of the stove for the dozenth time and, as soon as it was light, had taken a walk down to the elevated station, where cops were taking measurements and dusting for prints and questioning bystanders. He was bored, of course, which was probably why he cooperated with the officer who asked if he lived nearby. When Elwood gestured toward the apartment window, the officer became quite enthusiastic.

"That's perfect," he said.

"Well, it could be better," Elwood shrugged. "The toilet sucks. What I mean is, it leaks."

"I'm not talking about what's in the apartment," the officer said. "I mean the location. It's a perfect spot for you to have seen what happened last night."

"Oh, that," Elwood replied. Actually, he had seen nothing but a group of people milling about on the platform, but it seemed a shame to let the opportunity pass without giving the man some information. He was mentally formulating an account of how he had passed two hooded men carrying flamethrowers when the officer gestured toward the upper window of the condemned building across from the track.

"They said somebody up there fired something like a recoilless rifle or rocket launcher," he volunteered. "You didn't happen to see anything, did you?"

Elwood nodded sagely.

"Can you give me a description?"

Poor guy, Elwood thought. He seems so sincere. Surely it wouldn't hurt to give him a few crumbs to consider. "Black woman," he said after a moment of cogitation. "With red hair, but it may have been a fright wig."

The officer wrote it down. "Anything else?" he asked eagerly.

"Yes. She was wearing a Nazi armband."

"Nazi armband. Good. I mean, that's a description that should eliminate a lot of suspects right off the top. What's your name, sir?"

"Cheat O'Toole," Elwood replied without a moment's hesitation, calling on the all-purpose fictitious person he and Jake used.

"Is 'Cheat' a nickname?" the officer asked. "Or is it short for something?"

"Yessir," Elwood replied. "It's short for 'Cheater.'"

"Thank you. And if I need to talk to you again, you live in apartment—"

"Two-C," Elwood said, naming the floor below them. He turned and headed for the entrance to the hotel.

The conversation with the police officer recalled to mind the promise Jake had made about Viking House. As soon as he saw his brother's eyelids flicker, Elwood brought up the problem, but it only caused Jake to grunt and roll over against the wall. Finally, Elwood managed to shake him awake. "Listen, Jake," he said. "It's Monday, man."

"So fucking what?"

"So I got to go to work and I want to talk with you first."

Jake shook his head. "Work?"

"Yeah. My job, remember?"

"Dammit, your job is helping me find the rest of the band," Jake said angrily.

"Relax. I just gotta put in one more day."

"What for?"

"Clean out my locker. Steal some more stuff. And pick up my last paycheck. It looks like we're gonna need it."

"You should have done that last week before I got out."

"No," Elwood replied. "This is Monday. There's a special run of cans coming off the line. I want to be there. I *have* to be there. Believe me, I know what I'm doing."

Jake shrugged. "Okay. Take it easy."

"I'll meet you at the union hall at four-thirty," Elwood said, starting for the door. Then, turning back, he added, "And that's the last time you sleep in my bed."

"I should have stayed in prison," Jake muttered, pounding the greasy pillow, "for all the respect I get."

"That reminds me," Elwood said. "You promised that guy to check in at Viking House or give him a call, right?"

"Yeah, but I lost his name and phone number."

Elwood shook his head. "No, you didn't. You rolled it in a ball and threw it in a corner downstairs. Chances are it's still there."

"I don't have time to fart around with that screw," Jake said.

"He'll throw you back in the joint."

"No, he won't," Jake replied. "I been thinking about him. All he wants is somebody to scare the shit out of. If I act scared, he'll get his rocks off and I won't have to bother with all that crap."

"I wouldn't count on that."

"See you at the union hall," Jake said, rolling over and closing his eyes.

"That's right," Elwood couldn't resist saying. "We have to find some way of getting ourselves hired by the Jovial Club, don't we?"

"Piece of cake," Jake murmured.

Ten minutes later, Elwood and the Bluesmobile were winding their way along Lake Michigan on Highway 90, heading south toward the Illinois-Indiana state line. Traffic was heavy, a slowly moving parking lot of shimmering fumes and shortening tempers. Finally everything just ground to a complete standstill.

"Goddamn," Elwood seethed, craning his neck to find a way out. But even the shoulders were no help; they were the extra-narrow kind, barely wide enough for a pedestrian. While trapped in the dilemma, however, he suddenly spotted a sign he probably never would have seen at his normal rate of speed. It was on a Ramada Inn marquee, in letters that were large but did not particularly stand out. The sign read:

WELCOME EXTERMINATORS

DANCING—MURPH AND THE MAGICTONES

"Murph Dunne," Elwood said. "Yeah, it's got to be them."

Murphy "Murph" Dunne and Tom "Bones" Malone had been members of the Blues Brothers Band since its inception, both being thoroughly professional musicians who knew no other trade. Moreover, they were Chicago boys who had no illusions about the need to head east or west in order to succeed. They, among all of the original band members, would be most likely to settle down in some local niche, Elwood reasoned. Of course, Murph was a common name. The Magictones could be the creation of someone else. But if that were the case, why had Elwood been stopped at this particular spot on what was normally a racing strip?

"Goddamn," Elwood whispered. "I'm starting to believe this 'mission for God' shit."

Having noted the location of the Ramada Inn, Elwood

was pleased to see that traffic started moving quickly again, an act so coincidental it could only have been divinely inspired. A sense of well-being washed over him as he pushed the Bluesmobile into the left-hand lane and opened her up to a modest eighty. At such a relaxing speed and in such a good frame of mind, he found himself noticing scenery he normally missed: the sun in the east, silhouetting the smokestacks, coal towers and factories; the bright flames belching from foundry stacks; a horizon coated with red, purple and yellow smog. The ride passed quickly, Elwood leaning back and closing his eyes as Jimmy Rushing finished singing "Good Rockin' Tonight."

The Propellants Packaging Company had been constructed less than five years ago, but, like many factories of its type, it seemed to date from a much older era. Painted battleship gray, its cinder-block exterior was relieved only by small sections of dark windows heavily meshed with wire. Behind the dumpy structure was a large employee parking lot made of lumpy, thin-skinned tar, but Elwood invariably avoided the long walk by taking one of the executive spaces directly in front of the building's main office.

This morning all of the spaces were taken, a situation Elwood had been faced with before. He solved it as he had solved it in the past—by pulling onto the grass and screwing on a set of doctor's license plates he carried for such emergencies. Having to go to so much trouble was a pain in the ass, he had to admit, but it beat walking.

The plates in place, Elwood took a large black briefcase from the car and entered the plant, punching in along with several other latecomers. Strolling to his locker, he removed his jacket, put on a long white lab coat, took off his hat long enough to strap a filter mask over his nose and mouth, put the hat back on again, then entered the assembly room, where several dozen employees in similar masks and gowns were inspecting aerosol spray cans that were moving along an endless maze of narrow conveyor belts.

As Elwood walked down the main aisleway between the rows of cans, a loud buzzer sounded and the belts started rolling.

"How they doing this morning?" Elwood asked a woman near the end of the line.

"Pretty good," she shouted back, over the sound of the gears and motors.

Too bad, Elwood thought. He needed a good run of dented cans or poorly printed labels—anything to give him a couple of cases worth of empties. For the better part of an hour, he strolled back and forth along the line, noting unhappily that there were no major malfunctions. Several times he paused to look longingly at the propane cannister, with its gauge indicating FULL. That was the prize he wanted to get at, preferably during lunch hour or a break, when most of the other employees would be outside. If the operation continued so faultlessly, however, he might have to take matters in his own hands.

Rarely had the Traffic Division and the Department of Parole and Probation worked so well together. In fact, there was no single instance in Chicago police history when either division had helped the other at all. But now, in one stroke, that had all changed. Burton Mercer was proud of the part he had played, as was Detective Sergeant Wade Fiscus, but for the record, both were willing to describe it as a team effort.

"Amazing," Fiscus said. "We've been looking for this Elwood Blues scofflaw for years. He has more than two hundred tickets now, but we've never been able to track him down."

"And exactly how did you and Mercer here get together?" Fiscus' supervisor asked.

"Well," Fiscus replied with a smile, "when the two arresting officers—or the two officers who *tried* to make the arrest—came back with the address of Elwood Blues as Wrigley Field, that was something I more or less expected. It looked like just another of his bum steers. Then the computer spit out the conviction record of his brother, Jake, who was released from Stateville on Saturday. Turns out he went straight to the Bond Hotel to live with Elwood."

"The thing is," Mercer added, not wanting to lose his share of credit to a mere computer, "Parole and Probation isn't required to enter information about a person coming *out* of prison. Under normal circumstances, Jake Blues's destination after release would never have gotten into the computer, except that I thought someone might have use for it. It was a long shot."

"But it paid off," Fiscus said. "Now we know where to find Elwood Blues, and you can bet we'll be waiting for him."

"We'll also be waiting for Jake," Mercer said. "He's violated some of his parole terms already."

The supervisor smiled. "Good. Play it smart, though. Take both of them together if you can."

"You bet," Fiscus said.

He could hardly wait.

At last the waiting was over. By adjusting a nozzle here and a dial there, Elwood had managed to throw the entire hair spray operation into disarray. The line was still and cans littered the aisleways as Elwood and Max Wendish, another older inspector and troubleshooter, surveyed the damage.

"What's the problem?" Elwood asked, knowing perfectly well which set of valves was out of alignment.

"Same old thing," Max muttered, attacking the network of hoses, lines and tanks with a wrench, resetting a dial. "Too much hair spray compound, not enough propane. This system is bad. Ever since they spent a million bucks to switch from fluorocarbon charging, they can't get it right."

Elwood nodded. "That's what I thought, too."

Max hit a valve. "There. That should be good for a couple thousand hits, anyway!" he said, sliding out from beneath the belt.

The first setting wasn't quite right, Elwood noted happily, the word NO appearing on the pressure-gauge panel as soon as the line started again. More cans were swept off the belt and Max made another adjustment. "That oughta do it," he said.

The operation was better from that point on, but Elwood was pleased to see that he had more than enough spray cans to fill the trunk of his car. First, under the pretext of cleaning up, he loaded the rejected cans into cardboard boxes and moved them to one side. When the rest of the employees went to lunch, he slid the boxes over toward the door of the charging room, waited until no one was in sight, then dragged the boxes over next to the propane canister. Keeping a careful lookout for supervisors, he loaded up the cans until the needle on the gauge was literally bouncing off the mark reading EXCESSIVE PRESSURE. When he was finished, he tested one of the cans by holding a cigarette lighter into the spray as he pushed the nozzle. A jet of flame roughly equivalent to that of a flamethrower shot out of the can, striking the opposite wall and making a large black spot.

"Perfect." Elwood smiled.

The final step was loading the cans into his car, which he accomplished with the greatest of ease. Instead of trying to sneak out with the boxes, he enlisted the help of a fellow worker. "Hey, Wally," he said. "Could you help me carry some of these rejected cans out to my car?"

"Sure," the young black man said.

Together they carried the stuff out to the Bluesmobile, looking as if they had every right in the world to do so. No one even questioned them when they passed through the main lobby.

"Thanks a lot, Wally," Elwood said as they walked back toward the building. "If you'd like to have a few Molotov cocktails, I'll meet you after work, okay?"

"Molotov cocktails? You mean them cans?"

"Yeah. They're so full of propane they could blow up a battleship."

Wally smiled. "I didn't think you was stealin' dented cans for nothin'," he said.

"You never know when you're gonna have to blow up 'The Flying Fortress.'" Elwood laughed.

"Maybe I'll take a few," Wally said.

"Sure. Four o'clock."

Elwood made a pass by the company canteen, and bought a cheese sandwich from one of the vending machines. Sitting alone at one of the tables, he methodically removed the cheese, threw it away, and ate the white bread, being careful not to accidentally swallow any of the part made soggy with dressing.

Later, after a couple of routine hours on the assembly line, he decided to call it a day. Removing his mask and gown, he tossed them into a corner and strolled into the office of Jeff Sorrell, the manager. Sorrell, a bulky man with straight black hair continually falling over his eyes, looked up with a bit of a start, Elwood having surprised him playing pocket pool at his desk.

"Yeah?" he asked sharply.

"I have to quit," Elwood said.

"Why is that?"

Truthfully, Elwood had not given much thought to having to cite a reason for leaving, so he said the first thing that came into his head. "I'm going to become a priest," he intoned.

Sorrell smiled proudly. "You really feel strongly about it, huh?" he asked. "Well, I'm proud of you, Blues. I'll call payroll and have them send your check right up. Won't take but a minute."

"Thank you, sir."

"Good luck, Elwood."

"Thank you, sir, and God bless you."

"Goddamnit," hissed the blonde, slamming her fist against the genuine leather upholstery of the Jaguar as the familiar figure of Jake Blues strolled out of the Bond Hotel. For the better part of five hours, the two men in the plain car across the street from the fleabag had remained seated, their eyes glued to the hotel entrance. Now there was no doubt they were staking out the place waiting to nail either Jake or Elwood or both.

Or, she thought with a twinge of panic, were they on the lookout for the mad bazookist?

In either case, their presence spelled bad news. Not until they left would she be able to make another attempt at fulfilling her greatest earthly desire, and daylight was fading fast. All day their presence had frustrated her. How long, she wondered, did they intend to hang around?

"Goddamnit," muttered Burton Mercer, shaking his head wearily as Jake Blues came out of the building alone. "Where's the other one? I thought they were both in there."

"Maybe they were," Fiscus said. "Maybe Elwood Blues the scofflaw is still up there."

"What do you think we should do?" Mercer asked. "I'd sure hate to pick up one and scare off the other."

"Yeah."

"Maybe we should just follow him."

"I don't know," Fiscus replied. "Sooner or later, they'll both end up here. But if we tail one of them and he gets suspicious, we could blow the whole operation."

"There's something to what you say, Wade."

"Thanks, Burt."

"Maybe we'd better just stay put."

"Right. When in doubt, do nothing."

"It's great working with a real pro for a change."

"Goddamnit," Jake Blues sighed as he stepped outside, for the first time realizing that the gray atmosphere he had noticed from his room was in reality a light mist. It was ten blocks to the American Federation of Musicians union hall, and he was late. There was nothing for him to do but walk. Pulling the collar of his suit coat higher around his neck, he cursed silently as he began the long trek.

Behind him, the plain car with two men did not move. After a minute, the Jaguar parked two blocks from the Bond Hotel slowly moved away from the curb.

Constructed in 1942 during the Petrillo era, the American Federation of Musicians (Sub-Local 200) union hall was known to trivia addicts and a small coterie of architecture fanatics as one of the first truly round buildings ever built in Chicago. No one could say exactly why the structure was shaped the way it was—although a few hypothesized that musicians even then objected to squareness in any form. As innovative as the building was, however, even those who worshipped difference for difference' sake agreed that Sub-Local 200 was truly ugly, a monstrosity that set a standard unmatched until the Sam Rayburn Office Building came along more than two decades later. Constructed of beige brick punctuated by art deco glass panels, with a low rounded roof, it resembled nothing so much as a mud-streaked turtle. Inside, the union hall was less offensive, consisting of a large circular hall around which branched a series of hallways, offices and wickets. At the moment, this being a Monday afternoon, the hall was crowded with musicians carrying cases of every size and shape. Some walked briskly, as if knowing exactly where they were heading; others wandered; still others chatted with acquaintances; a few even stood still, listening to the public address system barking out information in a style as crisp and fast as a Seafarer's International Union call:

"I'm looking for one A-card progressive drummer, three weeks, downtown. I need a B-card electric bass rock player, one month out of state. I got a card for two A-card disco saxophonists. I need one permit-holding country steel guitar player for a two-week gig in Saudi Arabia. Who wants to talk to me?"

Close by, another pair of men, both long-haired, wearing army jackets and square, rose-colored glasses, were examining a cigarette.

"It's the first Colombian pot I've seen in months," the first man said.

"How much?" asked the second.

"Two hundred an ounce."

"No shit? That's great. I'll take some."

"Okay, but not here. Tell me where you're playing and we'll make a drop."

"Hey, dig those two, will you?"

The two musicians paused to stare at Jake and Elwood Blues, who had entered together and, both dressed in the same dark glasses, ties, and dark suits, were moving with resolute steps toward the main office.

"Wow," said the first musician. "They look like hitmen. Probably here to collect some back dues or puncture eardrums."

"Or maybe they're limo drivers," a nearby man offered.

"No, they're definitely cops," said the second musician. "You don't get a shine on a suit like that with the Mafia or just driving."

As the group of interested spectators grew, it inevitably came to include one who knew more than the others. "No," said the knowledgeable one, who was about thirty-five, with shaggy brown hair, "They're musicians. The short one's a vocalist and the taller one plays the harp."

"No kidding? Who are they?"

"They used to have an act called the Blues Brothers. You see those glasses, hats, and the suits?"

"How can you *not* see them?"

"Anyway," continued the knowing one, "they wear that stuff onstage and off. They never wear anything else."

"Wow," said the first musician, "they must really be into it."

Although they moved with measured steps, their eyes straight ahead, both Jake and Elwood were aware that they were being watched as they moved across the main hallway of the building.

"See?" Jake said out of the corner of his mouth, "they haven't forgotten us. It's like in the movies when the top gunfighter shows up in town. All the low life starts to think about running for cover."

"You sure that's it, Jake?" Elwood asked.

They paused for a moment at the bulletin board, a montage of business cards, job postings, items for sale, and pleas for help of one sort or another. As they read over the listings, they suddenly heard a loud voice bellow behind them.

"Blues Brothers!" it rasped, the tone decidedly angry rather than nostalgic.

"You see?" Jake said. "I told you they remember."

They turned to face a dark, husky man in a black pinstriped suit, white shirt, black tie and tinted glasses. His pudgy finger was pointed accusingly at them.

"Don't tell us," Jake said quickly. "We'll get the name in just a minute."

"I'm Louie the treasurer," the man announced.

"Isn't that what I said, Elwood?" Jake nodded. "It's Louie the treasurer."

"Get out," Louie said. "You can't come in here and use the union's facilities until your dues are paid up. You bastards know that. And you also know you still owe us for your last job."

"Come on, Louie," Elwood pleaded. "Give us a break. My brother here just spent three years in jail. He just got out."

"Then he owes three years' dues if he wants his card back," Louie replied shortly.

"Hey, look—" Elwood began.

"You!" Louie interrupted. "As I recall, you never even got your status. Last time you went out, you were on a temporary permit. As I also recall, you never even came to an audition or an orientation meeting. So get out."

"Hey, man," Jake said hotly. "Why don't you take your fuckin' union and sew tags on clothes? You think Robert Johnson ever belonged to a dipshit union?"

As he spoke, he started pounding on the bulletin board. Tacks, pamphlets, cards and papers fell noisily to the floor, scattering in all directions. Louie glared angrily at Jake, seemed about to lunge at him, then bent down to start picking up the mess.

"Goddamnit, I said get out," he hissed. "I'll blackball you two assholes. You hear that?"

"We'll be back with a fleet of lawyers," Jake said.

They started for the door, leaving a puzzled and amused group behind them.

"Why the hell did you do that?" Elwood said. "The guy

was mad enough without your screwing up the bulletin board."

"I had to," Jake said, sotto voce. "I saw something I wanted and didn't know whether we'd get back in here. So I had to do something to distract him."

"What?" Elwood said.

Jake lifted his right hand partway out of his coat pocket. Elwood could see a packet of cards.

"What is it?" Elwood asked.

"New bookings. And guess what just happened to be on top? The Jovial Club, Calumet City."

"You serious?"

"Yeah. Maybe now we can figure a way to get ourselves in there Friday, after we get the rest of the band together."

"You mean *if*."

"Mission for God, remember?"

Elwood was beginning to feel despondent. "But it's the third day you've been out," he reminded Jake, "and we've got exactly one member accounted for—Willie."

"That's better than nothing."

"Sure, and all it cost me was a set of tires."

"You said they were old anyway."

"Yeah. But I'm beginning to wonder about this mission."

They had crossed the floor and were in the main lobby. Looking back, they saw that Louie was no longer glaring in their direction but had gone back inside the main office. Jake paused, took the cards out of his pocket and examined them. Then he smiled. "Wow, we're in luck."

"What?"

"The Jovial Club starts a new act Friday. So all we have to do is substitute the Blues Brothers for them and we're in business. I'll bet we could raise the five grand in a long weekend there, especially if we can talk the manager into giving us a little advance."

"And how are you figuring to talk the . . ." Elwood looked at the card, ". . . the whatever that group's name

THE BLUES BROTHERS

is . . . how do we talk them out of giving up their gig?"

"I'll think of something," Jake promised.

As he continued to sift through the cards, Elwood suddenly let out a little yelp.

"Go back," he said. "There. That's it. Look at that. Murph, Tom and the Magictones. The Ramada Inn, 1001 East 156th."

"Yeah, so what?" Jake murmured.

Elwood related his experience on the highway earlier. "It's just a hunch," he said. "But something tells me that's Murph and Bones Malone."

"Okay," Jake said. "Let's go out there right now."

"You don't think I'm crazy?"

"No. Don't be crazy."

Across the street from the union hall, the blonde woman debated the pros and cons of sudden violent action. Having trailed Jake all the way to his destination without having a good opportunity to line up a field of fire, she now had a relatively clear shot. In the back seat was the Browning Automatic Rifle, fully loaded, in position to be propped against the open window and fired from a distance of no more than fifty yards. But what might happen if she missed again, or if the miraculous intervention of traffic should save the lucky Jake Blues? Would it be the narrow escape that finally convinced him to disappear or, at the very least, be much more cautious? Considering the fact that in her car trunk was the paraphernalia to seal his fate absolutely and for all time, was it not foolish to risk an attempt that had any possibility of failure? Sighing, she leaned back against the rich upholstery and watched the two men walk to the Bluesmobile and drive off.

"All right," she said resolutely. "You made the decision. Now get to work."

Starting the car, she made a quick U-turn and headed back toward the Bond Hotel.

Jake, meanwhile, had selected a Memphis Slim cassette

and was immersed in the sumptuous tones of "Lucille" as Elwood headed the car in the direction of the Ramada Inn. They made no conversation during the ten-minute drive, each man enjoying the music in his own particular way.

"This is the place," Elwood said finally, pulling the Bluesmobile into the parking lot next to the sign advertising the Magictones and welcoming the exterminators.

The Ramada Inn was as empty as a dry shotglass and twice as sad. The lounge consisted of a Mediterranean-type decor with embossed velveteen wallpaper, tiny round tables with glass-enclosed candles, and big husky waitresses in fishnet stockings and miniskirts. Less than four people were in the room. Jake and Elwood took a table at the back.

Directly across from them, against the opposite wall, was a small stage with orange curtains. A four-piece band— organ, drums, electric zither and electric guitar—was playing, the tune an up-tempo percussive version of "Di Mi, Quando, Quando, Quando." The band members were dressed uniformly in ruffled shirts, bow ties and burgundy tuxedos. All were dark, swarthy, Latin-looking.

The light, which shone directly down on them from atrociously placed ceiling spots, was hardly conducive to quick identification, but Jake thought the singer—obviously either Murph or Tom—looked vaguely familiar.

"What do you think?" he said to Elwood.

Elwood nodded. "It's the same voice. Or damned close. But the skin color and that rug . . ."

"I think it's Murph," Jake nodded.

A moment later, the vocalist finished the song, waited a moment until the polite applause died away, then said in a deep and soothing voice, "Thank you, thank you. You're marvelous, marvelous. I'm Murph and these are the Magictones—Rafael, Claudio, Wageel, and José. I regret to say that Tom's got the bug and can't be here tonight . . ."

"It's him!" Elwood said.

Jake nodded. "Yeah."

"For those of you who are with us for the first time, we extend a very warm welcome to the Armada Room of Indiana's newest Ramada Inn," Murph continued, "right here at Exit 128 of the Tollway. Okay, that's our introduction. Now you know who we are and where we are and who we love to see—you. So please come back any time after five o'clock weekdays and six on weekends. Now, from Murph and the Magictones, here's how we feel about you—a little bit of an oldie from the seventies..."

The band broke into a Mediterranean version of "Feelings," Murph singing two verses before standing aside and snapping his fingers in time to the crescendo that ended the piece. Polite applause spilled out from the audience as the stage lights went out and cash registers and waitresses returned to action. When the lights came on, Murph and the Magictones were gone.

"What a shame," Elwood sighed. "Look at that shit."

"Yeah, such a fall from being with the Blues Brothers Band," Jake said. "But a guy's gotta make a living, I guess."

"But that awful wig. Does he have to wear that?"

"Everything else here is plastic," Jake replied.

"Yeah."

"Well, let's go rescue him," Jake urged.

Backstage, or in the cramped alcove immediately to the rear of the miniscule stage, Murph and the men calling themselves the Magictones were having a hushed, frenetic conference. Rafael, Claudio, Wageel, and José stood together, almost shoulder-to-shoulder, facing Murph. The quartet's attitude was one of uniform belligerence; Murph's was one of wounded helplessness. Now he released a long sigh. "Hey, I'm doing the best I can, guys," he said. "That's all I can do."

"Two weeks no pay, boss, not good too much," said Wageel.

"I'm still making payments on your amplifiers, Wageel,"

Murph replied. "I'm paying the money to make you guys sound *good*. Come on ... I'm not gonna stiff you. You're eating, aren't you?"

"That cause we work in place with food," Wageel said. "We steal from kitchen."

Murph let it pass. "Look, guys," he continued. "You're all doing what you enjoy, right? You're doing what you're good at. Now, how many people can say they do that? It's a dream come true. You're playing music in a free country, entertaining people ... American people ... people who were *born here* ... people who don't have the *Immigration and Naturalization Service looking for them* ..."

"No show, boss," Wageel said. "We quits you."

A waitress pushed aside the heavy drape that served as a doorway to the alcove. "Couple guys out here want to see you, Murph."

Murph was grateful for the interruption because it gave him a moment to think, but was understandably wary of being visited by strangers. God knew, it was unlikely they were talent scouts or even ordinary well-wishers in this entertainment wasteland. That left Internal Revenue agents, cops, or jealous boyfriends or husbands, none of whom promised much happiness. "What do they look like?" he asked the waitress, signaling to the Magictones to stay put.

"I don't know," she said. "They're both wearing dark glasses and shiny, dark suits. They look like very young undertakers, if you ask me. Or maybe CIA guys."

"Okay, let them in. They don't sound dangerous," Murph said. Then, turning to the four swarthy musicians, he smiled. "Hey, why don't you maniacs go to the bar and have a drink? Put it on my tab. Give me some time to think this over ..."

Wageel nodded, a signal for the others to do likewise. Conferring in Spanish, the four walked through the doorway just as Jake and Elwood entered.

"Hi, Murph," Elwood said.

The effect on Murphy Dunne was instantaneous. With a laugh, he slapped his palms together and bounded toward them.

"Well, son of a gun, I don't believe it!" he shouted. "You madmen, I don't believe it. Elwood, baby! Jake, you monster! Ha! It's just incredible! Ha, ha . . . I love you, you maniac . . ." As he spoke, he grabbed Jake's hand, pulled him toward him, and pummeled him about the neck and shoulders.

"Easy," Jake protested. "I'm allergic to hair spray."

Murph laughed. "Hey, you maniac," he said. "What are you doing out so early? I thought they gave you three to five . . ."

"Parole," Jake said. "Good behavior. They took pity on me because none of my so-called friends visited me."

"Good behavior!" Murph repeated, ignoring the last remark. "You party animal. Amazing! Good behavior! That's like giving Jack the Ripper a prize for having the gentle touch." He gave Jake a punch on the shoulder, then turned to Elwood. "And how's your brother, the quiet half? I'm asking you because I know he can't answer. He's a robot, right? You never talk, do you, Elwood?"

"Never," Elwood replied.

"That's what I said," Murph laughed. "Say, you look great, guys. I mean, you had the suits done and everything. Other guys have their suits pressed, you have yours massaged, right?"

"We're here to talk business," Jake interrupted. "If you don't want to be serious, we'll just have to start talking about that hairy thumbtack you got stuck in the top of your head."

"Not bad, not bad," Murph replied, his hand moving toward the stiffly coiffed black wig he wore. "Actually, I hate this thing, but it goes with the act. So does the makeup."

He rubbed a finger across his cheek, removing a streak

of dark tan coloring. "That's why Tom's not here. You remember Bones, naturally."

Jake smiled. "So we struck oil twice," he said.

"What's the matter with Tom?" Elwood prodded.

"The makeup causes him to break out something terrible," Murph explained. "So once or twice a week, on slow nights like tonight, we let him take off."

"He still play a mean horn?" Jake asked.

"The meanest."

"Good. Because we're putting the band back together," said Jake. "The Blues Brothers are gonna live again."

Murph laughed. "Ha! You monster! How? Put the band back together? It's not possible. Forget it."

"Like hell we will," Jake shot back. "We've already lined up a gig. We got Willie—you remember 'Too Big' Hall—and Matt and the Duck. And it's not just a club gig, either. It's a recording gig."

Murph's eyebrows shot upward. "You got a recording gig? With the Duck?" he asked. "Huh! I wonder why he didn't mention it? I talked to him just last week."

"You talked to the Duck?" Elwood said quickly.

"You know where he is?" Jake demanded, his question barely a split second behind Elwood's.

"Ha! Ho!" Murph laughed. "You guys are good! You got a recording gig with the Duck! But you don't even know where he is. Ha, ha! What a couple of maniacs! But I love you. I love you guys!"

"Okay," Jake confessed. "We lied about the Duck, but the rest is true—about the gig and all. That's why we have to have you, Murph. Because you are the band, man, the nerve center, the arranger, the backbone, the pulse. The whole band used to revolve around you . . ."

"Hey, you're getting my ankles all wet," Murph said. But the boys knew he loved it.

"Come on, man," Jake urged. "Help the Blues Brothers *live* again. You gotta join us."

"And you gotta be kidding," Dunne replied.

"Why?" Jake challenged. "Is this really all that great? I mean, this ain't the most fantastic dressing room I've ever seen. And that stage. It's not big enough for a ventriloquist act."

"Hey, I can see," Murph replied. "You think I like living in this plastic motel, jammed under fifteen decks of freeway? You think I like being a lounge lizard playing *every* night to a bunch of transients stuck here because of the foam-rubber convention? You think I like it? Well, you're wrong. I *love* it! This is my life now. It's awful but it's secure, you know."

"You mean you won't come back with the band?"

"Did I say that?" Murph smiled. "No, I didn't say that, Jake. This is my life now . . . but if everybody else from the original band does it, then of course I'll do it. Are you crazy or something or don't you just get out much? Hell, I wouldn't miss it for a year's free dry cleaning."

"And how about Tom?" Jake smiled.

"Shit, he'll do it just to get out of the blackface."

Elwood and Jake smiled.

"Duck called me last month," Murph said. "Said whenever I come down to Farmer City to be sure and have supper with him. I say, 'Sure, Duck, I go through Farmer City at least once a decade.'"

"What's he doing?" Jake asked. "Is he playing? What's his address or phone number?"

"Man, you are a nervous little sonofabitch," Murph said. "I got a number where he works. It's some burglar alarm company down in Decatur. Now doesn't that blow your mind? The Duck, installing burglar alarms! Let me think now . . . it was Ray-Ban Alarm Company . . . Ray-Lette . . . Ray-Gun . . . damn, I don't know, I forget now. I wrote it down someplace. Anyway, it started with 'Ray.'"

"How about the other guys?" Elwood said. "You seen any of them?"

"He spoke," Murph squeaked, feigning shock. "It's a miracle. He actually spoke. What did he say, Jake? I was so excited to hear him speak, I forgot to listen."

"He said what about the other guys from the band?" Jake replied patiently. "You seen any of them?"

Murph nodded. "Sure. Mr. Rubin... the incomparable Mr. Fabulous... Angel Lips... he's the maitre d' downtown at the Belle Cuisine Restaurant. It's very chic."

"Well, it's sure worth a trip if we can get Mr. Fabulous," Jake said. Then, shaking Murph's hand, he added, "Thanks a million, man. Our first gig is this Friday night at the Jovial Club, Calumet City. We'll see you and Tom, right?"

"We'll be there. You maniacs!"

The boys turned to go. Waving to the still-conferring Latins outside the alcove as they left, they threaded their way through a polyester crowd already somewhat larger than when Jake and Elwood had first entered.

Sticking her head around the corner of the building, the blonde noticed in the fading light that both cops seemed to be fast asleep in the front seat of the car. Their heads were thrown well back against the seats, and from her vantage point their eyes seemed to be closed. That was the rub, though—the "seemed." Because cops had been known to pull a fast one or two, the blonde decided to stay put until darkness set in. Only if the Blues Brothers arrived momentarily would she retreat to her car before it was completely dark.

As the El rumbled overhead, she glanced down the length of the Bond Hotel's rear wall, wondering idly how much of it would spill onto the tracks as a result of the explosion. Her handiwork, as far as she could tell, was perfect, consisting of more than enough plastic gel nitro placed all along the already-rotting support sections of the building. In the middle nitro pod was an electronic detonator set to activate the *plastiques* in rapid sequence from a safe distance by remote control.

Another half-hour passed. In the unmarked police vehicle, Wade Fiscus watched the sun set behind the El tracks, wondering idly how long the stakeout would last. He still held the Chicago Police Department record of twenty-seven consecutive days without relief, by virtue of the time in 1967 when he had covered the apartment of Shelley Wengel, the notorious hijacker of municipal sanitation trucks. Unknown to Fiscus, Wengel had gone to Bermuda and been eaten by a shark just two days after the stakeout began, an unfortunate occurrence that had rendered the then-young officer's tenacity largely irrelevant. The police commissioner had allowed the record to stick, however, despite the valid protest of former record holder Officer Carley Watts, who charged that only a stakeout ending in an actual arrest should count. (Watts' previous record of twenty-four days, seven hours, had been established in 1947 outside the home of Chicago pornographer Nameer F. X. Freeman, whose specialty was taking a job as a window cleaner and scrawling huge obscenities in soap on the sides of skyscrapers.) Now, a decade and a half later, Wade Fiscus had no such patience; he wanted the Blues Brothers to show up as soon as possible so they could throw both of them in jail. Some other police officer could have the stakeout record, for all he cared.

With a slight smile and the comfortable feeling that he had achieved genuine maturity as a law-enforcement officer, he watched the long-legged blonde at the rear of the Bond Hotel as she made what seemed to be a final inspection of something tied to the building's support and then slunk away in the growing darkness, holding an object similar to a television remote-control switch.

He wondered for a moment if she was up to no good.

Then, with a shrug, he dismissed the thought from his mind. She was probably just another loiterer.

A minute later, he was fast asleep.

Jake and Elwood motored down the broad neon-lit thoroughfare of Rush Street just as the evening was getting under way. Groups of people, fashionably dressed for disco or dining, strolled past the stores, strip clubs, arcade rooms and sidewalk cafes. One particularly striking building was of newly restored brick, two stories high, with a broad, sloping roof and dormers. Reproduction gaslights illuminated the entrance, above which was an antique gilt sign reading LA BELLE CUISINE.

Elwood eased the Bluesmobile into a parking space reserved for the handicapped next to the restaurant, and the boys got out.

The interior of the establishment was as restrained and elegant as the outside, consisting of a large foyer furnished with Louis XV reproduction armchairs of gilded wood, and loveseats each wide enough for one and a half persons. The wall was papered with pastoral scenes of young eighteenth-century couples picnicking in the woods.

As Jake and Elwood entered, the maitre d' was in the process of seating a very straight, well-to-do Mom, Dad, and their children, a boy of about eight and a daughter in her twenties. Gracefully holding the chair for Mom, the maitre d' turned his attention to Dad, saying, "Might I say, sir, that you have a lovely family, and although I'm sure the waiters we have assigned to serve you this evening are more than competent, I urge you to summon me if I can be of any assistance in any capacity."

The incredible thing about the obviously rehearsed and

often-recited speech was that somehow the man made it sound sincere.

"Well, thank you," the Dad said, smiling.

The matire d', a slick, matinee-idol-smooth man in his middle thirties with prematurely graying hair, nodded his head sharply, bringing a very gay young man to the table with menus. He distributed them with rather more than an average flourish.

"This is Kent," the maitre d' announced. "I concur with his selections this evening. We serve an excellent vichyssoise, not too salty, not too creamy, made with leeks. I suggest it as the beginning of what I hope will be an excellent dinner."

Bowing slightly at the waist, he smiled and strode back to the reservation desk. The phone was ringing and he answered it, barely noticing the two dark-suited men in sunglasses standing in the background, the larger one ogling a nude wood nymph on the Fragonard wallpaper. As he took the reservation, the maitre d' wondered who the pair were, finally concluding that from their manner and dress they were either policemen or agents from the Health Department, inspecting for roaches.

He sighed as he hung up the telephone.

"Mr. Fabulous!" Jake said, extending his hand.

The maitre d' winced. "Oh my God." It had been months since someone had addressed him by that old nickname. He had never been particularly fond of it, and now was even less so. His head swiveled quickly about, as if to discover how many patrons had heard the remark. Fortunately, most were out of earshot.

"It is him, ain't it, Elwood?" Jake said in a loud voice. "It is Alan Rubin, right?"

Al, the maitre d', forced a smile to his lips. "Yes," he said. "It's me. But the name's Rubini. Alfonso Rubini."

"Wow," Jake said. "When did you get to be a duke of something?"

"This is a very high-class place," Al said, his eyes darting from side to side. "I had to spruce myself up a little."

"Still play the trumpet?"

"Of course. Uh... I thought you were still in prison," Al said. "Are you out on parole or something?"

"No," Jake murmured, leaning closer. "I busted out. Had to kill a guard. I thought you might be able to hide me."

"Jesus!" Al muttered.

The telephone rang. A bit glassy-eyed, Al picked it up and forced a smile to his lips. "La Belle Cuisine," he said. "Yessir... You're from out of town and you heard... Isn't that wonderful?... Well, yessir, we do pride ourselves on our French cuisine... And our wine cellar. No sir, Mayor Daley doesn't eat here anymore... he's dead, sir."

"That's the place—the wine cellar," Jake said.

"No!" Al replied quickly, then, with an embarrassed smile, returned his attention to the telephone patron. "Excuse me, sir. I was speaking with somone else. Yessir, we have an excellent wine cellar... Yes, private dining rooms are available, too...."

"That's not bad," Jake said. "They'd never think of looking for me in a private dining room."

Al waved him off, but Jake persisted, reaching out to grab at the lapels of his expensive jacket. "Please, Al," he urged. "They're right behind us! For God's sake, help!"

"Take your hands off me!" Al ordered. "Oh, sorry, sir. I didn't mean you... Thank you. What is the name, please?"

"Jake Blues," Jake interrupted.

"Jake," Al repeated automatically. "Pardon me again, sir. No, sir, I know it's not Jake. You said Henry Rizzoli... A table for eleven-thirty at eight. I mean, for eight at eleven-thirty. Yes, thank you, sir."

"Al, when you're a killer on the lam, you'll do anything to get help," Jake said.

THE BLUES BROTHERS

"You're bullshitting me, aren't you?" Al asked, a bit nervously. "You're really out on parole, right?"

"You'd have known the answer to that if you'd been like the others and come to see me once in a while," Jake replied coldly.

"Aw, come on," Al sighed. "I thought about it, Jake, but it's a real pain in the ass to go all the way out there."

"A real pal, isn't he, Elwood."

Elwood nodded.

"Well, we want to talk to you about something," Jake said. "Something very important."

"All right, but as you can see, I can't talk now. I'm on duty."

"When are you off?"

"When the restaurant closes. Two o'clock."

"That's a while off. What do you think, Elwood? Maybe we'd better have dinner while we're waiting?"

Elwood nodded again.

"There's a little place up the block," Al offered. "A nice reasonable Italian place. It's called—"

"Oh no," Jake replied archly. "We'll eat here. Nothing is too good to celebrate my early release from the clutches of the state."

"No, that wouldn't be so good," Al stammered. "Tell you what, I'll get somebody to take over for me for a half-hour and we'll go outside for a drink or coffee. Okay?"

"No, it's not okay," Jake said. "We seek a full meal and all the compliments of the house. Come, Elwood, let us adjourn ourselves to the nearest table and overlook this establishment's board of fare."

He moved toward the dining room. Elwood followed.

"No, wait," Al pleaded, just as the telephone rang. "Good evening, La Belle Cuisine. Could you hold on just a moment?" Putting down the phone, he looked around wildly for someone who could take the call. By the time he got the attention of the hatcheck girl, Jake and Elwood had already seated themselves next to the family of five Al had just taken care of.

"Take care of this, will you?" Al said, when the girl reached the reservation desk.

"What do you want me to do?"

"Handle it, for Christ's sake. If it's a reservation, take it. If it's somebody who wants street directions, give them."

The words were barely out of his mouth when a loud, shrill whistle shattered the serene, soft baroque musical background of the restaurant. Taking two faltering steps forward, Al did not have to guess where the sound came from. Jake, desiring the services of a waiter, had simply put his fingers in his mouth and whistled for one. So effective was the signal that no less than three waiters were at Jake and Elwood's table before Al arrived.

"How about a menu?" Jake said.

"Please, Jake . . . Mr. Blues," Al said softly, smiling. "Let me show you to another table."

"This one's fine," Jake replied.

"It's also reserved."

"So show them to the one you were gonna put us at."

"I can't do that. The party requested this table."

"We'll eat fast, won't we, Elwood?" Jake promised.

"That's what I'm afraid of," Al muttered.

One of the waiters arrived with a pair of menus, which were unusually large even for expensive restaurants.

"To start—" Jake said, munching loudly on a stalk of celery between words. "To start, we'll have a bottle of your finest champagne and six shrimp cocktails."

"Very good, sir," the waiter said, starting to leave.

Jake reached out to grab him by the seat of the trousers. "Hold on a second," he said. "That was just for me. For my brother here, you can bring a double order of white toast."

He released the waiter, who left with wide eyes.

Al started to say something, then noticed the hatcheck girl signaling, and left.

"You'll like the white bread they have here," Jake said to Elwood in his most sophisticated manner. "They grow only the best."

"I do look forward to it," Elwood replied.

A moment later, the waiter returned with a bottle of champagne, which he held in a napkin so that Jake could examine the label. "This is our finest, sir, a Roger Steuben, Blue Label—"

"That's fine, pal," Jake said.

As he sampled the champagne, Jake beat out a hot rhythm with his fork against the tabletop. Both Mom and Dad at the next table glared at him but it had no visible effect on his noisemaking, which actually became worse when Elwood joined in.

Al, meanwhile, had managed to enlist the services of another employee, who took over the reservation desk so that Al could handle what was obviously becoming a dangerous situation.

"Hey, guys," Al said, moving to their table. "Do you think you could—"

"That's a hell of a way for the maitre d' to address his clientele," Jake said archly. "Guys. Not 'sir' or 'monsieur'? What's the world coming to, anyway? Next you'll want to ride in the same bus with us."

"Seriously," Al said. "The food here is really expensive. The soup is ten fucking dollars . . . Come on. Let's go outside. I'll buy you a cup of coffee."

"No need for that. Sit down and have coffee here. It's on us. This whole meal is free."

"Jake, it isn't," Al replied miserably. "I don't have the authority to give you a free meal. It's not my restaurant."

"It's not? All right, then, we'll make it your restaurant. Where's the owner?"

Jake started to stand, but sat down again when he saw

that the waiter had arrived with the shrimp cocktails. Dipping three of the jumbo shrimp into the sauce, he jammed them into his mouth and chewed loudly. "Luscious," he slurped, licking his fingers noisily, emitting a loud pop as each broke free of his lips. Elwood began tossing shrimp, which Jake gobbled midair, seal-like.

"God, Jake," Al moaned. "Why are you doing this to me?"

"Sir!" a deep voice called out. "Waiter! Sir!"

Al turned to look into the narrowed eyes of the Dad at the adjacent table. He forced a weak smile. "Yes, sir," he soothed. "I hope your salads are all right?"

"The salads are fine," the father replied, glaring at Jake and Elwood with unalloyed loathing. "It's just that . . . we'd like to move to another table, if you don't mind . . ."

"Oh," Al murmured, feigning surprise. "Is something the matter with this one?"

"You know damned well what's the matter," the man shot back. He cast another murderous look at the Blues Brothers. Jake waved a shrimp at him.

"You mean these gentlemen are disturbing you?" Al asked, stalling for time in the hope that he could think of a place to put them.

"Of course," the man said. "They're not only noisy, but they smell bad."

"Hey, Elwood," Jake repeated in a loud voice. "The old guy says we smell bad."

"And the glare from their suits is hurting my daughter's eyes," the man added, undaunted by Jake's truculence.

"I'll see if I can locate another table for you, sir," Al said apologetically.

Casting a nervous glance over his shoulder, he moved quickly to the reservation desk.

Jake popped another trio of shrimp into his jaws and slid his chair over closer to the adjacent table. "We been having a little discussion," he said, dropping several drops of the sauce onto the tablecloth of their neighbors. "Mister, we want to buy your daughter."

"What?"

"You got wax in your ears?" Jake said. "We'd like to buy the kid. How much you want for her?"

The man's lips opened, but no sounds emerged except a frantic gurgling.

"Come on," Jake urged. "I know what you're trying to do. You think you'll get a higher price by holding out. Okay. We'll give you a thousand for the wife and two thousand for the pretty young girl." He reached in his pocket and withdrew a moldy-looking wallet.

"Waiter!" the man shouted, rising unsteadily to his feet and clutching the end of the table. "Waiter! Sir! Waiter!"

Everyone was looking their way, a few faces reflecting bizarre amusement, the vast majority horror and shock.

"Don't make a fuss," Jake rasped. "We'll go to five thousand each, but not a nickel more."

"Waiter!"

Al rushed from the reservation desk to the scene. Grabbing Jake by the shoulders, he spun both him and the chair back to his own table and thrust his face close to Jake's. "Goddamnit, Jake," he hissed. "I'm telling you to cut it out once and for all. If you don't, I'm heading right for that telephone and calling a cop. We have very good relations with them. They'll have a man here in less than a minute, I promise you!"

Jake cast one final glance at the man, then looked at the floor. "My best friend, the pulse, the backbone, the nerve center of the Blues Brothers Band, would turn me in like a common crook," he said mournfully. "I can't believe it."

"You better believe it," Al warned, noting with relief that the man at the adjacent table had picked up his fork and was about to resume eating. "I don't know what kind of a trip you're on, but you're not going to make an asshole out of me."

"Okay," Elwood said softly. "He'll cool it, Al. Just don't turn him in. He just got out, you know."

Al sighed and nodded. Sitting at their table, he waited until the restaurant resumed its normal sounds. Then, turning to Jake, he asked, "What did you come here for?"

"Do you know where Blue Lou is?" Jake responded.

"Marini? I don't know. I haven't seen him in months. I don't know, really."

"I still want to buy that kid," Jake whispered, staring wildly at the girl next to them.

"Cut it out, Jake," Elwood cautioned.

"The last I heard, he was going to night school in Champaign-Urbana," Al said. "Why?"

"Al, we're getting the band back together," Jake smiled. "We're gonna play again. And we need you. Because you're the pulse... the backbone... the lips of the band..."

"Not a chance... No way." Al shook his head.

"Look, we already have a gig. It's this Friday night at the Jovial Club, Calumet City. You gotta be there, Al."

"I can't. I really can't."

"If you say no, Elwood and me will come here every day for breakfast, lunch and dinner," Jake warned.

"I'll be there," Al said, "the Jovial Club, Calumet City."

"Friday night," Jake said, standing and draining the champagne directly from the bottle. "Now, if you'll pardon us, we must be going."

Ignoring the stares of the restaurant's shocked patrons, he weaved his way through the large room, picked up a bowl of mints at the reservation desk and tossed its entire contents high in the air, catching one or two mints in his mouth. Then, gesturing to Elwood to follow, he moved to the front door, peeked out in the manner of one determining whether the coast is clear, and quickly darted into the night.

chapter five

"Four down and four to go," Jake exulted, as they headed south in the Bluesmobile on Interstate 94. "We got Willie and Mr. Fabulous and Tom and Murph. That leaves the Duck, Blue Lou, Matt and Steve. This is a mission for God. No shit."

He was feeling unusually good, the champagne having taken effect even before they headed into the cool night and the exhilaration of Big Joe Williams singing "Gamblin' Man" and accompanying himself on the old twelve-string. Volatile by nature beneath his dour exterior, Jake was either way up or way down, and now he was way up. "Stop the car," he said suddenly.

They were in the hammer lane, with no exit ramp in sight. "Stop? What for?" Elwood asked.

"I feel like telling somebody how we're doing," Jake said.

"Who's to tell?"

"I guess old Curtis is the only person who'd understand," Jake said. "Look for a telephone."

"You're crazy. It's late. He'll be in bed."

"Gotta tell somebody," Jake murmured, beating his palms against the dashboard in rhythm to the music and the sound of his own words. "Gotta tell somebody."

Elwood shrugged and swerved right, darting between some fast-moving traffic to get into the right lane. A minute later, they were on a side road and had located a phone.

Elwood waited while Jake made the call.

"What did he say?" Elwood asked when his brother returned to the car.

"He was impressed. Said he'd get all the kids together and send them door-to-door with circulars and stuff, advertising our gig."

"What did you tell him?"

"I said sure, hop to it."

"But we're not even sure we can crash that Jovial Club, Jake. You may be sending them on a wild-goose chase."

"No sir. This is a mission for God. Somehow we'll get that gig and the place'll be jam-packed and we'll be a great success and they'll be throwing money at us."

"Man, you sure are high."

"Tell you what," Jake said. "We got nothing else to do. Let's drive down to Calumet City and sort of case that place. Just see what it's like, how much room they got. You know, no big deal. Just get acquainted with the layout."

Elwood threw the Bluesmobile into gear and headed back out toward the freeway. "What the hell," he said with a shrug. "I don't guess it can hurt."

It was just after daybreak when Curtis was awakened from a deep sleep by loud and persistent rapping. This is the second time tonight, his fogged brain reported as it slowly yielded to the conscious world. Of course, the earlier telephone call from Jake Blues had been enjoyable once Curtis got the cobwebs out of his head, and he had fallen asleep afterward concocting schemes and methods of helping them publicize their upcoming gig.

The rapping upstairs, on the other hand, promised less enjoyment; people seldom pounded on a door in such a heavy-fisted manner unless they were authoritarian types or self-appointed crusaders of some sort. Having listened to people's rapping for several decades, Curtis had come to the point where he could differentiate between the nervous knock of a returning runaway, the rapping of someone seeking information, and that of an ordinary official, such as someone from the Board of Education. The rapping he now heard, instinct told him, belonged to none of the usual cases. Even worse, it would not go away until someone personally attended to it. Slipping into a pair of work pants and a denim shirt, Curtis made his way to the side entrance.

He opened the door a crack, and immediately recognized the man who belonged to the Illinois Nazi Party. Dietrich Albrecht smiled briefly and superciliously upon seeing the old maintenance man. "Good morning," he said stiffly. "I realize it's early, but I'd like to show some friends around your building, which I understand is up for auction."

"Well, I don't know," Curtis replied.

"You see," Albrecht continued, as one explaining a basic math problem to a child, "these gentlemen have to be at work early, and this is the best time of day for them to come here. I've checked with Mr. Garmish of the Bureau of Assessments for the city, and he said it would be all right."

Curtis looked past Albrecht, counting four others in the background waiting to come inside. There was no way of checking with the Bureau of Assessments at this hour, of course, but Curtis saw no reason to cause trouble. Perhaps if he allowed the Nazis to have a quick stroll around, they would leave without incident. He decided to check with Sister Mary Stigmata.

Opening the door partway, he said, "Why don't you come in while I ask the Mother Superior?"

"Very well," replied Albrecht. With a sign to his partners, he moved into the hallway and watched as Curtis closed the door.

"I'll only be a minute," Curtis said.

"Thank you," Albrecht said. He followed along with Curtis until it became evident that the black man had no desire to take him along for the interview, at which point the young Nazi dropped behind and pretended to examine some watercolors painted by the orphans, which were arranged along one wall of the corridor. He was careful to note where Curtis went, however, and when the coast was clear, he followed.

Fortunately for Albrecht's proclivity for spying, Curtis found Sister Mary in one of the small offices nearby, which were separated from the main hallway only by a six-foot-high partition. In the early-morning quiet, the conversation between the older nun and the black man carried with near-perfect clarity into the area where Dietrich Albrecht was eavesdropping.

"Some of them Nazi fellas are back to look at the building," Curtis said. "I told 'em it's early, but they been pounding on the door for ten minutes and I figured letting them look might be the best way to get rid of 'em."

"Well," Sister Mary replied, "I agree with that, Curtis, but I'm not sure that I want this place to go to the likes of them."

"Don't you worry, Sister Mary. This place ain't goin' to nobody, so we can show it to whoever wants to see it."

"Why do you say it's not going to be sold? Unless a miracle happens, this place most assuredly will be auctioned."

"No, ma'am. No way. I got a phone call last night from Jake Blues, and he said they got themselves a gig and they'll have that back tax money in time to save this building."

Sister Mary's voice had an edge to it. "Jake and Elwood Blues? Save this orphanage? Why, I'm surprised they're still in town. I thought they would be in Las Vegas or Atlantic City or some other sin city by now."

"No, ma'am. They're still here. At the Bond Hotel. They told me how to get in touch with 'em, so you can see they're sincere about this thing."

"I see nothing of the kind. They're just a couple of ne'er-do-wells, as far as I'm concerned. And I want no part of their stolen money. I won't have this place tainted by that, much as I love it."

"But that's just it, Sister Mary. They're gonna save us honestly. By playin' that beautiful blues music next Friday night. They got a gig at the Jovial Club."

"I've never heard of such a place—"

"It's in Calumet City."

"I don't care if it's in Siberia. They're two of my boys and I love them dearly. But I absolutely refuse to have any financial dealings with them until they've proved they're on the straight and narrow."

"Well, you'll see," Curtis replied. "Now what should I do with those Nazis?"

"Give them ten minutes to look around," Sister Mary sighed. "Be very polite, but if they insist on staying around longer, call a cop and we'll see that they're tossed out on their . . . their fat behinds."

"Yes, ma'am."

Moving quickly to his former position opposite the watercolors, Dietrich Albrecht wore an expression of barely suppressed glee on his lean face as Curtis walked up the hallway toward him. Ah, he thought wistfully, if only the German spy network had been this efficient and clever during World War Two things might have been different. The bittersweet thought made it easier for him to assume a properly dour mien when Curtis arrived.

"Mother Superior says it's all right to take a quick look around," he said. "But not long."

"Danke," Albrecht said with a smile.

A minute later, he and his cohorts had assembled in the main hall and were happily exploring the large room's possibilities.

"The windows are perfect!" exclaimed one of them, clasping his hands across his breast. "And over there we put the flag of the Weimar Republic, which I have in my basement. And here's where he stood. Ach! It's so like the real thing, it's scary."

"Not only that," Albrecht said. "This whole complex is perfect. We have factories on either side of us, which means we won't have to worry about two sets of windows being broken by radical pigs. We can brick up the back and keep the front well guarded. It also helps that this is a ghetto. The bleeding-heart liberals will think twice before they come down here to picket."

The others nodded in agreement.

"Well, what do you think?" Albrecht asked. "Is it worth an all-out financial and physical effort to try and get this place? Personally, I believe it is. After all, *Man lebt nur Einmal*."

Yet another group nod, although a couple of the faces appeared confused at the German phrase.

"Then we'll do it," Albrecht said, clicking his heels slightly in happiness. "Gentlemen, I must add that I really think this is the beginning of something almost mystical. In just such a room, the career of our *Führer* began. If we can have a new beginning of his thoughts and ideas in such a room as this, who knows? Today, Illinois . . ."

The others sighed wistfully and started to move toward the door.

As they walked in the direction of their cars, Dietrich Albrecht took one of the men aside, spoke briefly with him about topics of relative unimportance and then, when the others had left, said, "Walter, there is one thing that could be troublesome." After telling him about the conversation he overheard, he concluded, "I thought that you and I might take a drive over to this Bond Hotel and make a few inquiries. Perhaps we can learn something about these Blues scum, find out if they have the power to hurt us. Personally, I believe it's all a joke. No one would pay real money to hear such trash, certainly not enough money to save the orphanage. But we must be thorough if we're to succeed, *nicht wahr?*"

The man known as Walter nodded solemnly.

"So I suggest that we, as they say, check out these so-called *Blauenbruder*."

"*Ja, mein Gruppenführer.*"

The dawning of a new day outside the Bond Hotel was vastly different from the same event in other areas of Chicago and its suburbs. As night gave way to day in other sections of town, increased activity could be seen as people awoke, cooked breakfast, hauled out trash, warmed up their cars, brought in the newspaper, kissed their children off to school, and eventually left for work themselves via bus or automobile.

In sharp contrast, no such montage of activity could be seen around the Bond Hotel. If a drunk had fallen against the side of a building sometime during the night, chances were he remained there until at least midmorning; as few residents of the establishment had regular jobs, no outpouring of persons on their way to work could be seen; no self-respecting newspaperboy would have ventured into the neighborhood; and trash collection was nonexistent. A vertical pile of rubble on a decaying moonscape of shattered glass and neglect, the Bond Hotel knew no seasons and no time of day in terms of human activity. Only the relentless pounding of the El train provided evidence that any form of life existed.

Wade Fiscus awoke with a start, rubbed his eyes, and was dismayed to see that Burton Mercer was dead to the world. Whose watch had it been? Had the Blues Brothers slipped into the hotel while they napped? If so, had they left again or were they still there, ripe for the taking? Nudging Mercer awake, Fiscus decided to be honest about the situation. "I was asleep," he said. "And so were you, Burt."

Mercer looked at his watch. "It's just a little after seven," he announced coldly. "I was off from six to eight and you were on. Or supposed to be on."

"Yes, but when you didn't wake up at four o'clock, I decided to stay on," Fiscus muttered weakly.

"You should have made me wake up," Mercer replied. "Instead, you improvised and look what happened."

"I was just trying to make sure you got some sleep, Burt."

"It's no good, Fiscus. Now we're in a hell of a fix. One of us is going to have to go in there and find out if those hoods are in."

Fiscus nodded. "You have the best excuse," he said. "You're the parole officer."

"I don't get it."

"Well, you could be there just to tell him something, maybe even something that would benefit him. But a Traffic Division officer would never be there for a good reason. Even the stupidest desk clerk would know that."

"All right, Fiscus. I'll go. It's a case of my making up for your mistake, but a good law-enforcement officer learns to put things like that second to getting the job done."

"Thank you, Burt."

Mercer got out of the car, stretched his legs and walked over to the Bond Hotel. The lobby was deserted, the same elderly man sleeping behind the Plexiglas wall, totally oblivious to the morning news emanating from the television set.

Mercer rapped several times on the divider, and flashed his badge when Lloyd finally opened his eyes.

"Yeah?" the old man said.

"Has my friend come back yet? You know the fellow. Jake Blues. The ex-con."

Lloyd shook his head.

"I'm not here to roust him," Mercer said. "There's a paper he has to sign so he can go to work. I think I've got him a good job in a parking garage."

Lloyd nodded. "I'll tell him you were here."

"Well, if you'd really like to do me a favor, I'd prefer that you didn't tell him," Mercer smiled. "It's not often we're able to get an ex-con a job so quick, and I know Jake'll really be happy. If you don't mind, I'd kind of like to surprise him."

"Got you," Lloyd said. "I'll keep my mouth shut, then."

"Thanks."

Congratulating himself, Mercer strolled back to the car and got in. As he did so, the blonde parked half a block to their rear yawned and once again looked down at the electronic device on the seat next to her. She had remained awake every minute of the long night and she was exhausted. But as grainy as her eyes felt, she knew she retained the power to stay awake until the Blues Brothers returned. If necessary, she would resort to the pills she had in her purse. They would give her another twenty-four hours of wakefulness. Beyond that, she dared not think.

Nor did she have to, for at that very moment the Bluesmobile rumbled into view, made a sharp right turn into the alleyway beneath the El tracks and disappeared. The deep-throated idling sound continued for another minute, followed by a roar and squeal of rubber and brakes. Then silence. Another minute later the two brothers appeared, walking slowly in the direction of the hotel.

When they pushed aside the door and entered the lobby, the blonde glanced at her watch. She would give them a minute to bullshit with the desk clerk and another thirty seconds to climb the stairs to their room. That was the minimum. Depending on how patient she felt, she would blow them to kingdom come any time after that.

As the two men passed the unmarked police car, Wade Fiscus slowly raised his head to observe them. "There they go," he whispered. "Do you think one of us should go in the front and the other cover the back?"

"Once they get in their room, it's a fifty-foot jump onto the El tracks," Mercer replied. "No, I think we'll just give them time to get in their room and that'll be it."

Fiscus nodded. "Good. They're going inside now."

"All right. We'll give them another minute or so and then move out."

In the lobby of the hotel, Lloyd looked up from the dirty book he was reading when Jake and Elwood entered. They looked tired. "Hi, boys," he said. "Hard night, eh?"

Jake nodded. "We been at the Jovial Club, Calumet City, listening to some bad disco acts."

"Too bad."

"Any calls for us?"

"No, no calls. That parole fella showed up, though. Said he had a job for you, parking cars."

Elwood smiled. "Jake parking cars. That would be dangerous. He's a bad driver."

A look of panic crossed Jake's features. "Goddamn," he said. "I don't want a job. Did he say when he'd be back?"

"No," Lloyd replied. "But I kinda have the feeling he's around here someplace."

"Probably staked out the place," Jake muttered. "Damn it, I didn't report to that House of Danish, either. He's probably got a hard-on for me instead of a job."

"We'd better bug out," Elwood said. "Thanks, Lloyd."

Taking Jake by the sleeve, he led him through the lobby, down a set of stairs to the basement, and out the back way. They were barely out of sight when Mercer and Fiscus entered the lobby. Mercer looked meaningfully at Lloyd, who rolled his eyes toward the top of his head, as if signaling that the boys had gone upstairs.

With a nod and a tight smile, Mercer walked briskly across the lobby and took the stairs two at a time. Although slightly winded, Wade Fiscus was able to keep up. He was grateful, however, when Mercer paused outside the room, listened for a long moment at the door and then shrugged. "I guess they sacked out already," he concluded.

With that, he backed off against the opposite wall, got

a head of steam up and lashed out at the door with both feet. It caved in quickly and artistically, just as they do in the movies.

"Okay, boys, you're under—" he began.

But the room was empty.

"Goddamn!" Fiscus shouted.

Rushing to the window, he noted that it was locked from the inside. "How do you like that?" he said. "They never even came in here. They must have—"

At that moment, the blonde woman twisted a dial, pointed the remote-control detonator at the Bond Hotel and watched breathlessly as the needle moved rapidly toward the red line. A split second after it crossed the line, a gigantic series of explosions tore the guts out of the lower rear section of the building, a great ball of fire and smoke surging upward, enveloping the El tracks and platform.

The top floors of the hotel sank downward as if pressed by a giant unseen hand. Rotted planking and timbers, with here and there a ruptured series of pipes and gas lines, slowly tumbled into the void left by the total blowout of the lower part of the building.

Throwing himself frantically toward the open door when he heard the explosion, saw the flash, and felt the floor beneath him shake, Burton Mercer grabbed the knob just as all support dropped from under his feet. He screamed as a quick downward glance revealed nothing but dust and timbers spiraling downward into an apparently bottomless abyss. But he was able to hang onto the doorknob long enough to swing his feet upward and catch both heels on the swaying planking of the hallway. Another superhuman thrust of his body brought him flush against the wall, to which he clung with both hands, turning his face away from the open chasm so that he would not have to look into it.

"Burt . . ." he thought he heard.

Only several yards away, Wade Fiscus was beginning a fantastic downward ride, his tiny fists frantically clutching a water pipe that was pitching wildly over the El tracks. He was momentarily suspended in an upright position, like a pole-vaulter. All around him, debris was sliding away toward the smoke-covered ground. Stoves, furniture and beds—one with two people in it—descended into the dusty maelstrom as if in slow-motion. High in the air above the chaotic mess, Wade Fiscus felt his stomach lurch as the pipe began to bend near the bottom, sending him whirling back toward the open-ended building and downward. He closed his eyes as a collision seemed imminent, but the pipe abruptly ceased its sideward motion and hung once again in an upright position, shaking Fiscus like a flag in a stiff breeze. His hands burning, he allowed himself to slide down the pole for ten or fifteen feet, and for a split second he thought he would be able to escape without further injury. The next thing he remembered was being hit by a falling chair and landing with a resounding thump on top of the pile of debris.

From their close vantage point at the base of the elevated train platform, Elwood and Jake turned to watch the explosion, neither of them saying anything for the better part of a minute. Then, as the dust settled, Elwood grunted. "Can't figure that one out, can you?" he said. "The building's old, but you wouldn't think it would go all at once, would you?"

Jake shook his head. "Maybe somebody tried to light a stove," he said.

Fifteen minutes later they were on the tollway, the tape player going full blast, Elwood clipping along as rapidly as traffic would allow.

"Lotta trucks on the road today," Jake observed, as a trackless trailer grazed the front bumper of the Bluesmobile in passing. "Must be some kind of truckers' protest."

"No," Elwood said. "Just regular, normal truck traffic for this time of morning."

"Lotta trucks," Jake said again.

"Yeah, well, according to the latest issue of *Highway Engineering Quarterly*," Elwood began, "there are—"

"The latest issue of what?"

"*Highway Engineering Quarterly*. It's a magazine I read. You can pick it up at the newsstand in Marina City."

"Good," Jake said, without noticeable enthusiasm. "Is that what you've been doing for the past three years? No wonder the band split up."

"Well, not every minute of that time," Elwood replied. "But I read it regularly, you know. Anyway, it says that seventy percent of all vehicles in America are commercial vehicles."

"No shit," Jake yawned.

"I thought that would impress you," Elwood said, not dignifying Jake's sarcasm. "In the latest issue they had an article about accident statistics for commercial carriers at specific peak hours."

"Excuse me if I don't sit straight up and get excited," Jake muttered, turning up the volume on the tape player.

"They mentioned this very section of the tollway," Elwood said, undeterred. "They said it's one of the most heavily traveled tollways in the country. They talked about the causes of commercial traffic accidents right here on Loop 294 southbound between I-57 and I-55."

"Right here?" Jake exuded. "Golly, it kind of gives you goosebumps."

"They had statistics to prove that I-294 on weekdays between five o'clock and ten o'clock in the morning averages more truck accidents than any other stretch of highway in America."

"Did they say why?"

"Mostly failure on the part of some operators to secure their loads correctly," Elwood replied knowingly.

"Not speeding?"

"No."

"That sounds like a bunch of shit to me."

"The statistics said—" Elwood began.

"They said you're a robot," Jake shot back. "You're just like everybody else—ready to believe anything you read. Everybody's ready to believe statistics. Mention a few statistics and you can hose anybody."

"Sorry, Jake," Elwood shrugged. "I didn't mean to upset you."

"I'm not upset," Jake retorted. "I'm just being logical. I mean, here we are, right now, on 294, it's between five and ten o'clock on a weekday morning, there's a lot of commercial traffic out, and I don't see any accidents because operators 'didn't secure their loads correctly.' Matter of fact, the closest thing to an accident I've seen is when you just missed that trackless trailer. Maybe *your* load's not secured correctly, man."

"Well, you're the biggest load in this car," Elwood returned.

"Shit," Jake muttered.

As they spoke, their attention was drawn, as if by magic, to a trailer immediately ahead of them. Caught in a passing pattern, cars whizzing by to their left, Jake and Elwood could do little but wait for an opening. Meanwhile, they noticed that a long-shackled padlock had been inserted sideways through both pieces of the rear door latch, but not locked. The jolting movement of the trailer along the highway caused the lock to vibrate and, even as they watched it, the tumbler fell down and the lock bolt slipped from beneath one piece of the latch. A moment later, the latch bounced upward and the door lever inched out, then flopped back loosely as the door opened slightly.

Traffic seemed to be momentarily clear to their left. Craning his neck to peer through the rear window, Jake yelled, "Pass, Elwood! Go ahead, asshole! You got an opening."

Elwood remained obdurately in the right lane, behind the trailer. "No," he said. "I'd like to see what happens here. And I'd like you to see what happens."

As the trailer picked up speed coming over the crown of a hill, the right rear door continued to bounce open, wider and wider, until it finally yawned fully open. Inside the trailer could be seen boxes piled in layers of four to a row, each boldly labeled: GE MW 3000 MICROWAVE OVEN. With ghoulish fascination, both men watched as the heavy boxes gradually crab-walked toward the rear of the trailer, then, one by one, began falling onto the highway, splintering with resounding impact as they struck the concrete or, in at least three cases, the hood of the Bluesmobile.

"You see?" Elwood said calmly. "If I wasn't such a good driver, a thing like that could make me swerve into the next lane and cause an accident."

"A fluke," Jake muttered, wincing as another box bounced off the hood, slid up against the windshield and remained briefly before crashing into the left lane. A moment later, they heard a squeal of brakes and the sound of a collision behind them.

"You see?" Elwood smiled. "That last carton was just too much for traffic to bear. Guy on my left swung over to avoid it and hit the car next to him."

"All right, all right," Jake mumbled.

Passing the half-empty trailer, they scorched the road for a couple of fast miles before running into another congested area. Directly ahead of them was a flatbed trailer loaded with rolled-steel construction reinforcement bars, held in place by retaining bands that were old and rusty. Two of them, in fact, had already snapped and were hanging loosely over the side of the truck.

"See that?" Elwood said.

Even before Jake could reply, they saw several more retaining bands snap as the load shifted. One by one, then at a faster pace, the steel bars began to slide out of the piles, spilling like huge matchsticks onto the road. Guiding the Bluesmobile with consummate skill, Elwood was able to move against the grain of the avalanche, riding on top of the bars lengthwise as they clattered onto the concrete. Soon the boys were even with the trailer and out of danger, but they were able to see behind them a picture of utter chaos, the bars spinning like gigantic lethal straws in a hurricane, striking a windshield here, slashing a tire there, causing dozens of cars to fan out in disarray. "Looks like Korea," Elwood remarked. "We gotta come back and drive this stretch of road more often."

"Yeah, well, I still don't believe in statistics," Jake snorted, lighting a cigarette, rolling down his window and leaning his arm on the sill.

They passed a pair of slow-moving trucks and were drawing up parallel to a dirty-looking tank-trailer rig with red letters along its side reading HIGHLY CORROSIVE. Jake took a deep puff of his cigarette and closed his eyes, able to enjoy the music for the first time in several miles. Neither he nor Elwood noticed the thick stream of vile yellow liquid leaking from the front filler cap of the truck. Then, as it hit the airstream, the yellow gunk poured in their direction like someone turning a hose on them. Hissing and eating a smoking path up his sleeve jacket from the wrist to the elbow, the chemical brought Jake out of his relaxed world with a bang.

"Jesus Christ!" he shouted.

With a grunt of annoyance, Elwood turned on the windshield wipers, but instead of clearing his vision, the rubber blades promptly disintegrated before his eyes, the smoking bits of black rubber mixing with the amber spray to form a hideously viscous compound that stuck to the glass like glue.

"All right, all right!" Jake shouted. "You're right, dammit! That magazine's right, dammit! I admit it! Now just get me the hell off this section of road, okay?"

Elwood craned his head to the left, the better to see around the glutinous streaks on the windshield. "It'll be all

THE BLUES BROTHERS

Sister Mary Stigmata casts Jake and Elwood from her office and orders them not to return until they have redeemed themselves.

In the orphanage basement where he lives, Curtis urges Jake and Elwood to go see the Reverend Cleophus James.

Reverend Cleophus of the Triple Rock Baptist Church.

Opposite page, top: Jake and Elwood bargain with Ray for instruments at Ray's Music Exchange.

Murph and the Magic Tones perform in the Armada Room of the Ramada Inn.

Right: The Nazi Party leader pursues Jake and Elwood with a murderous vengeance.

Matt "Guitar" Murphy's wife warns him to think about the consequences of his actions.

Jake and Elwood perform at Bob's Country Bunker.

Curtis rallies the orphans to help publicize Jake and Elwood's concert.

Parole officer Burton Mercer alerts the Illinois State Police about Jake and Elwood's concert.

The mystery woman confronts Jake and Elwood in the tunnel under the Jovial Club.

To placate the impatient Jovial Club audience, Curtis performs a song.

With police forces surrounding the auditorium, Jake and Elwood and the Blues Brothers Band give their concert.

In the high-speed pursuit of Jake and Elwood, police cars crash and pile up in the street beneath the El tracks.

To evade the Nazis, Jake and Elwood's Bluesmobile leaps over their car.

In pursuit of Jake and Elwood, troops invade Daley Plaza and converge on the Cook County Building.

In the Cook County Assessor's office, soldiers finally corner Jake and Elwood.

Inside Joliet Prison, Jake and Elwood with the Blues Brothers Band.

right soon," he said casually. "In a few minutes it'll be after ten o'clock."

"Stop there," Jake said when the Bluesmobile neared the first public telephone booth after entering the city limits of Decatur.

Elwood pulled to the curb and Jake immediately attacked the Yellow Pages. Turning first to "Burglar Alarms," he was told to look under "Alarms," which he did only after tearing out the first page and throwing it away. Running his finger down the list, he came to the name of a company that sounded right. "Ray-Dex Alarm Company," he read aloud. "217 Industry."

Tearing the page out of the directory, he stuffed it in his pocket and returned to the car. "Murph said the Duck was working for an alarm company named 'Ray' something," he said. "I think I found it. At least it's the only one with 'Ray' in it."

"Why'd you throw away that first page?" Elwood asked, putting the Bluesmobile into drive and heading onto the main road.

"I looked under 'Burglar' first and it told me to look under 'Alarms,'" Jake explained. "So I figure the next person won't waste his time if the 'Burglar' page isn't there, right?"

"Jesus," Elwood said softly.

They located the small plaza where Ray-Dex was situated, and Jake went inside. He returned in less than a minute and indicated that Elwood should head east.

"So—does the Duck still work there?" Elwood asked.

Jake nodded. "Yeah, he works for them, only he ain't there now. He's out on a call. They told me where. Some high school just outside of town ... East Decatur Senior High ... 27 Kimway Drive."

"What's he doing there?"

"I don't know. Fixing their burglar alarm system, I guess."

A quarter-hour later, they pulled up to the front of a traditional brick school constructed during the late 1940s, four stories high and shaped in the form of a T.

"Drive around the building," Jake said.

They spotted the van bearing the words RAY-DEX ALARM SYSTEMS halfway around the block near the school's large recreation ground. Several yards away from the truck was a thick utility pole, at the top of which was fixed a large, bell-shaped public warning siren of early 1950s vintage. A stepladder leaning against the base of the pole led to a platform around the top on which a man stood. He was busily moving the siren from one side to the other.

"That must be the Duck up there," Elwood observed.

"Can't see too well with the sun against us like this," Jake replied. "But the hair looks shaggy enough."

They parked the car behind the Ray-Dex van and walked over to the base of the ladder. From that vantage point, they were able to see that the young man pivoting the siren and adjusting something in the control box with a screwdriver had a thick red Afro, was smoking a pipe, and had the pink complexion of a newborn babe.

"Hi, Duck, you're looking real good!" Jake shouted.

The figure stopped working, squinted at Elwood and Jake, then threw his hands out in a welcoming gesture. "Hey, come on up," he said warmly.

The Blues Brothers scrambled up the ladder and onto the platform.

Duck grinned. "Jake, I thought they promised you three to five years in the pen."

"I escaped an hour ago," Jake explained.

"Well, buddy," the Duck said, "you can be damn sure up here ain't the best place to hide."

"Murph said you called him," Jake began. "Told us you were living down here. We figured we'd sort of drop in . . . say hello . . . drop by and see how you were doing, you know. Murph couldn't make it. Said to say hi and sorry he couldn't come down."

Elwood marveled silently at the transformation that came over Jake when he was around Donald "Duck" Dunn, their former great bass guitarist. Most people did not awe Jake and he could take liberties with them, bullshit them, treat them like groupies clustered about him, the star. With the Duck it was different. For some reason, Jake had an inordinate respect for the husky musician with the steady stream of cracker patter. Duck *was* Soul; as rock-steady as the thundering bass he played. Thus Jake's personality, usually so ebullient, became restrained and almost considerate around the Duck.

"Well, I guess Murph's awfully busy now that he's playing those big hotel chains," Duck said.

Jake nodded. "He's doing great . . . real great . . . I mean, he's *living* at a Ramada Inn."

"I know. I called him there."

"Oh, right," Jake muttered. "Right. He told us. He was the one who said you were down here . . . so we figured we'd come down and see how you were."

Thinking Jake was not in the proper mood to convince the Duck that he should rejoin the band, Elwood decided to stall for time in the hope that Jake would get a better handle on the situation.

"So what's the story on this?" Elwood asked, examining the siren's control box.

"It's just one of them public warning sirens they put up in the fifties," the Duck said. "They were built in case of a nuclear air raid. A kind of courtesy device so that people would have time enough to kiss their asses goodbye."

The boys laughed.

"Is something wrong with it?" Elwood continued.

The Duck shook his head. "I'm usually a burglar alarm man. But the company has a contract with the government... Civil Defense. So I have to come up here once a month and do a test."

"Great," Jake said. "I just get out and everybody's warming up for the big flash."

Elwood rotated the siren. "Could you sing through this thing?" he asked.

"If you had an older model mike," the Duck replied. "Low impedance, cardioid type..."

"Excuse me, I'll be right back," Elwood said.

He backed away to the edge of the platform and began to climb down the stepladder.

After a moment of silence, the Duck said, "Jake, if there's anything I can do to help you out... you know, a little money, some grub... a place to stay..."

"Well, as a matter of fact there is something," Jake said, seizing the opening.

"Shoot."

"Duck, I want to pull the band back together. All of us. Willie, Murph, Matt, Blue Lou, the Colonel... all of us. Playing like we used to."

"Well, I don't know about the Colonel," the Duck said. "He's mended his ways, I think. After you got plucked, he quit playing pool, quit playing guitar, quit drinking and moved back with his people... back with his father on the Hutterite colony."

"And what about you, Duck?"

"I don't know, Jake. I just don't know."

Jake put his hand on the Duck's shoulder. "Listen," he said sincerely. "We can do it, Duck. We've already got Willie and Murph and Bones and Al Rubin. But we need you. You... you were the nerve center... the backbone

... the pulse ... your bass was the band. We need you ... we can't do it without you ... we have to get the band happening. No kidding, God wants us to. If we don't get it happening, a lot of fine kids will lose their home and I'll never be able to go straight and never sing again. I'll roam the streets, a silent fugitive with a lost dream..."

"Hey—" the Duck interrupted.

"I'm sorry," Jake murmured. "I shouldn't come here and dump my bag of snakes in your lap. I'm not going to lie to you. I came because I really just wanted to know if you'd ever consider coming out on the road with us again."

"Shit, yeah!" the Duck replied. "You bet! Why'd you go through that song and dance, anyway? All you had to do was tell me where, when, and how much ... if any ..."

They were shaking hands when Elwood appeared at the edge of the platform, an old EV. 666 P.A. microphone in his hand.

"How about this?" he asked, handing the mike to the Duck.

"Okay, but I'm gonna have to splice it. Is that all right with you?"

"Sure."

As the Duck bent down to his tool box, Jake suddenly frowned, then looked intently at Elwood.

"That microphone," he said slowly. "I've never seen it before. Is that ... Is that the mike you traded the Cadillac for?"

"Yeah," Elwood smiled.

"You monk!"

"So it's being put to a good use," Elwood said. "What's all the fuss about?"

The Duck handed the mike to Jake. "Here," he said. "You want to sing?"

Jake nodded. The Duck put his hand on a switch, then looked at the Brothers. "Let me know when you're ready," he said.

"What's a good number to sing?" Jake mused. "Something appropriate, I mean."

The Duck smiled. "What's appropriate for an air raid siren? Why not 'Dig Myself a Hole'?"

"You're a genius," Jake smiled.

He waited until Elwood produced his harp, then gave the signal for the Duck to give them volume. After a brief surge of feedback that caused them all to wince, the system settled down and Jake began to sing the Arthur Cruddup classic dealing with a nuclear holocaust.

By a marvelous acoustical fluke, the reproduction was perfect, Jake's words booming into the surrounding community with perfect clarity, as if some unseen visitor from space were singing to the whole world. The accompanying harp added an eerie touch, as did a slight quavering tone created by the system as it neared overload. One by one, windows in the area began to open, and heads looked outside to discover where the heavenly voice was actually coming from. Cars that had stopped at red lights remained there after the lights turned green, their occupants too awed by the sounds to notice that they were free to move. Pedestrian traffic at a nearby shopping center came to a standstill, young and older adults collecting in tight groups to gaze at the sky and ask each other if anyone knew the source of the strange music. One young religious couple, believing the end of the world was being signaled by this classic tune, got out of their car at a crowded intersection and started dancing. Police sirens began to wail in the distance, adding to the nightmare quality of the event. Inevitably, a few persons started to run, trying to escape the sounds from above; their panic generated even more tension, so that before long the entire neighborhood was crisscrossed with people of all ages racing in all directions.

Then, as suddenly as it began, the bizarre incident came to a conclusion with Elwood's poignant harp solo simulating the howl of the siren itself. All was quiet once again, except

THE BLUES BROTHERS

for the police cars *wherp-wherp*ing in the direction of the utility pole where the three young men were gathered.

"You guys better hustle," the Duck warned. "Those cops'll be here in a minute or two."

Jake nodded as Elwood started down the pole. "Two things first," he said. "Where did you say Cropper was?"

"He's over in Indiana. In the Hutterite village at French Lick. You'll have to ask exactly where it is, though."

"Okay. Now what about you, Duck?"

"What about me?"

"You're with us?"

"I told you yes. Now get your ass moving down that pole, Jake Blues, or I'm gonna have a hard time hosing the cops with a story they'll believe."

"We have a gig Friday night," Jake said, swinging his leg over the side. "At the Jovial Club, Calumet City."

"Right."

"Don't forget, now."

The Duck smiled. "Don't worry, I'll be there. I just hope you and Elwood are."

The Bluesmobile rumbled up just as Jake's feet struck the ground. A half-minute later, they had burned two fast right turns and were out of range of the police.

Elwood slowed the Bluesmobile to seventy-five as they tooled through a quiet residential neighborhood. "Are we being followed?" he asked.

Jake shook his head. "No . . . I imagine the Duck is covering us right now, though. Weaving a web of bullshit around those cops so thick they'll never get it all off."

"Did you ask him about playing in the band?"

"He's in," Jake replied.

"Good."

"That's five in and just three to go."

"Even I'm getting excited now," Elwood said. "It would be even nicer if we really had a gig."

"I told you to stop being so negative."

"I'll try. Where's the Colonel?"

"Somewhere near French Lick, Indiana."

"Somewhere. That's a good clue."

"It's in a religious settlement," Jake explained. "The Hutterites. How many of them can there be?"

"That's a haul from here," Elwood said.

"Maybe we'd better try to get Blue Lou first. Mr. Fabulous said he was going to night school in Champaign-Urbana."

"That's only about fifty miles from here."

"Let's check it out," Jake said, leaning his head back, popping a cassette in the player and propping his feet against the dashboard.

A leisurely three-quarters of an hour later, they pulled off Interstate 72 and were soon driving down a university campus street lined with clean, antiseptic modern buildings. Ahead of them loomed a structure of gray concrete that rather resembled a bunker minus machine-gun slots. "That's it," Jake said. "Information center. Pull in that space marked 'Dean' and we'll ask about Blue Lou."

"Think it's worth putting on my doctor's plates?" Elwood asked after they had parked the car and gotten out.

Jake shook his head. "Chances are this Mr. Dean is gone out to lunch," he said. "Let's chance it."

As they sauntered into the building, several students turned to look at them, hardly bothering to disguise their curious gazes; others directed furtive glances at them from behind books or at their rears after they had passed.

"What do you think?" one student asked another. "Narcs?"

Elwood and Jake ignored the flurry of excitement they left in their wake.

Directly, they found a door marked REGISTRAR, marched into the office and rapped on the counter top until a secretary hastily got off the telephone to help them.

THE BLUES BROTHERS

"You gentlemen must be here to perform the autopsy," she said, super-sweetly.

"No, ma'am," Elwood replied. "Why do you say that?"

"Oh, just because the last time I saw outfits like that, they were worn by men from the county coroner's office who were here to perform an autopsy for the medical students." She smiled again in a very supercilious way. "Nothing personal, of course."

"We want to find out if a man goes to night school here," Jake said, getting right to business.

"Yes to that question," the woman replied. She had straight blonde hair tied in a bun and wore large glasses, but was obviously no laggard, especially when it came to holding a grudge.

"I'm sorry we had to interrupt your personal phone call," Jake said. "It's just that this is important."

"Then you're cops," she said.

"Could you please just give us the facts, ma'am?" Elwood asked. "We're trying to locate a night school student."

"What is his discipline?" the woman asked.

"Very little," Jake said.

"I meant, do you know what subjects he's studying? We keep students filed by subjects first and name second."

"Sorry, we don't know what he's studying. Or if."

"Then his name is—?"

"Blue Lou."

"Last name is Blue and first name Lou?" she said with a frown.

"No," Jake said. "We just call him Blue Lou."

"L-E-W or L-O-U, may I ask?"

"Pardon?" Jake asked.

"His name is Marini, miss," Elwood said. "Lou Marini. Louis Marini. M-A-R-I-N-I."

"Now we're getting somewhere," the woman said. "Just a moment and I'll see if he's registered."

She went to a desk with a computer console, sat down and punched several keys.

"How do you like that?" Jake asked in a deliberately loud voice. "She says she's gonna help us and starts watching TV instead."

A moment later, the woman got up and returned to the counter. "Yes," she said, looking at the printout provided by the computer. "We do have a Louis Marini registered here as a part-time student."

"Good," Jake said. "Where does he live?"

"Well, I don't see an address here," the woman replied. "But even if it were here, we're not allowed to give it out."

Jake's jaw fell.

"However," the woman added, "we do show that Mr. Marini has taken temporary employment through the student job bank."

"Employment?" Jake interjected. "You mean . . . he's working?"

"Hopefully."

"We really need to find him now, ma'am," Jake said urgently. "You see, we're artificial limb salesmen from Chicago—"

The woman arched her eyebrows. "You sell prosthetic devices?" she said.

"Yeah."

"I guess it figures, at that."

"Anyway, ma'am, several months ago Mr. Marini ordered new legs from our company . . ."

The woman studied the printout. "It doesn't say anything here about a disability," she said.

"Well, he needs a new set," Jake continued. "We came all the way down here to fit him with new legs. We got a couple of brand-new ones for him. Plastic, with simulated hair and everything. The best."

"If he keeps using the old ones, he'll damage himself," Elwood added.

"I don't understand how he got job placement," the woman murmured.

"Well, he can sit at a desk," Elwood said.

"But this indicates he's a night watchman!"

"Impossible!" Jake almost shouted. "How can he have a job like that? He can't work. He can barely hop! If this gets out . . . If it gets out that the school put a man like that to work as a night watchman, I hate to think of the bad press. Tell us where he's working so we can talk some sense into him."

"It says he's working for Bulmer Developments, Concessions Road 6, Blossomville," she said quickly.

"Thank you, ma'am." Elwood grabbed Jake's arm and led him away from the counter before he could say anything more.

Finding Concessions Road 6 was not as simple as it sounded, largely because the housing development being created by Bulmer Developments was not yet open to the public. After receiving conflicting directions that sent them from one side of Urbana to the other, the boys eventually ended up in the middle of a vast, open mud flat. It was dusk, the available daylight fading fast, and no structures of any sort were visible.

"Christ," Jake muttered as the Bluesmobile sloshed through the heavily rutted road. "I thought you said you knew where we were going, Elwood."

"You're supposed to be the navigator," Elwood replied.

After wallowing through another quarter-mile of liquid highway, the Bluesmobile came to a break in the road, a small creek with two-foot-high banks on either side. The boys got out and examined the situation.

"Look at this shit," Jake said, shaking his head. "We'd better go back."

"Are you kidding?" Elwood laughed. "We can make it through here, no trouble at all."

"You're crazy!"

THE BLUES BROTHERS

"This car can go anywhere," Elwood proclaimed. "This ditch is nothing for this car. I might as well stop for a dog pissing on the road. We can drive right through like a tank."

He returned to the vehicle, backed it up about ten yards, revved the motor and rocketed forward, blasting through the sludge and landing with a mammoth impact in the middle of the creekbed. Cursing under his breath, he gunned the motor, spun the wheels, rocked the car back and forth, succeeding only in rendering it completely immobile.

"You robot!" Jake shouted angrily.

Elwood got out, exiting via the window onto the hood. With his hands on his hips, he stood looking down at the hopeless situation.

"You oughta drown in that dog piss," Jake taunted.

"I really thought I could make it," Elwood murmured thoughtfully. "If I had it to do over again, I would."

"Asshole!" Jake thundered.

Stuck in what resembled a World War One battlefield, they wandered about for an hour until well after sunset. Only the fact that the sky was clear and bright with summer stars made their situation less than totally miserable.

"Very nice night," Elwood said once.

Jake didn't answer.

A minute or so later, they spotted a thin sliver of light far in the distance.

"Civilization!" Elwood shouted.

"Probably just a witch-burning," Jake muttered.

"That's what I said—civilization," Elwood said. "Come on, let's hustle."

They slogged through mud until a small aluminum office trailer was but yards away from them, a warm and welcome light shining from within.

"Listen," Elwood said, stopping in his soggy tracks. "Music. Do you hear it?"

"No, I see it," Jake replied.

He pointed to the silhouette of a man playing a saxophone, the sounds of which were reasonably cool—in fact, not bad at all.

Even as they stared at the person, however, the music stopped and the figure moved toward the door of the trailer. Jake and Elwood quickly hit the dirt like a pair of well-drilled Marines, their lunges carrying them just below a beam of light flashed outside from the open door of the trailer.

"Oh no," Elwood whispered. "It's a cop!"

Covered with mud, looking like a pair of raccoons caught in the garbage, Elwood and Jake cowered lower and lower to avoid the beam of light. But it followed them, finally shining in their eyes and holding them like an accusing ray of guilt.

"Shit," Jake muttered.

The light went from one face to the other. Then a familiar voice called out, "Jake? Elwood?"

"It's all over," Jake moaned. "It's a trap set by that goddamn parole officer. They been waiting for us."

"Jake, is that you, man?" the voice asked. It didn't sound like the voice of a cop. "Hey, come on in . . ."

Elwood and Jake crawled out of the ooze, mounted the stairs of the trailer and went inside. The interior was a construction office with drafting tables, an oil stove, a cot, and a coat rack on which hung variously colored hardhats. Next to the door was the familiar figure of Blue Lou Marini, mustached, long hair in a pony tail, incongruously clad in a gray uniform with a shoulder patch reading SPARTAN SECURITY.

"Hey, what are you guys doing out there?" Lou asked. When the boys continued to stare at him, he added, "Hey, it's me—Lou. Remember? Blue Lou Marini."

"Damned if it ain't," Jake whispered, awestruck.

"Sit down," Lou offered, closing the door. "What's happening, anyway? You look a little spaced."

"We got lost," Jake explained, pointing a finger at Elwood. "*He* got lost. We were looking for you."

"Then you ain't lost."

"Yeah."

"You came all the way out here just to see me?" Lou smiled. "Must really be something heavy. Did you come to pay me for my last gig back in . . . I forget the year . . ."

"Well, we came to work out a deal with you," Jake hedged.

"Let's have some coffee," Lou suggested, moving to a corner of the trailer that was obviously his, consisting of the cot, a desk with his horn lying in its open case, scattered clothes and other belongings giving the small area a lived-in look. Putting the coffeepot on the stove, Lou said, "Hey, I thought you were still in jail, man."

"I escaped a couple of hours ago," Jake said.

"Really! Well, you're welcome to hide out here for a couple of weeks. Nobody'll find you here."

Jake's eyes suddenly came alive. "Forget about that coffee," he said, reaching into his side coat pocket and bringing out a pint of Key Largo wine.

"Allll right!" Lou smiled.

Jake cracked it open as Lou produced some paper cups. The three wheezed back the vicious sweet wine.

"That's great stuff," said Elwood.

"We heard you was going to school," Jake remarked.

"Yeah," Lou said. "I became a student to get a job through student placement. Except I haven't made it to class lately. I've been on twenty-four-hour guard out here for a couple of months. I live here, rent-free, no neighbors. I can practice my horn and nobody hassles me. So I don't miss school that much."

"It's just as well," Jake said. "We told them you were a double amputee, so they might not be too anxious to have you back."

"Why'd you say that?"

"Just for conversation."

Lou shrugged. They swilled down another round of the cheap wine.

"It was nearly dark by the time we got out here," Elwood said. "Just what exactly is it you're 'guarding'?"

"It's just a construction site," Lou said.

"Looks like the end of the world."

"Yeah."

A few minutes later, Lou reached into his desk drawer and brought out a plastic bag.

"Do you guys mind if I have a smoke?" he asked.

The boys shook their heads. Lou slid an office chair over to the desk and proceeded to roll a fat, European-style five-paper joint of gold marijuana. Using a match, he heated and crumbled a black lump into the mixture, twisted it up and inserted a cardboard filter.

"Do you guys still get high?" he asked. "It's been a while. A lot of people don't get high anymore." Exhaling a lungful, he added, "Medical reports say it's bad for your health."

"A lot of things we enjoy are bad for our health," Elwood said.

Jake nodded. "A lot of things we need. Like alcohol . . ." He took a long pull on the wine.

"Fluorocarbons," Elwood said.

"Bacon," Lou offered.

"Sugarless gum," Jake said, reaching across to take a puff of the joint.

"Kettles with lead heating elements," Elwood continued patiently.

"Eskimo pies . . . TV dinners," added Lou.

"Diet sodas," Jake said.

"Asbestos insulation," Elwood murmured softly, luxuriating in the first glow of the joint.

"Toothpaste in aluminum tubes . . ."

"The glue on the backs of stamps . . ."

"Folding chairs . . ."

"Who said folding chairs?"
"I didn't..."
"I didn't..."
"And I didn't..."
"Anyway, nuclear waste..."
"What about it?"
"Is something else that's bad for us... that we need..."
"Aspirin..."
"Cheerios..."
"Cap'n Crunch..."
"Distilled water..."
"No shit? Distilled water?"
"Will kill you..."
"All kinds of things are bad for you..."
"X-rays..."
"Yeah, things around us every day. Let's not talk about it."
"Fingernail polish..."
"I said, let's not talk about it."
"Yeah... Sure... Cracker Jacks..."

They fell asleep not long afterward, Jake's last contribution being a meticulously articulated "Roumanian alphabet soup" before passing into the world of deep snoring and Rapid Eye Movement.

chapter six

Jake awoke from the night's sleep in heavy pain. His head throbbed from the cheap sweet wine, both his cheeks seemed glued together from the inside and his eyes felt as if they were focused on the backs of his eyelids. In addition, the memory of the dream still lingered.

The good news was that the dream was only a dream, perhaps a forewarning of things to come. In the dream, he and Elwood and the rest of the Blues Brothers had performed—disastrously. The sound—which he could hear yet with only the slightest effort—was flatulent and listless, without character or drive, a mere shadow of a ghost of an outline of their former greatness. Instead of everyone being the pulse, the nerve center, the backbone, every man was a follower in search of a leader, a hack musician faking uninspired variations to an erratic beat. The audience knew, of course, and sat on its hands, too mortified for the Blues Brothers' sake to boo, hiss or walk out.

Jake experienced a great sense of relief when he realized he was still in the trailer, that the day of the band's comeback was still in the future rather than the past. True, it was Wednesday, only two days before the monumental gig he still had not yet arranged. Yet even as he enjoyed the feelings of relief, he was tortured by new waves of doubt.

First, of course, they had to convince Blue Lou that he should join them. Jake sensed that doing so would not be too difficult; yet he wanted to strike quickly, get the day moving successfully. Shaking Lou gently, he managed to rouse him in less than a minute.

"Come on, Lou," he urged. "Elwood and me have to get moving soon. And I want to talk with you about something before we go."

Lou's words came out thickly. "I . . . I thought you said you wanted to hide out here awhile," he murmured.

"No," Jake said. "C'mon. Let's go outside for some fresh air."

It was just after dawn. Lou shivered. "Fresh?" he repeated. "You mean freezing."

"It'll do us good."

"Okay."

A minute later, they were trudging along on mud that was crusty on top as a result of the night's chill, which made for adventurous walking in that some sections were as firm as rock, while others gave way like quicksand. Ahead of them, in whatever direction they looked, they could make out low, flat roof outlines of new houses, silhouettes that had blended into the treeless landscape the night before, but which now gave a surreal quality to the scene. It was as if some deity had wiped all life from the face of the earth and then dropped dozens of plastic model houses onto the muddy soil.

"What is this place, anyway?" Jake asked.

"Cherrywood Hills, they call it," Lou replied. "Champaign-Urbana's newest planned community. There are over five miles of streets and well over three hundred prefabricated houses in here."

"That term 'planned community' makes my flesh creep," Jake said. "It makes me think of a bunch of robots."

"You got it."

"Where are they all now?"

"Man, these houses are brand-new," Lou explained. "Most of them are presold, but none of the owners can move in. Two months ago, there was a big tradesman's strike—electricians, carpenters, sheet-metal workers. The plumbers and heating contractors went out in sympathy, so

THE BLUES BROTHERS

a lot of these houses aren't even finished inside."

They moved up a board pathway to the first of the homes and stepped inside. The foyer and living room area was a tangle of plaster, nails, insulation and wire, a mess that looked as if it could never be put in shape.

"Well, here it is," Lou announced sarcastically. "The model home you've always dreamed of owning. Cherrywood Hills' exclusive Mediterranean model, a three-bedroom, custom-designed split-level at an affordable $93,000."

"Are you serious?" Jake asked, aghast.

"Of course. Where you been the last few years?" Then Lou smiled. "That's right. You been in the slammer. I don't guess they talk much about the price of new homes there."

Jake grunted.

"Anyway," Lou continued, "this is standard housing for the middle-income class. Ninety-three G's."

"It ain't right," Jake said. "Nobody's gonna pay that."

"Are you kidding? Half of these places are sold already."

"Goddamnit!" Jake shouted, suddenly picking up a large piece of wallboard and heaving it against the ceiling. As soon as the dust had settled, he threw a handful of nails against the picture window, shattering several of the small panes.

"Hey, man, what's the matter?" Lou demanded. "You trying to get me fired?"

"No," Jake muttered, sighing. "It just pisses me off that people can pay that kind of money for a piece of shit like this, and the kids at St. Helen's may get their asses thrown on the street for a lousy five thousand. It's just not right."

"What's St. Helen's?"

"An orphanage."

"Oh. Yeah, I guess the world's full of crap like that," Lou said. "Anyway, the strike won't be settled for another month, so if you guys want to hole up here, it's fine. I'll make runs for supplies and stuff."

"No, we gotta keep moving," Jake said. "We have to

go to Indiana and find the Colonel."

"The Colonel? Cropper? You're going to see Cropper?"

"Sure," Jake said, nodding.

"I thought he was still living with Matt."

"No. We're looking for him, too. You know where he is?"

"Last I heard, he was working at the Soul Food Cafe on Maxwell Street."

Jake smiled. "Hey, that's great to know. If we can find Cropper over in Indiana and Matt on Maxwell Street and you throw in with us, we'll be ready to go."

"What do you mean?"

"We're putting the band back together again," Jake said.

"How? With what?" Lou asked skeptically. "*On* what? I mean, I dig you and Elwood . . . personally . . . but, like, you still owe us money from the last appearance."

"Money!" Jake shot back. "Is that all you can think of? Here Elwood and me are carrying out a mission for God—"

Blue Lou couldn't help laughing.

"I'm serious!" Jake returned. "We're getting the band together again to help a bunch of orphans. It's a mission for God and you think it's just a joke."

"I'm sorry, Jake," Lou said softly. "I didn't mean to laugh. It just took me by surprise, that's all. Hey, relax, man. You did stiff us. From a professional standpoint I'm just being straight with you."

"You got me high so you could be straight with me. Thanks a lot," Jake said.

They returned to the trailer in silence.

Elwood was awake and, having found some near-frozen bread in the refrigerator, was munching happily away. Jake remained outside, walking in tight circles while Lou came inside.

"Sleep okay?" he asked.

Elwood nodded. "Something the matter? Jake looks shittin' mad."

Lou shrugged. "He said you guys were going to put the band back together and I asked about our pay from two years ago. That set him off, I guess."

"He's been touchy lately," Elwood said.

"Maybe I shouldn't have mentioned the money."

"Well, maybe not," Elwood replied. "Jake only remembers the good things, you know. How great we all sounded, the songs, the laughs. He's managed to forget the unpaid bills."

"I mean it about you guys staying here."

"It's nice of you, but we gotta get the car outa that mud and move on."

"Do you want me to come back with the band, Elwood?"

"Are you kidding? We sure do. Like Jake says, you're the pulse, the backbone, the nerve center. The reason he's so pissed is he can't imagine how we're gonna make it without you."

"When do you think it will happen?"

"This Friday night. We got a recording gig at the Jovial Club in Calumet City." As he spoke the words, Elwood marveled at the way they rolled off his tongue. Obviously he had heard the lie repeated so often that he now believed it himself.

"No kidding? Hey, I'll be there."

"Great."

"Now let's see about getting you guys outa that mud."

As they stepped out of the trailer, Elwood gave the thumbs-up sign to Jake along with a wink. His brother's mood brightened immediately. A few minutes later, the three of them were riding a big, yellow snorting Cat DJ-10 bulldozer in the direction of the Bluesmobile, which from a distance resembled a surfacing blue whale.

"Well, you guys did it up right, anyway," Lou said, surveying the car's messy dilemma.

"Yeah."

"Help me get these chains on," Lou said, scrambling

down from the cab. It was a messy quarter-hour, but soon the bulldozer eased the mired Bluesmobile onto solid ground. Elwood got inside and turned the key in the ignition. The engine roared to life.

"All right!" Jake shouted.

Before they drove off, Lou came over to the window. "Elwood told me about your gig Friday night and I'll be there," he said. "If it's all right with you."

Jake smiled. "Look, if you can make it, it'll be great," he said. "If not . . . well, I'll kill you."

"I'll be there," Lou laughed.

With a blast of the horn, Elwood sent the Bluesmobile sloshing noisily across the spongy surface. Soon they were on a macadam road, then a six-lane highway. The weather, which had been threatening at first, cleared, the clouds giving way to a blue sky. The land had a clean, just-scrubbed look, the light rain of the previous night still clinging to the trees and grass, accentuating the greenness. Traffic was light and the drive was a pleasant one, especially so after they left the main road to enter a farming community complete with horses and buggies, old-fashioned barns with hex signs, and red-roofed houses.

"This is the place," Jake said as they passed a small rectangular sign reading FRENCH LICK. "I guess the best thing to do is stop somebody and ask."

Presently they neared a buggy driver wearing a chest-length beard, black half-Stetson hat, black frock coat, and white collarless shirt. Elwood slowed the Bluesmobile as Jake leaned out the window.

"Hey, pal," he said. "We're looking for the Colonel . . . Colonel Steve Cropper."

The buggy driver smiled and shrugged.

"The Cropper place," Jake said.

"Try the Elder Cropper," Elwood suggested. "They're big on that term, I hear."

"The Elder Cropper?" Jake said.

The driver put his hand out, indicating south, but his expression was not too convincing.

Jake nodded. "Thanks, pal."

"Must be one of those seasonal vows of silence," Elwood said, gunning the car.

At a nearby gas station, they were given a good clue as to the whereabouts of the Cropper family. Following the rather complicated directions, they came to a dead-end community of three or four houses next to a washed-out creekbed. The largest home was a well-built two-story clapboard structure with a covered wooden porch and a red roof. Jake got out of the car and knocked on the door. A Hutterite woman in a black and white outfit answered.

"Excuse me, ma'am," Jake said, removing his hat. "Could you tell where I might find the Elder Cropper?"

The woman pointed to a man walking down the road toward the house, a rugged, strong-looking type of about fifty, with a gray beard.

"Thank you, miss," Jake smiled. He waited for the man to amble onto the porch, then asked, "Elder Cropper?"

The man nodded.

"I'm a friend of your son," Jake went on. "The Colonel . . . I mean Steve . . . Stephen . . . your son."

With a quick, firm shake of his head, the man looked at Jake and opened his lips very slowly. For a long moment, Jake wondered if the words would ever emerge. They finally did, deep and resonant, the way Moses' words from Mount Sinai might have sounded.

"Know ye now and remember the Elder spake but once," the man intoned. "The son hath long returned from the veil of wickedness. *Thou* shalt not cause his abandonment. Begone, thou scion of Satan, for neither he nor the Elders desireth thee. Begone!"

With that, he turned and entered the house, slamming the door behind him.

Jake trudged back to the car.

THE BLUES BROTHERS

"What'd he say?" Elwood asked.

"Somethin' about the Hell's Angels," Jake replied.

"Was that the Colonel's old man?"

"Yeah."

"Was the Colonel home?"

"I don't know. The old man didn't give me time to ask. He's a powerhouse. He wouldn't have let me inside anyway."

"Well, let's cruise the property," Elwood suggested.

The lines of the Cropper property were fairly well defined by a series of neat fences and dirt trails giving access to the various fields. Jake and Elwood made a quick tour, but had no luck until they spotted a young man plowing a corner of one field with a team of horses.

"Damned if that don't look like him," Jake said.

"Yeah," Elwood agreed.

Spotting an opening in the fence, he headed the Bluesmobile across the newly carved furrows, the car bumping gently as they neared the figure, who seemed straight out of the nineteenth century.

"If this ain't the Colonel, he's really gonna be pissed," Jake said.

"Listen," Elwood replied. "It could be the Colonel and he'll still be pissed."

Their subject, who was totally immersed in his work, was a clear-eyed, stern-looking man of about thirty, with shoulder-length hair and a full beard. He wore a collarless shirt, high black pants and black suspenders. His sleeves were rolled up, his hands and arms coated with sweat, the soaked shirt clinging to his back. Around his neck were draped the leather reins of the team.

"It's the Colonel," Jake said in a loud voice.

The young man turned, and started as he saw the car bearing down on him. Instead of smiling with recognition, he looked at the two visitors as if they were about to attack him.

"Get that car out of my father's field," he ordered. "I just plowed these furrows."

THE BLUES BROTHERS

"This looks like a tough one," Jake said to Elwood. "I'd better turn on the charm."

"We can probably do even better than that," Elwood said. Turning off the ignition, he got out and unlocked the trunk. In the meantime, the young man had dropped the reins and was in the process of kicking at the car's grille.

"I mean it!" he shouted. "Move it or I'll start taking it apart! I'll do it! I swear it!"

Working quickly, Elwood reached into the trunk and brought out an old guitar case. He opened it and brought out a Telecaster guitar. Holding it above his head as a priest might brandish a crucifix to ward off evil spirits, he moved slowly in Cropper's direction. The rays of the sun caught the metal of the guitar, and it shone with a holy light of its own.

The light seared, golden, into Cropper's eyes. His hands flew to his face, covering his eyes.

"It's yours," Elwood said soothingly. "Here, Steve. You thought she was gone, but she lives. Here."

The sun's rays bouncing powerfully off the pickup plate, Elwood extended the instrument in the direction of the young man. Cropper took two steps backwards. "No," he stammered.

"We have come to return her to you . . . and you to her," Elwood intoned mystically.

He held the guitar outward until Cropper's hands started to move toward it. Then, drawing the instrument slowly back to his own body, Elwood edged closer to the Bluesmobile, his eyes noting the intensity in the Colonel's expression. In fact Cropper seemed mesmerized, his movements almost wooden as he lurched toward the guitar, feet stumbling slightly over the rough ground but taking him inexorably toward the object.

"It's yours," Elwood whispered. "Soon you will be together again. Soon . . . soon . . ."

Gently he opened the rear door of the Bluesmobile and slid the guitar onto the back seat, pushing it to the far side. Cropper, still seemingly in a trance, followed, getting into the car so that he could finally reach out and touch the object that so fascinated him.

As soon as the Colonel was inside the Bluesmobile, Elwood slammed the door, ran around to the driver's seat and started away.

Clutching the guitar to his breast, Cropper seemed to snap out of his hypnotic trance, shook his head and reached for the door handle to get out. Instead he encountered only a metal stump.

"It's a police car," Elwood said over his shoulder. "No door handles, so you can't get out, Colonel."

The Colonel looked down at the guitar, a tear forming at the corner of his left eye. "What do you want of me?" he asked slowly, wiping the moisture away with the back of his hand.

"We want to talk to you," Jake said. Lighting a cigarette, he offered one to Steve.

"No, thank you," Cropper said. A split second later, however, he sighed and said, "Well, maybe I will."

Jake handed him the smoke. They rode in silence for several minutes. Then Elwood pulled the car over on the shoulder of the road. "I guess this is far enough away from the old homestead so we can talk in peace," he said.

Steve Cropper continued to look at them as if they were strangers, rather than former compatriots. "Bringing me my old Telecaster is one thing," he said finally. "But baiting and caging me like an animal is another. Whatever you want, you can't expect me to cooperate if you treat me like that."

"You know what, Elwood?" Jake said. "I kinda think Steve here has changed. Permanently. I think maybe we were wrong to drive all the way here to enlist his help in this mission for God."

"Mission for God?" Steve murmured.

Jake nodded. "You see, we thought you would be the first to go for it."

"How can I go for anything if you don't tell me what it is?" Steve asked.

Jake outlined their position and plans. Steve listened attentively but displayed no overt enthusiasm.

"I'm sorry," he said. "It doesn't seem right."

"Yeah," Jake shrugged. "Let's go, Elwood. Let's let him go. He can't even understand what we're trying to do."

"Sure I can," Steve returned. "But do you guys have any idea what it's like keeping a strict religious way of life after years of smoking, hustling pool, drinking, gambling and guitar playing? I had to make a real commitment and it's not easy to leave . . . just like this."

"Yeah," Jake replied shortly, obviously upset that Steve had not accepted their mission and joined them with loud hosannas. "You can get out if you want. Elwood and me got to get back to Chicago."

Cropper could not seem to make the plunge. "Look," he said in a high, fragile tone of voice, "you know what it's like to be confined, Jake. You were in prison all that time. Well, I was also confined. If I go back to that field, I'll be going back to a kind of prison. Oh, it's not a prison with walls or anything, but a mental prison. You know what I mean? And the worst thing is, even with all the agony I go through, they still don't really accept me . . ." He looked down at the floor and took a long drag on the cigarette before continuing. "I mean, I love my Elders and their way of life, but I'm different. I chose a different path. Sometimes they don't understand why I ever left and I have to pray hard to absolve myself of the guilt . . . guilt which I honestly shouldn't be feeling . . ."

Jake's expression softened and he nodded. "Yeah," he said. "Well, go work it out with them."

But Steve continued, as if he were talking to himself, "And they still insist on speaking the olden way, with the *ye*'s and *thou*'s . . . and sometimes I feel like saying, 'Hey, it's hard to communicate that way, at least for me. Can't we just talk like ordinary people?' I guess if I could communicate with them, I'd say something like, 'I'm not really a bad person, I love God and my fellow man, I'm grateful for your raising me to believe in the good. But I just chose a less disciplined path . . .'"

"Maybe you'd better come with us, Colonel," Jake said. "We can use you, and so can the kids at the orphanage. And if you still think it's wrong, Elwood and me will sure bring you back here."

Steve nodded soberly. Elwood threw the car into gear and scorched onto the highway.

"Yea, though I turn now my back with a hardened heart," Steve intoned, craning his neck for one last look at the Hutterite valley, "so must I long await my day of atonement."

So much had happened to Dietrich Albrecht during the past twenty-four hours. He had learned of the Blues Brothers' existence, seen their hotel demolished seconds after they escaped, received a telegram from the national leader of the Neue Nazi Party congratulating him on his acquisition (Dietrich had exaggerated in a recent letter) of an exact replica of the Munich beer hall in which Adolf Hitler staged his famous *putsch*, then remembered that Thursday was the anniversary of the death of that great storm trooper, Horst Wessel. At the last monthly meeting, he had suggested that a parade be held commemorating Wessel's martyrdom, if possible in the neighborhood of the orphanage that would soon be their new headquarters.

After a tour of the factory district he pulled up at the orphanage. Pausing for a moment in front of the building, Albrecht then slowly eased the car down the block to see how level the adjacent streets were, whether they contained many alleyways or fences from which missiles could be thrown, etcetera. He was just in the process of turning the corner when a couple of youngsters, one white and one black, approached the car.

"Look at this disgusting race-mixing," Albrecht whispered before they were within earshot.

"Check it out, check it out," the black boy said. "Friday night only in Calumet City. The Blues Brothers Rhythm and Blues Revue. One night only for the benefit of St. Helen of the Blessed Shroud Orphanage. The fabulous Blues Brothers!"

As he spoke, the white kid thrust a couple of handbills into the car. They read:

> DISCO SUCKS
> FRIDAY NITE ONLY, HEAR REAL
> *MUSIC*
> THE BLUES BROTHERS GENUINE
> RHYTHM AND BLUES SHOW AND REVUE—
> JOVIAL CLUB
> CALUMET CITY
> SAVE THE ORPHANAGE WITH YOUR $10
> DONATION AND HEAR THE BEST MUSIC!
> CALL 555–1739 AND
> ASK FOR SID

"Very interesting," Albrecht murmured. "They've certainly moved fast."

He drove up several blocks, looking for a telephone that had not been dismantled, finally locating one on the fourth attempt. He dialed the number.

"Hello," a voice said.

"Is this Sid?"

"You got him. Want to make a reservation for the Jovial Club Friday night, pal?"

"Well, yes, I was thinking of it. Is this the Jovial Club?"

"Sort of. I'm taking reservations for that particular night. It's being handled a different way. You see, if you want to see the Blues Brothers, I'll tell you where to go. You go there and give your donation and the man will give you a ticket."

"Very well. Tell me what to do."

"Do you know where St. Helen of the Blessed Shroud Orphanage is located?"

"Yes."

THE BLUES BROTHERS

"Okay. Go to the side entrance and ask for Curtis. He's the man to see."

"Thank you."

Dietrich hung up and walked slowly back to the car. "I don't understand it," he said to himself. "If they have a concert at the Calumet Club, why can't we just call the club itself?"

And then, like an SS directive, the thought hit him. "Maybe the Calumet Club doesn't know about it?"

"Ja!" Dietrich smiled. "That could be it. They're planning their own *putsch*, perhaps. But we've got to be sure."

With that, he returned to the phone booth and looked up the number of the Calumet Club.

"Yeah?" a voice answered.

"Is this the Calumet Club?"

"That's right."

"Pardon me for bothering you, but I understand you have a new group coming in this Friday night."

"Yeah."

"Could you tell me the name of that group, please?"

"Sure. Just a minute." The man was away from the phone briefly. "It's Waldo and the Wall-Walkers," he said.

"Very interesting," Dietrich said. "Thank you very much."

He hung up and returned to the car.

"Magnificent!" Dietrich laughed. "Well, now we have them. I'll call the manager of the Calumet Club and warn him about the Blues Brothers' plan to have a *putsch*. I'll say they're Jewish fanatics. *Ja*, that's it! They can be attacking the place because they're against entertainment on the Sabbath. We'll scare them off before they even get started. Maybe we should contact the police now, before this swindle gets off the ground."

As he drove past the orphanage once again, he slowed down at the side entrance. Two young people appeared to be handling a transaction with Curtis at that very moment.

"It looks like business is booming," Dietrich said.

"Seven down and only one to go," Jake beamed. "We're getting there, men. We're getting there."

Steve had lost a great deal of his melancholy and aloofness during the ride back from Indiana; Jake had been correct in assuming that all young Cropper needed was a good session listening to some all-time favorites. So they burned across the Interstate to the accompaniment of Big Joe Williams, Lightning Hopkins, Brownie McGhee and Lonnie Johnson, all joined by Elwood Blues on the harp and Jake on vocal.

"Pull over," Steve ordered, the first time they stopped at a traffic light. "Could either of you lend me thirty dollars?"

Elwood reached in his pocket for some crumpled bills.

Steve took them and darted into a nearby clothing store. He emerged less than a minute later, having discarded his Hutterite collarless shirt in favor of a tapered polyester shirt with a dark blue pattern. All the solemnity was gone from his face.

"And now," he said, "you can drop me off at Cosmo's Pool Room just two blocks down the road on the left."

"What for?" Elwood asked. "Hey, we asked you to come back so you could play that Telecaster, man, not pool."

"Sure, I understand," Steve said. "But we need money, don't we?"

"What makes you say that?" Jake demanded.

"Because you'd have told me all about the equipment we're using Friday night if you already had it. Listen, I may be a little slow and quiet sometimes, but I ain't stupid. You just got outa prison and the guys are scattered all over three states. I was still around after you went to the joint and they started peddling all the amps and mikes and God knows what else. I saw it go, man. I cried when Matt and Willie and Lou dumped some of that equipment. Anyway, am I right? Do you need it or not?"

"Sure, we need it," Elwood said.

"Then I'll be at Cosmo's. Drop in once in a while between now and Friday and maybe I'll have some green for us."

"You're all right, man," Jake said.

They stopped in front of the pool room and let Steve out. "Drop by later this afternoon," Steve said. "O ye of little faith, only through righteous hustling shall truth vanquish evil."

He turned and strolled confidently into the building.

"Where now?" Elwood asked.

"Well, we got a few choices," Jake said. "We could go back to the Bond Hotel and find out if anything's left of our belongings. Or we could try and find Matt. Or drop in at Ray's Music Exchange and see what kind of stuff he has for sale cheap."

"Makes sense to see if we can find Matt first, I guess," Elwood said. "That way we'll know if it's seven or eight we're buying for."

"Good thinking," Jake smiled. "Besides, I'm hungry."

They broke left and headed for Maxwell Street, a broad avenue in a transitional section of the city. It was teeming with people on the lookout for bargains, both sides of the street being lined with small specialty shops; some were legit, some handled stolen merchandise. On one corner were two old black men, playing guitars hooked up to amplifiers right on the sidewalk. A small crowd watched and listened.

"How do you like that?" Jake said. "Street Slim and Baby Boy Red, still playing Maxwell Street."

Elwood pulled into a parking space and they passed the musicians just as the number ended to a smattering of applause.

"Thank you, folks," the thinner of the two said. "That was the boogie, which I wrote."

The second man, with a round face and a flat nose, broke into a wide grin. "Never mind him, folks," he said in a high voice. "He's lying if he says that, 'cause the first boogie I ever heard come offa my mother's church organ and after that offa Pinetop Perkins' piano and offa Tampa Red's guitar."

"You callin' me a liar?" the first man demanded.

"Yes, sir."

They were instantly nose to nose. Loving it, the crowd urged one or the other to prove his case by bustin' the other in the mouth.

"Same old act, too," Jake said.

In the middle of the next block was a neon sign advertising the SOUL FOOD CAFE, a simple diner with the best and greasiest soul food in South Chicago. Behind the counter stood the establishment's only waitress, a large black woman in her forties, with flashing eyes and an animated face. Seven or eight customers sat at small chrome-and-plastic tables, while a trio of women at the counter had just been served a plateful of ribs and were diving in. Jake and Elwood entered and sat down at the counter.

"Can I help you boys?" the waitress asked.

"Got any white bread?" Elwood said.

"Yes."

"I'd like some toasted white bread, please."

"You want some butter or jam on that toast, honey?"

"No, ma'am. Just dry."

Shrugging, the waitress looked at Jake.

"You got any fried chicken?" he asked.

"Best damned chicken in the state."

"Bring me four fried chickens and a Coke."

"You want chicken legs or chicken wings?"

"Bring me four whole fried chickens and a Coke," Jake said.

"And some dry white toast, please," Elwood reminded her.

"Nothing to drink for you?"

"No, ma'am."

The waitress went back into the kitchen, where a broad-shouldered, intensely muscular black man in his late thirties was seated at a table, going over some figures on a sheet of paper.

"We got two honkies out there dressed like Hasidic diamond merchants," she said.

"Say what?"

"I said, we got a couple of honkies who look like they're from the CIA or something."

The man twisted his body to look through the door, but could not get the right angle. Instead of getting up, he merely relaxed against the back of the chair. "What're they wearing?" he asked.

"Dark glasses," she said. "Dark suits, real shiny like a baby's ass, and skinny ties that look like dead snakes."

A light of recognition came into the black man's eyes. He smiled. "What did they order to eat?" he asked.

"The tall one wants white bread toast with nothing on it."

"Elwood..."

"And the other one wants four whole fried chickens and a Coke."

"Jake! Shit, woman, it's the Blues Brothers!"

He was out front in five seconds, his large, handsome face wearing a wall-to-wall grin. When they saw him burst through the doorway, Elwood and Jake stood. The three then burst into spontaneous applause.

After the back-pounding was over, the black man said, "Jake, how you doin'? How was life in the joint?"

"It's bad. They serve a lot of kale and pepper steak."

"Yeah? Can't be as bad as them cabbage rolls at the Terre Haute federal pen."

"I guess they're all pretty bad," Jake conceded.

"Yeah. So what are you guys up to?"

"We're putting the band back together again, Matt," Jake said. "That's why we're here. Because we need you."

Matt turned to look over his shoulder, noticing the waitress who stood leaning against the kitchen door, all evil.

"Oh, man, don't talk so loud around here," Matt whispered. "My old lady, she'd kill me."

THE BLUES BROTHERS

"Kill you for what—talking with us?" Elwood asked.

"No. Bringing up the idea of my going back with the Blues Brothers. Or any musical group."

"But you don't understand, Matt," Jake said. "This is different. We're on a mission for God."

"Surely she'll understand that," Elwood added.

The waitress divined that the conversation was including her. Edging in their direction, she frowned and glared Matt down. "What in hell's they talking about?" she asked.

"Now don't get riled, honey," Matt began.

"Don't you 'don't get riled, honey' me," she said. "You got a guilty look on your face I don't like. Now tell me what you was talking about."

"About my playing my guitar a little—"

The woman's eyes narrowed as she folded her sizable arms across her equally sizable chest. "Oh no you don't!" she exploded. "You're not going back on the road. You're not playing in no two-bit sleazy dives anymore! You're living with me now. You're not going to go sliding around with your white hoodlum friends!"

"But, honey, this is Jake and Elwood," Matt explained. "The Blues Brothers!"

"The Blues Brothers!" the woman spat. "Shit, they still owe you money."

Jake tried to step into the breach. "Ma'am," he said, "would it make you feel better if you knew that what we're asking Matt here to do is a holy thing?"

"You see, we're on a mission from God," Elwood added.

The woman was not only unimpressed, she was livid. The veins in her neck stood out as her eyes widened and her hands rolled into tight fists. "Don't you blaspheme in here, you no-account honkies!" she shouted. "This is my restaurant and this is my man and you two are just gonna walk out that door without your dry white toast and your four whole chickens and a Coke and without your Matt 'Guitar' Murphy!"

The customers quite spontaneously broke into a sustained round of applause.

When it was over, Matt took a deep breath and looked the woman straight in the eye.

"Now you listen to me," he replied. "I love you, but I'm the man and you're the woman and I'll make the decisions concerning my life."

The woman did not back down. "You better think about what you're saying!" she shot back. "You better think about the consequences of what you decide to do."

"Oh, hush up, bitch," Matt muttered. Then, putting an arm around her, he said, "Look, honey, I'll be back. These guys want me to help them out on something and I don't even know what it is yet. But I'll do it because they always been square with me. An' then I'll be back to you because I love you and you always been square with me. Fair enough?"

She sighed. "Go on, dammit," she said.

A few minutes later they were in the Bluesmobile, heading for Ray's Music Exchange, less than a mile away.

"Eight down and none to go," Jake laughed. "Man, I can hardly wait for us to start jamming."

His smile faded when they noted some of the "sale" prices of musical equipment in the window of Ray's shop. "Hey," Jake complained. "Look at that. Have prices gone up that much?"

"You been away," Matt said. "It's been a crazy world out here."

"Chances are the shit's stolen, too," Jake continued. "Man, tell me this guy isn't paying a bundle for police protection."

He pointed to a sign in one corner of the show window. Printed in neat letters, it read:

SALE—STOLEN PROPERTY—HOT TVs—BRAND NEW

THE BLUES BROTHERS

"Well, let's see what the man's got," Elwood suggested.

They went inside. The shop was small but seemed even smaller because of the conglomeration of items that hung from the walls and ceiling and the sides of counters. Amplifiers were stacked from floor to ceiling; every conceivable type of musical instrument was in view. At the rear of the store was a counter enclosed in wire mesh. Looking around for a moment, the boys saw no one, so they proceeded to amuse themselves. Matt strolled over to a guitar and began playing B. B. King riffs; Elwood played some chords on a steel guitar; Jake found a harmonica and blew a succession of loud discords. The commotion soon brought them the attention they wanted in the person of the proprietor, Ray, a thin, elegant blind black man.

"Pardon me," he said. "But we do have a strict policy concerning the handling of instruments. An employee of Ray's must be present. Now, can I help you?"

Jake seemed surprised by the formal speech. "Hey, Ray, it's me," he said. "Joliet Jake. I once rented column speakers from you for my band, the Blues Brothers. And this is Matt 'Guitar' Murphy, the best guitar we had, Ray. The pulse, the backbone, the heartbeat of the whole band."

Ray smiled and nodded.

"Ray, we're here to buy stuff and we'd like you to give us your best shot because we're on a mission for God," Jake said. "We need a piano, mikes, amps, the works..."

"Excuse me," Ray said softly.

During Jake's brief plea, the proprietor's head had very gradually moved to his left, in the direction of a young man of sixteen or seventeen who, thinking he was not being watched, had removed a Fender guitar from the wall at the far end of the store. Having crossed the Rubicon, the boy dropped the hand holding the instrument to his side and, shielding the guitar behind his leg, began to move quickly but without panic toward the front door. He was about ten

THE BLUES BROTHERS

feet from it when Ray whipped a revolver from his jacket and fired three rapid shots in the boy's direction. They shattered the plaster less than six inches above the head of the would-be thief, who froze where he stood.

"Just put it back, son," Ray said in a strong, authoritative voice that carried easily across the store.

The boy, terrified, replaced the instrument, took one wide-eyed glance at Ray and rushed outside.

"Seeing a boy that young going bad breaks my heart," Ray murmured, replacing the weapon inside his jacket.

"Well," Jake said, grinning, "I guess I better put back that electric piano I slipped under my shirt."

"I guess you'd better," Ray laughed.

"Seriously, though," Jake continued. "We need a piano, and that one over there looks good."

"You have a good eye, my man," Ray said. "That's the best in the city of Chicago."

The four men walked over to the instrument. Elwood bent to look at the price tag. Shaking his head, he took Jake by the arm. "Maybe I'd better go and see how Steve's doing," he suggested.

"Good idea," Jake agreed. "So far, we don't even have enough for a down payment on this."

As Elwood trotted out of the store, Matt appraised the piano with a long, sensuous touch of his hand, then struck a few chords. "How much?" he asked.

"Two thousand bucks, it's yours," Ray said.

"But that's the price on the ticket!"

"Then we can both read."

"Hey, man," Matt persisted. "Don't you have any compassion for working guys? I mean, we done business here before. That should count for something, shouldn't it?"

"Tell you what," Ray said. "I'll throw in the black keys for free."

"Two thousand for that chunk of shit?" Jake protested. "Come on, Ray . . ."

Matt tickled the keyboard, pumped the pedals. "Yeah, come on, Ray," he said. "It's used. There's no action left in this keyboard."

Ray shoved Matt politely away from the instrument and sat on the stool. "Excuse me, gentlemen," he said. "There is nothing wrong with the action in this piano."

He struck an arpeggio of beautiful strength and character, then launched into a version of "Shake a Tail Feather" which was both scorchingly perfect and brimming with soul.

Jake sighed. Beautiful music had never made him feel quite so miserable.

The Colonel lined up the complex shot, took a deep breath, let part of it out, and made a clean sure stroke.

"Shit," he muttered as the nine ball hit the pocket with too much mustard and coughed itself back on the table. He stepped back with a shrug as his challenger moved toward the table, chalking his cue and studying the mix.

Elwood was at Steve's side. "How are you making out?" he asked softly.

"Not bad, considering," Steve whispered. "You gotta remember that some of these guys have been waiting two years for the chance to hustle me. I don't even know half of them."

"How much have you made?" Elwood said.

"About a thousand. Trouble is, I've lost about half of it. I got two hundred riding on this game and maybe three hundred left."

"Give me that three hundred, okay? It'll at least be a down payment on something."

"Sure," Steve said. He reached into his pocket and brought out a package of smokes and, along with it, a half-dozen fifty-dollar bills.

Elwood deftly slipped the green into his pocket, and moved back as the opposition pool player missed his shot.

"Thanks," Elwood said.

"Come back for me later," Steve told him. "I'm just starting to cook."

Elwood watched for another few minutes before leaving at the first good opportunity.

Now, thanks to Jake's brainstorm and a handful of dimes, the interior of Ray's Music Exchange was really jumping. Finally realizing that he didn't know exactly what each member needed for their gig—and secretly hoping that they would be willing to contribute financially—Jake had gotten on the telephone and called Willie, Murph, Al, Duck, Tom and Lou. When Murphy Dunne arrived, he immediately sat down at the electric piano and warmed up the place. The Duck arrived a few minutes later, took a bass guitar from the wall rack and added to the jam along with Matt and Jake, who joined on the vocal. It was a good enough session to bring traffic along Maxwell Street to a near standstill, pedestrians spilling off the curb almost to the middle of the road.

After the session was ten minutes old, Jake spotted Elwood moving through the crowd and quickly pounced on him.

"Where's the Colonel?" he asked.

"Still at the pool hall."

"Is he making any money?"

"He gave me three hundred."

"Goddamn," Jake muttered, shaking his head. "Three hundred! What the hell can we buy with three hundred?"

Elwood looked around for a moment, then reached for

an instrument. "What about this banjo?" he suggested.

"Shit," Jake said.

"What did you do, call the guys?" Elwood asked.

"Yeah. Couple said they'd be here, the rest told me what they needed."

"Think we can do it?"

"I don't know," Jake sighed. "Next time you see the Colonel, you tell him he's *gotta* win or we'll be going out as an *acoustic* dance band!"

Willie Hall broke through the crowd into the store, his arms loaded with an assortment of rifles and shotguns, in and out of cases. Seeing him, Murph stopped in mid-cadence.

"Hey, Willie!" he called.

"Hey, Murph. Jake. What's shakin', men?"

Murph got up and slapped Willie's hands, which appeared from beneath the small arsenal. "This maniac Jake told me we have a gig, but I didn't really believe him till now," he said. "So what's with all the hardware? You starting a war or something?"

"Good," Jake said. "I was worried about your getting here with that stuff."

Willie looked at Jake blankly. "Why?" he asked.

"Well, that neighborhood you live in," Jake explained. "I wondered how you'd be able to walk ten feet once they saw this stuff."

Willie smiled. "'Course, this ain't the way I carried it back there," he laughed. "Back there I made sure it was pointin' *out*."

Jake grabbed Ray by the arm. "Got a trade here for you, Ray," he said.

"Hey, you still got my Ludwigs?" Willie asked, dropping the guns on the counter.

Ray shook his head. "No, but I have some beautiful Rogers Dynasonics . . ."

Jake looked at Elwood. "Better get back to that pool

room and light a fire under the Colonel."

Elwood nodded and left.

"It looks to me like you fellows are going to need a lot of equipment," Ray said. "Maybe we can work out a good rate if you take over a certain amount."

"Okay," Jake said. "Let's total it up." He began to walk around the store. "How much for this small Ampeg?"

"Three hundred."

"This used strobe tuner?"

"Five-fifty."

"Goddamn. Counting the other things we talked about, how much are we up to?"

"Let's see. Two Peaveys, one Vox preamp, the piano, two mikes, cords, stands, two upright columns, the tuner..." Ray added up the figures. "Six thousand, seven hundred seventy-five dollars and nine cents."

"How about making it two thousand even?" Jake suggested.

Ray laughed.

"Then do you have any kind of long-term leasing arrangements?"

"Not as long as I think *you'll* need."

"We're doing a gig tonight," Jake said. "How about putting down our fee as a down payment?"

"That depends on what it is," Ray replied with a smile.

Jake made a motion to Murph, and took him aside. "Listen," he said. "Don't let any of this good stuff get away. I'm gonna try to get us a gig tonight so we can pay for it."

Murph looked at his watch. "That'll be good if you can do it," he said.

"You got a car?"

"Yeah."

"Let me borrow it. You stick around and see what happens when Elwood gets back. Maybe the Colonel can hustle us enough for a down payment. Just in case he can't, I'm

THE BLUES BROTHERS

gonna see if I can get us in business." He took out a crumpled piece of paper and stuck it in Murph's pocket. "If you want to make yourself useful, give the rest of the guys a call and tell them to keep themselves loose for tonight, okay?"

Dunne nodded, a bit nervously. "It's the new Datsun 280Z out front," he said. "Elwood says you're kind of a crazy driver, Jake. So you'll take it easy, right?"

"Yeah," Jake assured him, taking the keys.

A minute later he had started the car, ground it into first gear, bucked away from the curb, clattered into second and was away, just barely missing a delivery truck on the opposite side of the street. As he turned the corner, he looked back at the music store and thought he saw Murph standing at the front door, holding his hands over his eyes.

"Shit," he said, "I'm as good a driver as any of these assholes out here."

When he pulled up in front of the Wrigley Building, he noted that it was already late in the afternoon, almost certainly too late to find a prospect for that evening. But he had to try, at least, which meant that there was little time to fool with looking for parking spaces. He therefore pulled into a bus lane, turned off the engine and opened the hood. For effect, he peered inside, shook his head distractedly, then darted into the building.

The Tri-Lite Talent Booking Agency office was on the second floor, he noted with satisfaction, disdaining the elevator for the stairs. Less than a minute later, he was in the outer office of Maury Sline; it was a spacious room lined with pictures of various blues artists, great and unknown, theater posters, and even a few old circus advertisements. Jake walked briskly to the young female secretary who sat at a centrally located desk surrounded by plants.

"May I help you?" she asked.

"Where's Maury?" Jake countered, getting right to the point.

The direct approach seemed to throw her, at least momentarily. "He . . . he's in his office at the moment. Could you wait and—"

Jake was already past her. He rapped once on the door of Maury's office and went inside. The office was just about the same as he remembered it: walls filled with photographs of artists stacked frame-to-frame, a few framed records, both 78s and 45s. At the desk sat a man in his late forties, well dressed, wearing a lot of gold.

The conversation he was holding on the telephone seemed almost providential. "Nobody I have is going to want to drive all the way down there for a one-night engagement," he said.

"Hey!" Jake shouted.

Maury looked up, shook his head and returned to the phone. "Wait a minute," he said. "Somebody just came in. Hold that one open. I'll call you back."

He hung up. His smile was genuine as he stood and extended his hand. "Jake," he said. "Why didn't you phone and tell me you were getting out? I coulda set something up. I thought you drew three to five years."

"You'd have been better informed if you'd written me once or twice," Jake remarked acidly.

Maury shrugged, not noticeably devoured, or even nibbled at, by guilt. "Well, you know how I feel, Jake," he said. "I've never liked loitering around federal penitentiaries. For me they are frighteningly prophetic . . ."

"What the hell does that mean?"

"Never mind, Jake. What I mean is, this is a risky business. You know. Your manager gambles away your gig money and you end up in jail. The same thing could happen to me if I make too many mistakes, or even if people around me make mistakes. Anyway . . ." He gestured to a seat, which Jake took. "What can I do for you?"

"Well," Jake said, "I'm selling Girl Scout cookies and wondered if you'd like to buy a carton or two."

"What flavor?"

"For God's sake," Jake hissed, "why do you think I'm here? We're putting the Blues Brothers together again and need a gig. Lots of gigs, as a matter of fact."

"Listen," Maury sighed, "what are you guys gonna do? The same act, in those same suits, which haven't been cleaned since last time? You'll scare people away! Don't you guys ever wear blue jeans? Or leather? Or jogging suits? You remember Wayne Cochran and the C. C. Riders..."

"Sure. They all wore them red jumpsuits."

"Right. Wayne Cochran and his show toured fifty weeks a year in the late seventies. Now, it's practically no time later and they're deader'n dinosaur shit. What am I gonna do with you?"

"We'll go anywhere, play anytime, for anybody," Jake promised, trying not to plead in a whining tone.

"I book a lot of other artists," Maury said. "Not only blues artists, you know. I book show bands, country trios, rock bands, heavy metal rock bands, imitation fifties rock 'n' roll bands. Discos. They're all discos. The kids wanna dance with lights. Discos... singles, mixed singles, gay singles, these people like to dance with each other... or with themselves. You get the picture?"

"No!" Jake protested. "We *are* a dance band."

Maury sighed. "Discos..." he repeated. "They want string sections. How many pieces you got?"

"Ten, counting me," Jake said. "Anywhere within a two-thousand-mile radius."

"All right, Jake," Maury promised. "I'll see what I can do, and I think we'll work out something."

Jake smiled. "Good. There's just one other thing. We need something tonight."

"You serious? Why?"

"Couple reasons," Jake replied. "First thing is we need the money in a hurry. Second thing is we got another gig

Friday night and we need a tune-up."

"Where's your Friday night gig?" Maury asked.

"Never mind."

Maury smiled knowingly and looked down at his notepad. "There is one thing," he said. "But I don't think I oughta send you to this place so soon after you got outa prison..."

"Why?" Jake asked.

"Now it's my turn to say never mind. Do you want it or not? It's tonight and you'll make some money."

"We'll take it."

Maury pulled out a contract, shoved it toward Jake. "Just sign at the bottom and I'll fill in the figures," he said. He then scribbled some notes and directions on a piece of paper and pushed it across the desk to Jake. "This is the place."

Jake took the directions but did not sign the contract. Instead his eyes narrowed as he said, "How do we make sure that you won't rip us off?"

"What do you mean, 'make sure I won't rip you off'?" Maury replied. "Of course I'm going to rip you off. It's all clear, there in the contract...clear...simple...'the artist will be ripped off.' Guaranteed. Absolutely, positively..."

"Okay," Jake said. "Just so you aren't trying to hide something."

He signed the contract and tore off the bottom copy for himself. "I'll need this to prove we're in business for tonight."

"Hey, wait a minute," Maury protested. "You can't take that until it's signed by me and the figures are typed in. Hell, you could fill in your own figures and make a lot of trouble for me."

"Which is what I intend to do," Jake said. "Except for the last part."

He got up and kissed Maury on both cheeks, like a French general awarding a medal for bravery. "Thanks,

THE BLUES BROTHERS

pal," he said. "You're a lifesaver. We'll give you a call next week."

"Yeah. Let me know how you like Bob's Country Bunker. I'll call and tell them you're coming."

Jake waved and left. Upon arriving at the ground floor, he noticed that a traffic cop was standing next to Dunne's car. He hesitated a moment, then raced quickly out of the building, being sure to make as much noise as possible. The officer looked up just as Jake reached the edge of the curb.

"They need help in the bank!" Jake shouted, jerking his thumb spasmodically toward the Wrigley Building.

The officer stared at him blankly. "Jesus Christ, you asshole," Jake hissed. "Get in the fucking bank!"

"Yessir!"

He ran into the building, nearly knocking several pedestrians to the sidewalk in his haste. Just as rapidly, Jake slammed down the hood, leaped into the Datsun and blasted away from the curb.

A few minutes later he pulled onto a side street and, using a piece of carbon paper stolen from Maury Sline's receptionist on the way out, wrote some very impressive figures in the blank spaces of the Tri-Lite Booking Agency contract. With a smile of satisfaction, he carefully folded the document and put it in his coat pocket.

He arrived at Ray's just before five o'clock, noticing happily that parked outside was the Ray-Dex Alarm System van, a sure sign that the Duck was going along that night. The truck would come in handy for lugging equipment and people. In the store were seven band members, the only missing person being Tom "Bones" Malone.

"Well, we got us a gig tonight," Jake announced. "Where's Bones?"

"He's not coming," Murph answered. "Just doesn't feel like it."

"Do we have time to kidnap him?"

"Depends how far away the gig is and what time we gotta be there," Murph said, looking at his watch. "Don't see how we can have much time to spare, though."

Jake nodded grimly. "You're right. We'll have to pass on Bones for tonight and see if we can grab him tomorrow."

"Where are we headed?" Elwood asked. "I hope it's a couple hundred miles away so the Bluesmobile can get a workout. She seems a little sluggish."

"It's Bob's Country Bunker in La Crosse, Indiana," Jake read off the paper. "We have to be there by seven."

"Great," the Duck said. "That means we'll only have to bust our asses instead of pray for a miracle."

"It's a piece of cake," Elwood said, clearly disappointed. "Just down the road."

"Tell you what, Elwood," Murph offered. "We'll let you drive all the way in reverse."

Jake spotted Steve and waved. "How'd you do, hustler?"

"Picked us up a big K."

"K?"

"Thousand."

"Great." Turning to Ray, Jake reached into his pocket for the contract. "Now, counting the thirteen hundred dollars or so in cash we have here and the trade you're giving Willie on the guns—"

"Oh, that's an even swap for the drum set."

"Well, we're down to you for about five and a half K," Jake continued. "But maybe you could look this contract over and use it as a sort of down payment. I'll sign a note saying that the fee for the gig will go to you—"

Ray smiled. "It's all right," he said. "When the Colonel got here with the thousand, I decided to give you all a break. We'll work out a payment plan, okay?"

"Great," Jake said.

They had the gear loaded in the Duck's van in no time and were soon heading east on Route 30, the big road that swung about ten miles above La Crosse. "Hey, how come we never heard of this place?" Elwood asked.

"I heard you can get yourself killed in some of those dinky places," Blue Lou said.

"How so?" Cropper asked.

"Rough customers, you know. Not like at the Falls End Hotel or the Palace or the Jovial Club. I hear that bands die in these places. I mean really die."

"Nooo problem, we'll *own* the place," Jake assured them—and himself.

Bob's Country Bunker, which they reached just before sunset, was a long, wide, single-story cinder-block roadhouse, illuminated and identified by a neon sign with a rocking cowboy hat. The parking lot, quite a large one, was already half-filled with a variety of pickups, tractors, and four-wheel-drive vehicles. The musical convoy, which consisted of the van, the Bluesmobile and the Magictones' Datsun, pulled in together just as a couple of customers drove up in a Jeep. Blue Lou got out and shook out his long hair, running his fingers through it. The two young men in the Jeep, both red-necked individuals wearing peaked hats advertising De Kalb Grain, looked on and smiled.

"Pussy..." one of them called to Lou. "Hey, pussy..."

"Eeehuh," the second added. "Hey, little girl."

Blue Lou's expression darkened and he was about to shoot them the finger when Jake reached out to grab his hand.

"Now, now, Blue man, just a couple of music lovers," he cautioned.

Lou restrained himself and the band walked into the roadhouse, everybody taking a seat at the long bar across the front. Presently a hefty woman in a black wig and miniskirt placed coasters in front of them.

"Just driving through?" she asked. "Ya wanta see our supper menus? We make the state's best pepper steak."

Jake made a retching sound and spun around on his stool.

"What's the matter with him?" the woman asked.

"Nothing, ma'am," Steve Cropper said politely. "This here is Jake Blues and Elwood Blues, and the rest of us are the Blues Brothers Band. We'll be playing here tonight."

"Oh, terrific," she said. "My name's Claire, and me and Bob own the place. I'll go hunt up Bob for you."

A minute later a tall, husky, cowboy-shirted man with a rough, pimply complexion came around from behind the bar.

"Which one of you guys is the Blues Brothers?" he asked.

"Which *one*?" Jake said.

"We are," Elwood said, pointing to Jake and himself. "All of us. The whole band."

"Well, it's nice to have you, especially on such short notice," Bob said. "That chickenshit outfit that was here last night just took off without a word. We didn't even find out they was gone until one o'clock. Anyway, this here is my place."

"It's really fantastic," Willie said, pouring on the public-relations juice.

"Marvelous," Murph added.

Bob beamed. "I guess you fellas'll want to set up your steel guitars and stuff," he said. "Claire, honey, turn on the stage lights, will ya?"

The woman flipped a switch behind the bar and a bank of spotlights illuminated a stage at the rear of the far wall. It consisted of a slightly elevated platform with a wire cage in front of it—a seven-foot-high fence held in place by four-by-eight planks.

"Oh no . . ." Blue Lou muttered. "Chicken wire."

The group got up together and explored the area.

"What's with all the chicken wire?" Murph asked.

"Guaran-goddamn-tee ya it ain't for chickens," the Duck replied, testing it for strength. It seemed very solid, a forbidding layer of protection between the performers' area and the tables and booths for spectators.

"Hey, Bob," Jake called out. "How about losing the cage just for tonight?"

"Why?"

"Well, we like contact with our audience. The way this is, it's kind of a barrier."

"I really couldn't do it," Bob said. "You see, that's part of the fun here at the Country Bunker." He laughed and slapped Jake's shoulder. "Hell, by the time the end of the night rolls around, you'll be real glad that wire's there."

Steve Cropper was the first band member to speak. "Looks like it's the Christians versus the lions and we're the Christians," he smiled.

Jake shrugged. "Okay, let's set up for a sound check."

Bob reached into his pocket and drew out a folded slip of paper. "By the way," he said, "I'd like you to look this over before you go on tonight, see if it gives you any problems."

"What is it?" Jake asked.

"It's the list of the songs for tonight."

Overhearing the reply, the rest of the band paused to listen as Jake read from the paper.

"'Settin' the Woods on Fire,'" he read. "'Wreck of the Old 97,' 'From a Jack to a King' . . ." He folded the paper and smiled tightly. "All right, Bob. I'll talk with the rest of the band about this."

Bob nodded and went back to the bar. With startling quickness, the interior of the Country Bunker came alive as more beefy and rail-thin patrons arrived, most wearing peaked 'name' hats, work boots, vests and chain wallets. The noise level increased dramatically, one or two near-fights breaking out early in the evening. Blue Lou, the longest-haired and smallest of the band members, received an increasing number of taunts. Steve Cropper, eyeing the crowd, was obviously nervous.

"No wonder that group left in a hurry," Al observed.

"By the way," Murph said, hoping to divert the conversation from the mordant turn it seemed to be taking, "what do you guys think of that song list we've been given?"

"Man, I'm not sure I know 'Wreck of the Old 97,' or whatever that was," Matt shook his head.

"That list doesn't mean anything," Jake assured them in what he hoped was a convincing tone of voice. "They're just suggestions, requests. You know, things the customers expect to hear. But we'll do our regular set. Let's start with 'Gimme Some Lovin'."

The boys nodded.

"But first, get those beer cans off the set, okay? You guys musta gone through ten cases of beer already."

Matt shrugged. "So what? We can handle it. And besides, it's on the house, ain't it?"

Jake spread his arms helplessly.

It was shortly after seven o'clock and the natives were getting restless. Jake cast a glance in the direction of the bar. Bob nodded to him and indicated that he was about to turn on the spotlights.

"Here we go, gang," Jake said. "Get ready for the intro, Elwood, and let's give 'em hell."

A moment later the spotlight came on, followed by a raucous noise that was not so much applause as a combination of stomping boots, catcalls, whistles and shouted words melding together into an unidentifiable vocal avalanche, and glasses tinkling.

"Good evening, ladies and gentlemen," Elwood shouted into the microphone. "We're sure glad to be here in La Crosse tonight. We're the Blues Brothers Band from Chicago and we hope you enjoy our show. I'm Elwood and here's my brother, Jake."

The band hit a hot intro and Jake slammed into "Gimme Some Lovin'":

"Well, my temperature's risin' and my feet off the
  floor,
Crazy people knockin' 'cause they want some
  more..."

THE BLUES BROTHERS

Claire and Bob, at the bar, suddenly looked up from their drink-pushing.

"Hey, that's not a Hank Williams tune," Bob said.

At the same time, four mean-looking, weathered patrons shot glances first at the stage and then at Bob and Claire.

Jake, meanwhile, continued:

> "Well, I'm so glad
> you made it,
> Yeah, I'm so glad
> you made it..."

His voice was nearly drowned out by some cracker screeching, "Eeeeeyushit, whut're those damn freak peckerheads playin'!"

Bob's reaction was immediate. Like an air raid warden trained to move at the sound of a siren, or a fireman conditioned to react at the first scent of smoke, he reached out to his left and hit the switch at the end of the bar. The Country Bunker went black. A few chords of music continued, then died away in confusion. Shouts of glee and confusion arose from the patrons.

Onstage, the reaction was even more chaotic. "Why the fuck'd they turn out the lights?" Murph shrieked.

"Maybe they blew a fuse," Willie's voice replied.

"No, they put us in the dark on purpose," the Duck explained.

"What?" Jake yelled.

"Jake, you don't understand," Steve said. "This isn't the Tick-Tock Lounge or the Paradise Ballroom."

"What do you mean?"

"The owner wrote down the songs he wanted us to play on a piece of paper and we aren't playing them."

"The sonofabitch!"

By now their eyes had become accustomed to the semidarkness; there was some light filtering in from the other end of the room. But Jake was furious at the indignity of their situation. Throwing both feet out in front of him like an athlete executing the long jump, he hurled himself at the chicken wire, grasped it with his hands and began clawing his way to the top, yelling obscenities. Reacting immediately and almost joyfully, the patrons threw beer bottles, ash trays—everything that was not nailed down—in his direction, the noisy barrage bouncing off the screen and clattering to the floor. Several men even kicked back their chairs and started to move toward the climbing figure.

Willie tossed his drumsticks aside and sprang to the front of the stage, reaching out to grab Jake's feet. A second later, Matt and Steve joined him, the three finally managing to pull the maniacal Jake from his perch.

"Easy, man, easy," Matt soothed.

"Tranquilize yourself, boy," Steve said.

"Tranquilize, shit!" Jake yelled. "We're gettin' the hell outa here right now!"

Elwood turned his glance from Jake to Willie, who seemed to move in a stealthy manner that indicated that trouble was a distinct possibility. Turning his back to the audience, he reached into his pocket, withdrew a pearl-handled stilletto and pushed a button that brought a seven-inch blade flashing into view.

"What the hell are you doing?" Elwood demanded.

"Covering our rear," Willie said.

"The hell you are. Where's that song list?"

Willie handed Elwood the paper.

"Now put that shiv away," Elwood ordered.

By now the house was in a turmoil, some patrons furious with the band for playing an unfamiliar number, others furious with the management for turning out the lights, others angry with Jake for climbing the screen, and the rest just angry.

"You guys remember the theme from 'Rawhide'?" Elwood shouted. "Hey, Duck . . . Matt . . . Lou!"

"I remember it!" yelled Al Rubin, grabbing his trumpet and hitting a signature.

Blue Lou immediately picked it up, followed by Steve and Matt. In less than a quarter-minute, Duck was working on the bass line while the Colonel and Matt worked out a quick arrangement with country licks. Willie set an equine pace as Elwood sang basso.

> "Rollin', rollin', rollin'...
> Keep those dogies rollin'..."

Even Jake, having quickly regained his composure, added a few lines:

> "Don't try to understand 'em...
> Just head 'em up and brand 'em...
> Soon we'll be ridin' far and wide...
> Rawhide!"

The lights came on, a form of blessing that reinstated the band in the audience's good graces. Gradually the angry men who were standing returned to their tables and began stomping their boots in time to the music. Warming to the task, Jake and Elwood and the rest of the boys carried the song with great feeling. It sounded great. Even Bob relaxed against the bar and smiled at Claire.

When it was over, the audience clapped long and loud, stomping its approval.

"Thank you, thank you," Jake said. "That was the theme from 'Rawhide.'"

From that point on, it was more or less a typical evening at Bob's Country Bunker. While the Blues Brothers performed the classic Tammy Wynette number, "Stand By Your Man," a small red-haired man sat alone at a table, sobbing to the music. Two big men approached the table and motioned for him to leave but he declined, offering them the other two chairs. This was followed by one of the men lifting the redhead out of his seat and pushing him outside. A minute passed. Then the redhead returned with a screaming twenty-four-inch chain saw, with which he proceeded to cut the table in two, scattering the two interlopers and their lady friends in a shower of sawdust. A fight followed, beginning in the lounge and continuing out to the parking lot. It was all over by the time the band had rendered its extended version of the number.

"Thank you, thank you," Jake said. "Now let's hear 'Sink the Bismarck'!"

It was better than four hours of fun, although the music was at times a bit ragged. The Country Bunker crowd did not notice, but it worried Jake. Several times during the evening, he stood to one side and listened to the tones of the band, detecting a thinness in the middle horn ranges. Or it might have been his imagination. The acoustics at the roadhouse, like most places constructed of cinder blocks, left something to be desired. He tried not to be negative, but it bothered him. As the evening neared a conclusion, however, he yielded to the general good feeling. They finished with a repeat of "Rawhide," to long and enthusiastic applause.

"Okay, guys," he said as soon as the house lights went on. "Now let's get the fuck outa here."

Not needing to be reminded, the band immediately began breaking down the equipment. From the parking lot could be heard the squealing of wheels as happy patrons in four-wheelers, pickups and dump trucks did a few burns, donuts or other personal driving antics for their friends. Inside, a few toughs still hung around, Jake sizing them up as the type who aren't truly satisfied with an evening's entertainment unless it ended with some sort of fight. Keeping his eye on them, Jake directed the loading of the vehicles. Bob, the owner, sauntered over after a while.

"Shit, boy," he said with a grin, "that damn combo of yours is good. Best country sounds we've had in the Bunker for a long time, let me tell you."

"Thanks," Elwood said. "Sorry we couldn't remember

'The Wreck of the Old 97.'"

"Well, now ya know," Bob said. "Learn it for next time. Look, I already wired yer wages to yer booking agent up in the city."

"Thanks."

Elwood turned and started to leave, but Bob put out a hand that was gentle but firm.

"However, there is the matter of all that beer you guys drank," he said.

Elwood's expression was ingenuous. "Oh," he said. "When we first came in, the bar lady never charged us for the first round. We figured it was like complimentary . . . like . . . for the band, you know."

Bob laughed. "Oh no," he said, "maybe the first round, just to be sociable and get acquainted, but no more'n that."

"Well, okay," Elwood stalled. "I'll just go out and take up a collection from the boys."

"I'd appreciate it," Bob replied.

Before going out to the parking lot where the band was busily loading the equipment into the van, Elwood said, "Say, is there a good cheap motel around here?"

"Go north on 421 to Wenatah and keep looking to yer right for the Young America Motor Court," Bob said. "If you hit Route 30, you went too far."

"Thanks," Elwood told him with a smile.

By the time he reached the parking lot, the rest of the boys were already making plans to bed down for the night. "If we move the drums back, three can stretch out in the truck," the Duck was explaining to Jake. "It's insulated . . . nice and quiet. You'll sleep like the dead."

Elwood took Jake aside. "The owner wants us to pay for the beer," he said.

The band members within earshot gasped. "I'll bet we poured down at least a couple hundred dollars' worth," Steve laughed.

"We'd better get out of here," Jake said.

"I asked him where a good motel was," Elwood continued. "He told me about someplace called Young America Motor Court, north of here."

"Then we're heading west. But we gotta give the rest of the boys some time to get started." Jake turned to the others. "Duck, you and as many as you can hold get moving as soon as Elwood and me get back inside."

"Sure. Where should we meet up?"

"Know a place called Maiden?"

"Yeah."

"Wait for us in front of the Volunteer Firehouse. It might take us a while to lose them."

"Right."

"Okay," Jake said, glancing out of the corner of his eye. "They're watching me now, so I'm gonna point north. And you can start out heading that way and then double back. Got it?"

Also indicating north with his arm, the Duck nodded and mouthed a few words for the benefit of Bob, who was standing just outside the Country Bunker entrance with a half-dozen rednecks.

"Let's go," Jake said.

He and Elwood strolled back to the club. The others got in the van and were on their way, the Duck moving with deliberate slowness, by the time the two had reached Bob and his cohorts.

The owner had a bunch of bar chits in his fist. "Boys, on that beer, totals up to two hundred and thirty-eight dollars. That's with ten percent off because you're the band."

Jake shrugged. "Seems fair enough." He disdained examining the chits. "We'll take your word for that." Then, looking at Elwood, he said, "Where you stashing the big bills these days, man?"

"Same place," Elwood said, the men having worked out their patter by prearrangement. "Behind the speakers in the car."

"Well, go get it. Or drive over here," Jake said.

"Be right back."

"Bob, we loved playing here," Jake said as they waited for Elwood to bring the car across the lot. "Maybe we can work out something again in the future."

"Sure thing," Bob said.

They chatted about music until Elwood arrived. Jake got in the passenger's side, very pointedly leaving the door open. "Hey, Elwood," he said. "We still got them traveler's checks?"

"Sure. In the glove compartment."

Jake looked at Bob. "You take traveler's checks?"

"Guess so. Why not?"

Jake reached into the glove compartment, patted his jacket for a pen, then took the one offered by Bob. The huskies hovered around but did not crowd the car, their suspicions allayed by the open door. As Jake began to write in the bogus checkbook they carried as standard equipment, Elwood leaned across behind him to shake Bob's hand. "Nice to've met you, sir," he said.

"Mutual," the owner said.

As soon as he released Bob's hand, Elwood grabbed the door handle and slammed it shut, simultaneously tromping on the accelerator. With a shriek of burning rubber, the Bluesmobile leaped almost vertically into the air, then blasted forward, scattering the trio of quick-reacting crackers, who managed to make a grab for some part of the car or driver. In a matter of seconds they were on the main road, heading north at well over a hundred. Behind them, they could see three sets of headlights.

"Think they got a chance?" Jake asked, turning almost completely around to look through the rear window.

"You just keep looking out that window," Elwood smiled. "I'm gonna make those lights disappear like when you turn off a TV."

The road ahead was a straight section of uncluttered

highway. Elwood simply floored the Bluesmobile and it was greasy speed and saltwater taffy. By the time they crossed under Route 30, there was no sign at all of their pursuers.

"Damn," Jake said suddenly.

"What is it?"

"I forgot to give ol' Bob his pen."

chapter seven

"Where now?" Elwood asked, after they had doubled back and met the boys in the Ray-Dex van.

Jake answered the question with a question. "Where else but the housing project? One of those houses would be a good place to sleep. And then, first thing in the morning, we can start rehearsing. We need a quiet, private, secure place. A top-secret location known only to the members of the band."

Blue Lou was asleep in the back of the van, his arms and legs curled around his guitar, the smile on his face so peaceful that Jake hated to think about waking him.

"Think you can find it again?" Jake asked.

"Sure."

Two hours later, again mired in the middle of a landscape that resembled no-man's-land, Elwood sighed and threw the Bluesmobile into neutral. "Looks like we're stuck," he said matter-of-factly.

"You motorhead!" Jake shouted. "How can you do the same damn dumb thing twice?"

Jake struggled through the mud to the van behind them. "What do you think, Duck?" he asked. "Should we wake up Blue Lou and see if he can find a way out of this?"

The Duck shrugged. "Why not just sleep here?" he suggested.

"Makes sense, I guess," Jake said.

Four hours later, feeling as if he had rolled all the way up and down Pike's Peak, Jake awoke and was gratified to see that they were in fact stalled in some sort of housing project rather than an ordinary swamp. He fumbled in the glove compartment for a pint of bourbon he had stolen from the Country Bunker, took a long drink to get the juices flowing, and shook Blue Lou until the eyes finally opened.

"Yo," Lou muttered.

"Get out and see if this is Cherryhill Woods, will you?" Jake asked.

"You mean Cherrywood Hills?"

"Yeah."

Lou scanned the horizon and nodded. "Trailer's over there a half-mile or so," he said. "Wanta walk it?"

"No," Jake replied, then shrugged. "The hell with it. Let's go. Let the rest sleep while we get the bulldozer."

As they struggled across the pitted ground, Jake outlined his plans for the site, adding that he hoped this would not get Lou in trouble with his employers.

"Fuck them," Lou said. "As a matter of fact, if we're gonna stay here a day or two, rehearsing, we'd better make one of these places livable."

He stopped in front of a "Mediterranean" model, which had the word SOLD pasted over its sign—only partially obscuring the modest selling price of $99,700, including swimming pool. "Now this looks like a pretty good one," Lou said. "It's got all the work done, so it'll be sure to have juice and a refrigerator and water and all that shit."

"Looks big enough, too," Jake added.

"Needs some furniture, though," Lou said. "But we can take care of that in no time."

"Yeah? How?"

"Make a phone call."

"No kidding? All you have to do is make a call?"

"Well, you'll have to make it. The dealer might recognize my voice, but I'll tell you what to say."

"Let's go," Jake said.

When they reached the trailer, Lou found an address book and dialed a number for Jake. "Ask for Mr. LaGrange," he said.

Jake did so. While he waited for the man to pick up the phone, he placed his hand over the mouthpiece and looked to Blue Lou for instructions.

"Tell him you're Roy Pantalone from Bulmer Realty and you'd like him to deliver the first order for Cherrywood Hills."

Jake nodded. He spoke with increasing confidence as the call progressed. "Hello, Mr. LaGrange," he said. "This is Roy Pantalone of Bulmer Realty . . . Fine . . . How are you? . . . Excellent. No . . . Everybody's still on strike, but we do expect a group of potential buyers this week, and we'd like to begin furnishing our model units as comfortably as possible . . . Ah . . . Well, whatever you have down first on the order . . . Mr. Bulmer didn't specify. All he said was to get at least one home furnished right away. Today. This morning, if possible. You know how impatient he can be . . . Yes . . . Rugs, couch . . . lots of easy chairs . . ."

"Beds!" Lou urged.

"And some beds. At least ten . . . Thank you."

He hung up, looked at Blue Lou and smiled. "Perfect," he said. "Said the truck would be here first thing."

By the time they started the bulldozer and drove it to the van and the Bluesmobile, the rest of the band was up and stirring, if not exactly wide awake. Jake got them together and explained what they were going to do, adding that he hoped no one would have to leave for a day or two. The only one who hesitated was Murph, who thought about it for a few seconds before saying, "Sure, I'll stay. The Ramada Inn and those wetbacks can get along without me for a while."

They spent the next half-hour getting to the model home and loading their gear in the living room. But when they plugged one of the amps into a wall outlet, nothing happened.

"I guess it's not turned on," Lou said. "Duck, you're an ace with juice. You'd better come with me to the transformer box."

While they were gone, the rest of the boys inspected the house. One by one they arrived at the same conclusion, no one voicing it until a sudden silence found them all staring at the long wall separating the dining and living rooms.

Jake was the first to speak. "I know what you guys are thinking," he said, "and you're absolutely right."

"Yeah." Willie nodded. "It's got to go."

"Absolutely," said Murph and Elwood in unison.

"There's some tools outside," Steve suggested.

Jake went outside and brought in an armload of picks and shovels. Passing them around, he struck the first blow himself, driving a foot-long hole in the cheap wallboard, then thrusting the pick farther in and tearing out large chunks of material. Meanwhile, the others started to work on the opposite side, battering furiously at it from all angles. Soon they had worked their way down to the framework, whereupon someone produced a saw and began cutting through the two-by-fours. Working in shifts, the men had the area completely open in less than an hour, by which time the Duck and Lou had produced electricity.

"Hey, guys," Lou said, looking at the pile of shattered wood and plaster littering the floor. "This won't be so easy to hide, you know."

"Don't worry," Jake said. "We'll sweep it up and cover the whole thing with a rug."

"You didn't really expect us to play decent music against a baffle like that, did you?" Murph asked with exaggerated hauteur.

"No, I guess not."

They hurriedly plugged in their equipment, but before they could begin playing, Jake held up his hands for silence.

"Before we get started," he said, "I'd like to ask you how you felt about last night."

"Well, I think there's still a band here," Elwood said. "In fact, still a pretty good band."

Steve nodded. "Yeah, but it wasn't together. We were lucky we even finished close a couple of times."

Murph smiled. "Come on, we were playing for the first time in years, and it sounded to me like we never stopped."

"Then we're agreed it's still there but we can use a little work?" Jake summarized.

The others nodded.

"Well, let's rock," Jake said.

Matt took the cue and came down hard with a drum intro, but stopped almost as soon as he started. "Hold it, guys!" he shouted above the disorganized start. "Looks like we got company."

Sure enough, they could spot a large furniture truck with the lettering CHAMPAIGN FINE FURNITURE on its side, moving slowly over the rough track, wallowing from one side to the other to avoid the raised, uncovered sewer mains.

"Down the basement, everybody," Blue Lou shouted. "And take your equipment."

A frenzy of activity ensued as Lou walked slowly out to meet the truckdriver and his crew. Before long the house was loaded with expensive beds, sofas, rugs, chairs and tables.

"What happened to that wall?" the driver asked Lou at one point in the moving operation.

"Shoddy workmanship," Lou explained. "They're sending a crew here this afternoon to fix it."

"That's the worst-looking wall I ever saw," the driver remarked. "Look at them joists, Zeke, all hacked to pieces like that. Looks like they tried making it with scrap."

"By tomorrow, nobody'll ever notice," Lou said, seeing them out.

As they left, the furniture truck passed the Ray-Dex van driven by Duck, who had taken the opportunity to sneak off to the nearest Seven-Eleven store for food. Seeing the goodies, the band men suddenly realized they were starved and proceeded to pitch in right in the middle of the living room floor. Beer cans were thrown from one side of the room to the other, dousing the expensive furniture and rugs.

"Well, look on the bright side," Jake told Lou. "At least now we don't have to worry about covering up the remains of that wall with a rug."

Then he became serious.

"Let's get down to work, okay?"

They did, beginning with one of their old favorites called "Excusez Moi." It was a trifle ragged at first, but soon they got a free-rolling jam going. The tones got rounder and fuller, the chords tougher and more precise. Jake could feel them get better with every passing minute. His bitter years of waiting in prison now seemed worth the enervating frustration, self-recrimination and loneliness, even the gastric insubordination of the kale and pepper steak.

He drove them harder and harder, yet none seemed to mind. The beer cans piled up, the floor becoming a soggy sea of litter awash with remnants of snacks, hastily lit cigarettes that furnished one or two drags each before being discarded, and ground-up plasterboard and shards of wood. The place was a mess, but the music grew simultaneously hotter and cooler. By midafternoon, they were almost limp with fatigue. Jake was satisfied with their sound up to a point; he knew, however, that something was still missing.

"We got to get it perfect," he said. "It's not quite there yet."

"Maybe we really do need the Bones," someone offered.

"Maybe," Steve Cropper admitted. "But maybe it's just a case of not having enough volume."

"More volume?" Murph asked incredulously. "My head can hardly stand it now."

"Well, if we're gonna do this song over again," Steve continued adamantly, "I'd sure like to turn up. It's not that I can't hear myself. I'm at six now. I just want *everybody* to turn up."

"No, no, you maniac," Murph shouted. "It's too loud already. You want even more brain damage, you cretin?"

"It's not that it's too loud," Blue Lou interjected. "It's just that it's bouncing back too fast."

"This room is too small for the sound," Al said.

"The sound is coming back off the front wall," Lou continued. "But this is the biggest room in the development."

"What do you think, Jake?" Steve asked.

Jake stood for a moment, rubbing his Buddha-belly thoughtfully. "Well," he said finally, "I wouldn't mind kicking it up a few notches. Just to see if we can fill in the bridge."

Steve smiled. "Yeah, let's try one that way."

The Duck cranked up the master volume to nearly full, so that even the hum was intimidatingly powerful for those with weak eardrums.

What followed was lost in a veritable explosion of sound, the chords of the band bellowing and creating shockwaves in the room that were primitively terrifying—a mountain avalanche, a volcano. Standing closest to the picture window, Al noticed it shiver. Cranked up full, Al could barely stand the noise, and noticed that several other band members were wincing in pain even as they added force to the torrent of decibels; yet each man seemed powerless to disengage himself from the self-induced agony.

Incredibly, the sound became even louder. The picture window shuddered and noticeably moved, then bulged outward. Al felt as if he were watching a newsreel in slow motion, a single-frame study of an atomic blast as, bit by bit, the last molecules of wood and glass yielded to the concentrated force of musical energy, tearing into tiny fragments with a roar that overpowered even the sound of the jacked-up amplifiers. Al saw the mud outside the window spattered with countless bits of debris, felt the *whoosh* of cold air past his cheeks, heard the shattering crack of the facade exploding into the yard.

The music stopped—all except Willie, who continued to pound out his drum rhythms, totally oblivious to the blast.

"Hey, did you see that window?" Steve said finally. "It blew up like a frog under a school bus."

"It's good," Jake said. "You know I like it loud. That song works loud."

For a moment the entire crew silently regarded the irregular opening in front of them. "It's much better with that window gone," the Duck said. "Now we won't have to worry about the sound bouncing back at us."

A faraway gleam of light caught their eyes. Blue Lou put his sax against the back wall and walked quickly toward the front door.

"What's that?" someone asked. "The cops?"

"Probably not," Lou said. "It's a car up by the main entrance. I'd better hustle my ass over to the office so they won't come looking for me. It's probably the security people."

"Anything we can do to help?" Jake asked.

"Yeah," Lou called over his shoulder as he sprinted in the direction of the trailer. "Don't play another note."

He was out of breath by the time he reached the trailer, and was still a bit red-faced by the time he slipped into his uniform, barely seconds before the visitors arrived. The truck in which two men sat was a four-wheel-drive van with a sign reading SPARTAN SECURITY on each side panel. The driver, an older, florid man with glasses, wore a uniform jacket with British-style colonel's pips on the epaulettes. He looked at Lou and smiled.

"Hi there, Commander Strang," Lou said.

"How are you, Mr. Marini?"

"Fine, sir."

"Has it been quiet around here?"

"Yessir. Pretty quiet."

"You're lonely, I'll wager."

"Not especially, sir."

"Of course, it's only natural, out here in the middle of nowhere. Would you like to start working the airport next week?"

"The airport?" Lou stammered.

"Yes. We need somebody to sit in the Park 'n' Pay there.

At least you'll see some people."

"That's all right," Lou said. "I don't mind being out here. In fact, I'm really getting used to it."

Strang nodded. "Well, the trades are coming off the strike next week," he said. "That means they'll be back in here working, so we'll need you less here and more at the airport."

"Yessir."

"Have you seen any strange vehicles the past few days?"

Lou shook his head.

"Well, keep a sharp lookout," Strang warned. "We've had some reports of strange vehicles. You know how people are today. If we don't keep both eyes open, they'll probably find a way to sneak in here and steal a whole house, foundation and all."

Lou managed a laugh.

"Anyway, Marini, you think about the airport thing. We'll be dropping in now and again, so we'll see you soon."

"Yessir."

He saluted weakly as the two men waved goodbye, then walked back to the model home.

"Who was it?" Jake asked.

"My supervisor, Commander Strang. He's gone now," Lou said. "But they're liable to be back at any time. They're looking out for strange vehicles, so it's possible he could turn up in another hour or two."

"That's a good point," the Duck said. "You know, I've been thinking about our security here. Actually, we were pretty lucky to spot that car so far away. What we need is something that'll tell us somebody's coming and get our attention even while we're jamming."

"And what would do that, short of a nuclear explosion?" Steve asked.

"How about if I could fix it so that one of them street lamps went on as soon as a car passed through the main gate?" the Duck asked.

Jake shrugged, unimpressed.

"Then how about if I brought that street lamp so it was right about . . . here?" He held his hand above his head, less than six feet from most of them. "And suppose it glowed red?"

Jake nodded. "Now that would give us a good signal."

"And suppose I fixed it so's it winked on and off?"

"Foolproof."

"Okay," the Duck said. "Grab some shovels, boys. I got a Technitran electric eye in the van, a 2011-12 beam that should do just fine. We'll cut a hole in the roof right . . . there . . . and run a line from that junction box . . ."

"Wait a second," Jake interrupted. "How long will this take, Duck?"

"Couple hours, no more. Best thing is, it'll be ready by tonight when it'll really help."

"All right. But I've been thinking, too. While you're doing that, I'd like to go get Malone."

"Good idea," Murph said. "We can use him."

"Yeah," Jake said. "I hate to admit it, but we need another horn, we need the presence, we need the charts. We need Bones Malone."

"Well, he bought a house up in Libertyville," Al said. "I got the address here someplace."

He fumbled in his shirt pocket and soon produced a sheet of paper. Jake took it. "Elwood and me'll be back as soon as we can sell old Bones on the idea."

They grabbed a couple of beers and some food for the trip. As they started out the front door, Steve and Lou were studying the broken window and arguing animatedly.

"We can't touch it there," Lou was saying. "That's the main support joist."

"Sure we can. All we have to do is cut around here—"

"What are you guys doing?" Jake asked.

"We thought we could get better acoustics by taking out the whole front wall," Steve explained.

THE BLUES BROTHERS

"The whole roof'll cave in, I tell you," Lou said.

"C'mon!" Steve yelled. "I'll show you, okay? Get me the power saw, some four-by-eights, a bunch of eleven-inch common nails and a hammer. It'll be a piece of cake."

Jake shrugged and walked with Elwood to the Bluesmobile. Before they started, Elwood took one long look at the once-impeccable house, which now sported a gaping hole in its front, through which could be seen piles of trash and walls that were streaked with yellow and red and mottled gray. He shook his head.

"What is it?" Jake asked.

"God sure works in strange ways."

Dietrich Albrecht was ecstatic. *"Deutsche Jubellaute!"* he shouted above the din of traffic after reading the telegram. *"Freiheit!* We are free to march!"

The liberal protest had been denied, largely because of the influence of the American Civil Liberties Union, which Dietrich thought a nice ironic touch. Now the Illinois Nazi Party was free to celebrate *Sturmtrupper* Horst Wessel's martyrdom by holding its parade right in the neighborhood of the orphanage that would soon house the organization. Clad in brown and black shirts, holding banners and flags like the masses assembled at the historic Nuremberg rallies, the INP was but two hundred strong. Yet, as *Gruppenführer* Albrecht assured them so many times, one of them was equal to many of the enemy because they were organized, had a purpose, a cause, courage, and knowledge that the man next to them would not run from a fight.

Brandishing the telegram, Albrecht walked down the line of troops. "They have realized," he shouted, "that it is futile to deny us, that it is illegal, and, most important, that it is unwise. For soon they will have to deal with many more parades, not only here but in Washington and all across the nation. We are the wave of the future and they realize it. Therefore, *mein Kameraden*, march proudly as Horst Wessel did a half-century ago."

Having arrived at the spot where an eight-piece German band was stationed, he gave the downbeat that sent them squealing into a tinny version of the "Radetsky March."

"*Vorwarts, Kompanie . . .*"

"One, two, three . . . hup!"

Balanced precariously on the stirrup formed by Jake's hands, Elwood was able to get a clear view over the seven-foot-high fence that bounded Tom Malone's yard in South Libertyville. An introvert who always preferred being alone, "Bones" was not merely a virtuoso performer on the trumpet, trombone and saxophone; he also wrote and arranged music and could improvise melodies of any description on cue and at will. Despite these considerable talents, however, he had never enjoyed the luxury of feeling he had it made in the world of music. His days with the Blues Brothers Band had been enjoyable, although he thought the leaders were basically dangerous. After that, he had worked in television and radio, then with several advertising agencies, and finally had hit the nadir with his "blackface" routine at the Ramada Inn. At first, when Murph had asked him about returning to the Blues Brothers, he had looked upon it as a form of salvation; only hours later, his enthusiasm had waned. "It'll be just another wild gig or two, and then oblivion," he reasoned. "Why bother?"

At thirty-two—but looking younger—he wondered if he ought not take a safe job and stop trying to hang onto the fringes of music. After all, he had a family and owed them something. But the thought of a desk or an assembly line frightened and revolted him even more than the prospect of another evening as the tallest of the Magictones. Trapped by his own indecision, he found little comfort in the typical suburban relaxation of a late afternoon barbecue. He found even less satisfaction in listening to the ramblings of his guests.

"Excuse me," he said, starting for the kitchen. "I'm going to check on the food."

"Sure," said the man with black curly hair and aviator glasses as he turned to the two women who remained in his captive audience. "Anyway, there I was getting ready to drill the guy's teeth, and suddenly I remember where I've seen him before. I think to myself, 'So this is the jerkoff cop who beat my head open at the Democratic convention in 1968.'"

"Oh no," one of the women said. "What did you do?"

"Well, needless to say, I drove him crazy with pain," the man recounted proudly. "First I gave him oxygen without any nitrous, I used an old carbide burr on my drill, I poured the gold while it was hot and used an extra heavy mallet to pound it in."

"You sadist!"

"Crazy!"

"Jesus F. X. Christ!" Jake wheezed up at Elwood from their vantage point twenty feet away. "What the hell's taking so long? Is Tom there, for Christ's sake?"

"Yeah," Elwood said. "The guy was telling an interesting story and I wanted to hear the end."

"The end is I go through life with heel prints in my palms."

"Sorry."

He hopped down.

"So what'll we do now?"

"Let's go around the other side near the kitchen and see if we can climb over," Jake said.

As they worked their way around next to the fence, they

could hear the conversation in the backyard, which seemed to have taken a more serious turn.

"What's Tom doing these days?"

"With his music?"

"Yeah..."

"Well, I don't know. He's sort of freaked out lately. He's stayed home for the last few days. He won't write jingles anymore. He used to free-lance a lot of them, you know..."

"Golly, he was doing so well at that. I love the one he did for that cereal."

"Rocket's Frosted Flakes..."

"Yeah, he played all the woodwinds on that himself."

"Had a nice classical feel..."

"What's he do all day?"

"Hangs out. Helps take care of the kids. He's been writing... his own stuff..."

"I'm sorry. If there's anything we can do..."

"This should be about it," Jake said. Then, forming his hands into a stirrup once again, he helped Elwood pull himself over the top of the barrier.

Tom Malone looked up from the stove, where he was browning the burgers before taking them outside, just at the moment when Elwood's head suddenly popped into view.

"Jesus Christ!" he shouted, losing control of the skillet, which clattered to the floor, sending burgers in all directions.

Propping himself on the top of the fence, Elwood reached down to give Jake a hand. Tom, meanwhile, rushed out into the yard to calm his wife and guests, who thought the neighborhood was being taken over by Cuban Secret Police agents.

"My God!" one of the women shouted. "What are they—the Mafia? Tax agents? Jews?"

"No," Tom said. "It's all right, it's all right."

The larger of the two men was now in view, his bulk balanced delicately on the sharp points of the fence. As he hovered dangerously on his perch, one meaty hand pointed at Tom while the voice intoned an almost Biblical pronouncement.

"It's your destiny," Jake said meaningfully. "We are back in your life. The band is together, we're rehearsing right now. We have a tour booked. There's no use trying to get away, because your fate is staring you in the face."

"No, man," Tom sighed. "I can't go . . . I won't."

Hopping down to the ground with surprising agility, Jake continued while the others watched as though mesmerized: "Bones, you're a genius. We need your genius. We need you. Blue Lou and Mr. Fabulous and all the rest are calling for you—"

"It sounds like he's come back from the dead or something," the dentist managed to say.

"Jake," Tom murmured. "I have a family. I just can't leave them. What about my wife . . . my kids . . ."

"Maybe you'd better go," his wife urged.

"Listen to the little woman," Jake smiled. "Even she sees how clear your destiny is."

"But—"

Elwood put a hand on his arm. "The world of music calls you, Tom Malone. You can't deny it."

Tom looked helplessly at his wife.

"Go with them, Tom. Tomorrow if you like," she said, smiling.

"Tonight," Jake said.

Tom gulped, raced into the house and emerged less than a minute later with an overnight bag and several instrument cases. "I'll . . . I'll call as soon as I know something," he said, kissing his wife quickly.

"Tomorrow night," Jake said. "The Jovial Club, Calumet City. The return of the Blues Brothers, starring the pulse, the backbone, the heartbeat, Tom 'Bones' Malone. Bring your family and friends. It's a mission for God."

Taking Tom's other arm, he led him through the gate and to the Bluesmobile. They had left the city limits of Libertyville before Tom had a chance to think twice about his decision.

"You'll be home in a couple weeks," Jake said finally, as they pushed down 94 toward Chicago.

"I hope so," Tom replied. "She's an understanding woman."

"I got that impression."

"Yeah. I've been acting kind of weird lately. Not going to work, lying around all day writing, composing my own music. I was working on a piece for three hundred cellos. It'll never see the light of day. I gave it up after the introduction."

As they neared Morton Grove, Elwood snapped his fingers for attention. "Hey," he said. "How about stopping by St. Helen's and finding out how they're doing on the advances?"

"Good idea," Jake said, even as Elwood veered right across three lanes of traffic to catch the nearest exit ramp. By way of explanation, he said to Tom, "We've got some people at the orphanage sending out flyers and stuff to promote our gig tomorrow night. That's what we meant by a mission for God. What we're trying to do is raise enough money to help pay off the mortgage on the place."

"Well, I'm in favor of that," Tom nodded.

Elwood's expert driving brought them into their old childhood neighborhood within minutes, but less than three blocks away from the church, traffic became increasingly congested until they finally approached a police officer diverting cars down a side street. Elwood stopped, and rolled down the window. "What's the matter, officer?" he asked in his most self-effacing voice. "A fire or something?"

"No, those people won their court case and so they're having a parade," the cop replied.

"Those people? What people?"

"Ah, those bums with the armbands. The Illinois Nazi Party."

From the distance, they could hear the sound of music, an oom-pah-pah band blasting away at full volume.

Tom leaned forward, his eyes wide. "That music," he

whispered. "Those horns. I know that music."

"Yeah, it's an old folk song or Nazi storm-trooper march or something," Jake murmured.

"No. That music, that arrangement. I wrote that oom-pah-pah arrangement," Tom said. "Now I remember. I did it for a Finka Toys jingle. And those bastards are using it. Goddamn it! I didn't give a bunch of Nazis the right to use my arrangement!"

"Come on, move it along," the cop urged. "You're holding up traffic behind you, fellas."

Tom's complexion turned pinkish, then red. "No," he wheezed. "They can't use my music that way. We gotta stop 'em. They got no right to do that!"

"You heard the man, Elwood," Jake said.

Needing no further encouragement, Elwood put his foot firmly on the brake pedal and at the same time, tromped the accelerator. The Bluesmobile bolted to a near-vertical position under the restrained power, the back tires smoking, the front tires spinning in a curiously leisurely fashion. The police officer leaped backward as though yanked by an invisible cord.

"Wait—" he managed to say before sprawling to a sitting position. "You guys—"

Slowly and with great control, Elwood guided the roaring Bluesmobile into the intersection, its presence made more menacing by the fact that it was obviously proceeding under massive power, capable of bursting loose at any second. Clustered on the sidewalks, regarding the marching Nazis with vocal hatred, the pedestrians suddenly became aware of the Bluesmobile's entering the parade like a huge fire-breathing, rubber-belching dragon. A collective gasp could be heard as several of the more timid onlookers broke and sought cover from the infernal machine, which seemed ready to split into shrapnel, whirling pistons, and napalm. The marching Nazi Party members became aware of the apparition at the same time, especially the band members, whose mouths apparently dried up as soon as the gray fumes from the shrieking engine curled around the tailpipes and poured downstream toward them. One by one, the oompahs faded into astonished nonmusical burps. A tuba fell to the asphalt. The strutting Nazi immediately behind it, who had the misfortune of playing the bass drum, promptly tripped and fell headfirst into his own instrument. Once begun, the pileup could not be halted. Like swastika-marked dominos, the Nazis' once-orderly parade line became an erratic accordion of chaos, shouting, tripping, and goose-stepping that was rapidly turning into an orgy of ass-kicking.

"Flaggensalut!" Dietrich Albrecht called out from the rear, just as the marchers turned the corner at which he had managed to hang a black, white and red banner.

He saluted smartly himself, executing an eyes-right as he did so, but a split second after turning his attention from the men in front of him, he was felled by a flying elbow to the middle of his forehead.

"Gott im—" was all he was able to say before being pushed to the street and receiving a knee in the back. All around him he could hear sounds of confusion, not unlike the noisy retreat of an undisciplined army; men were yelping like dogs, whining like little boys, screaming like women. Was it the end of the world?

He heard the engine's roar, and looked up to see the Bluesmobile bearing down upon him, carving a path for itself through the parade like a bowling ball through a group of helpless tenpins. Reaching out to grasp a flagpole, he managed to rap the vehicle across the windshield before it tore past. At the same time, he caught sight of the occupants—a pair of identically dressed, dark-glasses-wearing individuals who for all the world looked like Middle Eastern fruit merchants. Yet there was something strangely familiar . . . the outfits . . . the glasses . . . the impassive features . . . Yes, it had to be!

"Blauenbruder!" Albrecht shouted, looking about for something to throw. *"Mutter—Mutter—Mutter* fuckers!"

He located a discarded baton just as the thundering car stopped, made a horrendous grinding sound that could only be a shift into reverse, and started backwards. Like a good soldier, Albrecht committed the license number to memory before heaving the baton at the car and hurling himself into the gutter. The crowd along the sidewalk laughed uproariously as the return trip succeeded in sending nearly as many Nazis sprawling as had the surprise initial pass. At the intersection from which it had departed, the Bluesmobile paused a second as the police officer stationed there wagged his finger in gentle reproof. Then, belching great puffs of gray exhaust, it roared out of sight.

"So this is what you call democracy!" Albrecht shouted. "Well, we'll show you what we think of your fucking democracy, you decadent welfare-state pigs! We'll show you in spades, you Jew-loving, mother-humping, fat-assed shitheads!"

He turned to face the sidewalk spectators, his hands balled defiantly into fists.

But no one seemed to be listening to him. Not even his own men.

Curtis answered the rap on the door, his eyes coming to life when he saw Jake and Elwood.

"Well, well," he said. "Nice to see you. How'd you get here, by the way? They got the streets blocked off for the parade, I hear."

"We found a way," Elwood smiled.

"Come on in."

"Curtis, this here's Tom Malone," Jake said. "You probably remember him from the old days."

"Sure do."

The two shook hands. Curtis led them down to the boiler room and again produced the bottle of bourbon. After they helped themselves to a drink, the black man opened an old shoe box and passed it to Jake. It was crammed full of money. "More'n three thousand dollars in there," he said proudly. "The kids have been bustin' their asses for that gig tomorrow night."

"Terrific," Elwood said. "Now all we have to do is—"

He paused. Both Curtis and Tom looked at him, their eyes registering puzzlement at first and then sudden understanding.

Tom managed to speak first. "There's no gig," he said.

"Not yet," Jake admitted. "But we're going to make it happen. You'll see. It's gonna be all right."

"Jesus Christ," Tom murmured. "It's Thursday. Late Thursday afternoon. Do you understand what that means?"

"It means it's only a little past noon on the Coast," Jake replied, holding his right index finger up all-knowingly.

"I don't get it," Tom protested. "It looks to me like you've pulled another sleazy scam, Jake. Sure, you got some money to help pay off the mortgage, but what's gonna happen when those people go to the Jovial Club and find out we're not there? They might come back and throw bricks at this place, or even worse, call the kids of bunch of cheaters. You shouldn't have done it, Jake."

Jake looked at Curtis, who avoided his gaze.

"Look," Jake said, "I've got an idea. I know you think I'm an asshole for waiting so long, but so help me, I've been thinking about this all week. I considered everything—kidnapping the group that's supposed to be there, building a detour in the road, even asking them if they'll go along . . ."

"Now there's an idea that hasn't occurred to you very often," Elwood said. "Telling the truth."

"But it's too risky," Jake continued. "If we get stuck

with some ambitious sonofabitch who says no, we may end up having to kill him. So I thought of something else. Just this minute, when I made that remark about the time on the Coast."

"So tell us?"

"I'll show you instead. Where's the phone, Curtis? Still upstairs in the hall? I don't want Sister Mary listening in."

Curtis smiled. "Never mind her. We can plug in down here, if you don't mind using alligator clips."

He led Jake to a beat-up headset held together by alligator clips, with a dial face apparently lifted from a telephone of the 1940s. "This is the best I can offer," he said. "But she works."

"Let me have it," Jake said. He fished in his pocket for a paper and dialed a number.

"Maury Sline, please... Jake Blues. Tell him this is urgent... Thanks... Hiya, Maury. Listen, I want you to find out two very important things for me right now ... Because I need help... And I still got that copy of the contract with the blank spaces, plus a pigeon who's ready to lend me two thousand just on the basis of *your* signature... That's right... My signature, but it says Maury Sline and you know damn well that when I blow town he's gonna come looking for you... Sure, he doesn't have a prayer, but you don't need the aggravation, do you?... Besides, what I'm asking will be a piece of cake for you... Okay... Got that old pencil and paper ready?... Fine... Now what I need to know, as soon as possible, like *now minus one*, is who is the agent for 'Waldo and the Wall-Walkers' and where they are now... Got it?... Then call me back... Or better yet, I'll call you in ten minutes... Yeah."

He hung up.

"What's the top club in L.A.?" he asked.

The boys thought for a moment, then Tom smiled and shook his head. "No, not a club," he said. "That's too easy for them to check. But if you were working for TV or one of the major film studios... Shit, they could try to give it a quick double-check and chase their own asses around the mulberry bush for three days before finding out they'd been had."

"Great!" Jake said.

"Tell them you're from Republic Pictures and they're doing a new musical," Elwood suggested.

"Yeah," Jake muttered. "I'd try that, but they might see through it." He frowned, thought for a moment, then smiled malevolently. "Never mind. I've got it. All we have to do is wait for Maury."

He looked at his watch, and waited until twelve minutes passed before dialing Maury again. When he was put through to him, he smiled broadly as he scrawled names and numbers on the side of a styrofoam cup.

"Thanks, Maury," he said finally. "Oh, and there's one more thing. This'll be even easier. Pick a major film studio and name me a top executive who's almost totally inaccessible... Good..." he scribbled some more, leaned back against the wall and sighed. "Maury, you've been terrific. I'm sure glad I don't have to use your name for criminal purposes. By the way, we knocked 'em dead last night at Bob's Country Bunker... Yeah, same to you, fella."

He hung up, spat on his palms and smoothed out the styrofoam cup for easier handling.

"One thing," Tom suggested as Jake reached for the dial face.

"Yeah?"

"Don't pretend you're their agent, okay?"

"Why not?"

"Because they'll know it's not the voice, for God's sake. Tell them you're the person from Hollywood who's been trying to contact their agent, and name him. That'll be enough."

"Christ, Tom," Jake marveled. "You're a fucking genius. A natural crook, a first-rate budding scam-man."

"It's just common sense," Tom said modestly.

"And now to business," Jake said. As the others watched nervously, he dialed a long-distance number and waited a maddeningly long time before someone answered.

Taking a deep breath, Jake suddenly transformed himself into the consummate con artist. "Hello," he said in a very suave voice. "I'd like to speak with someone with Waldo and the Wall-Walkers, preferably Waldo... You are?... Good... This is Milt Svargarar of Universal Pictures in Universal City... Yes, that's right... I've been trying to get hold of Ty Briscow, your agent, all day, but we either have the wrong number or he's out. Anyway, through a process that's too devious to go into at the moment—and it's really not that important—we found out where you're playing so we could contact you. Listen, Waldo, the deal is we'd like you and your group to be out here tomorrow morning for a picture we're doing. I'm not at liberty to say over the telephone what it is, but it's a big-budget rock 'n' roll, disco musical and we thought you'd be perfect for it... Gee, I wish we'd been able to contact Mr. Briscow about this, because I know you'd prefer leaving things like this to him... You see, the problem is, we're replacing a group that just hasn't worked out and it's all very hush-hush, and has to be done fast. What I mean is, we needed somebody today, but I talked the powers that be into waiting until tomorrow if I could get you and the Wall-Walkers... You can?... Well, that's fine... Don't worry about the financial end, because I'm sure we can work something out... Just put yourself on the first plane and we'll reimburse you when you get here... Now this is important. Please don't tell anyone what you're involved in until you see Miss Walls... That's Jeannette Walls, who's very important here and is handling the whole thing... If there's an emergency, of course, you can call here, but try to avoid it if you can... For God's sake, just show up sometime tomorrow and we'll fill you in completely... I'm really sorry to have to throw this at you, but I thought you'd like to have the opportunity... Yes... Milt Svargarar, but generally speaking I won't be too available until late tomorrow... Thanks very much... See you then... Oh, you're quite welcome... Goodbye."

The others applauded as he hung up.

"Goddamn," Tom said, shaking his head in awe. "Kiss me where I pee."

Curtis was cracking up with laughter. "If they ever try to find a Mr. Svargarar, they're gonna drive some poor telephone operator crazy..."

"Do you think they'll even bother to call the Jovial Club?" Jake asked.

"Now there's a thought," Tom said. "At what point do you get ready to move in?"

"We show up in the late afternoon and say we're the replacement group," Elwood said.

"No," Jake rejoined. "We're there first thing in the morning, so there's no chance he can find somebody else during the day."

"Another thought," Tom interjected. "Suppose they call the Jovial Club right now and the manager asks the group that's there tonight to stay one more day or so until he can find a new group?"

Jake looked daggers at Bones. "Damn you," he muttered. "How can a guy pull a decent scam with you around, Tom?"

"What do you mean?"

"I mean, some things have to be left to chance or it's no goddamned fun."

THE BLUES BROTHERS

As the sun set over Cherrywood Hills, Matt sat eating a grapefruit with the skin on, listening contentedly to Al and Murph jamming their adlibbed version of "Expressway to Your Heart." The Duck lay on his back next to the missing picture window, his eyes closed, hands folded across his chest, which was gently rising and falling. Willie stood a few feet away, throwing rocks at beer bottles. Cropper and Lou, having punched a hole in one of the upstairs toilets, were trying to repair it with gaffer's tape.

Suddenly the giant red eye hanging over the center of the living room began blinking on and off, its frenetic pulse reminding Matt of the Martian creatures in *The War of the Worlds*. "Red alert!" he shouted, even as he realized it was unnecessary. At the first burst of color, Al and Murph abruptly stopped their performance and the giggling from upstairs ceased. The Duck opened his eyes and sat bolt upright. "Damn," he said. "It really does work."

As one, they looked in the direction of the access road from the south, at the gate of which the electric eye had been so carefully rigged by the Duck. Slowly the cloud of dust rose, obliterating any signs of the vehicle creating it.

"Must be Elwood," Matt said. "He's the only white man I know who drives like that."

"Yeah," Steve agreed, having come downstairs.

A minute later the Bluesmobile lurched into view, and now the eyes of the men at the house strained to see if a third person was present. When they could make out the face of Tom Malone, they broke into loud cheering and applause.

"Now we got the full sound," Willie said. "Hey, help the man bring his horns in here and let's get something started."

Before it was completely dark, they were under way, playing at near-full volume, each man listening carefully not only to himself but to the overall sound of the band.

207

And as they continued, the music took on a new dimension, one of joy, for they realized that they truly were all together. *The* sound was back. Drunk with the nostalgia of themselves, they played long and hard into the early-morning hours.

Jake called a halt reluctantly. "I'd like to keep going, but tomorrow's a big day for us," he said. "Now let's get some sleep so we can start early."

Before turning in, he and Elwood and Blue Lou sat up awhile, discussing what had to be done before making the trip to Calumet City. "Hey, I hate to tell you this, man," Blue Lou said, "but if we're pulling out in the morning, that doesn't leave us much time to do something about this house. And we gotta do something, you know."

"Don't worry," Elwood soothed. "We'll fix it."

"I don't know how we can. The walls in every room are punched full of holes, and that picture window's blown to hell, and somebody used the toilets even though there's no water. The shit's caked on like putty."

Jake looked around in the semidarkness, and nodded. "Yeah, I gotta agree. This place is beyond repair."

"I guess there's only one thing to do," Elwood said.

"What's that?"

"We must adopt a scorched-earth policy."

"You mean burn it down?" Lou asked. A smile playing over his features indicated that he was more than a little intrigued by the idea.

"I just don't know," Jake said. "Wouldn't that be worse for you, Lou? If they found nothing, I mean? At least if they had the frame, they could recoup something."

"It depends," Lou murmured. "Maybe it would be better if just nothing remained. Absolutely nothing. Then I could deny there was ever a house here."

"But how can we do that?"

"I don't know," said Lou. "Elwood? What do you think?"

But all they heard was steady, heavy breathing, Elwood having sagged slowly into one corner of the room.

"Let him sleep," Jake said. "And you get some sleep too. We'll talk it over with the boys and figure out something."

Lou nodded and closed his eyes. Less than a minute later, he could hear the dull rumbling of Jake's snoring interspersed with sharp popping sounds.

Lou laughed. Jake Blues was, to his knowledge, the only person he knew who cracked his knuckles in his sleep.

Shortly after the sun cast its first golden rays on the twisted framework of the Mediterranean model home in which the band slept, Jake opened his eyes, belched noisily, closed his eyes again for about five minutes, and then suddenly bounded to his feet. Everyone else was dead to the world, so he inspected the house for food without success, added some of his own putty to the powder room toilet and returned to the living room, clapping his hands as loudly as possible.

"Everybody up!" he yelled, rather enjoying the expressions of displeasure and outright loathing he received from the slack-eyed troops. At first they tried to ignore him, but soon realized it was impossible.

"Why so early?" Willie asked, his voice sounding like a run-down Vegamatic.

"Because we gotta fire this house," Jake explained.

"Without two weeks' notice?"

"Come on, Willie," Jake said, kicking lightly at his supine figure. "Get your ass up."

In a quarter-hour, the men were upright and had heard, if not fully comprehended, the situation that faced them regarding the house and Jake's decision to burn it to the ground.

"Maybe we should just try dismantling it," Murph said. "Carpenters probably put these places up in fifteen hours, so we could most likely take 'em down in three."

"I think we should torch it," Al said.

"Torch it," the Duck agreed.

"I'll help, if you want," Al said. "I used to be a professional, you know."

"If we burn it, there'll be smoke," Tom interrupted. "The last thing we need is smoke signals."

"Yeah, it'd be easier to just phone them and have them take us all away," the Duck laughed.

"This would be a good time to have smoke, though, if we have to have smoke," Elwood said. "About this time of the morning, the factories start firing up their furnaces and usually there's a lot of colorful shit in the air until it gets burnt off the stacks from the night before."

"Just another fart in the breeze," the Duck noted.

"Hey, let's blow it up, man," Willie urged. "I've never blown up a house, not even one."

"You live in that project and you've never seen a house blown up?" Jake returned.

Willie shook his head. "I seen 'em dismantled brick by brick, but that took an hour or so."

"Well, if there's no dynamite around, it might be hard," Lou observed, looking around at them. "Anybody just happen to have some dynamite?"

"Only what we're rolling and smoking," Steve replied.

"How about that bulldozer you used to pull out the Bluesmobile?" Murph suggested.

Al nodded. "That might work."

Steve shook his head. "If you drive a bulldozer through this house, you'll mangle it," he said professorially. "Trusses and walls might get jammed together. Your pieces would be too big to move and hide. The whole place would end up looking like a dog's breakfast."

"Not only that," Tom added. "But it would be obvious who did it, since nobody else has the keys to that vehicle but Lou. It would be like signing a confession."

"Is everybody finished talking now?" Elwood asked.

The rest turned to look at him. Since no one spoke, he took their silence as an indication that he had the floor, so to speak.

"As it turns out," he said, "I don't have dynamite, but I have something just as good. In the trunk of the Bluesmobile, I got thirty or so aerosol cans of overpressurized propane. If we heat them just a little, they'll blow, quiet and quick. The way I figure it, that should make this place disappear very scientific-like."

"You been driving around with that in the trunk for how long?" Jake demanded.

"Since Monday."

"Jesus Christ."

"Well, like you said, Jake, you gotta leave some things to chance or it's no fun."

Jake sighed, rolled his eyes and led the way to the car. While he and most of the others unloaded the cans and began dragging their equipment out of the house, the Duck and Elwood planned the operation. First they had Lou bulldoze a trench in front of the house, into which the men tossed everything that would burn, including garbage, rugs, and furniture. Elwood then grabbed a bunch of twenty-five-ounce cans and began packing them in pairs into corners between the walls and roof truss. The Duck, meanwhile, picked up a section of electric baseboard heater and tore away the metal covering with a pair of pliers in order to expose the heater's tubular heating element. Pulling out the two power leads connected to it, he bent the leads into a coil, which he wrapped around an aerosol can of propane, then connected the leads onto the element around the can to the leads on the plug wire.

"What you doing?" Steve asked, taking in the Duck's rapid but intricate maneuvers.

"Making bombs."

"That's what I thought."

The preparations were finished in less than an hour. The ditch having been loaded with furniture, stoves, a refrigerator, kitchen cabinets and assorted garbage, Blue Lou deftly plowed dirt over it, pushing and backfilling until the burial ground was flush with the rest of the lawn. Plug wires hung down from cans packed into the roof trusses at the corners of all the walls. All the equipment had been stowed in the van or the Bluesmobile, and a final inspection made of the premises. Only one adjustment needed to be made when the Duck and Elwood were left alone in the living room.

"Okay," the Duck said. "Willie just signaled that the juice is off. Go ahead and plug them in."

Elwood inserted an extension cord into a wall outlet, and plugged four of the wired cans into it.

"Now let's haul ass," Elwood said.

The two jogged through the doorway to the spot a hundred yards away where the rest of the band waited. Raising his hand above his head, the Duck signaled to Willie at the power transformer farther down the road.

"Okay, let's heat 'em up!" he yelled.

At the transformer site, Willie threw the predetermined switch and felt a hum of power. Immediately his eyes, like those of the other men, turned toward the house.

For perhaps ten seconds, nothing happened. Slowly the band members began to look at one another—all except Elwood, who stood with eyes fastened on one set of cans. At first they seemed unaffected by the surge of power, then they began to glow pink, then red, finally exploding with a great flash of flame but surprisingly little accompanying sound. At the same time, other cans along the circuit sent out masses of red fire, the whole house becoming enveloped from first floor to roof in a matter of seconds. The wave of heat suddenly struck them, forcing the boys to retreat several steps.

"Goddamn!" someone yelled. "I never saw a house catch fire like that!"

Their faces registered shock and joy as the house seemed to melt before their very eyes—whole sections of walls, metal beams, wooden panels falling against each other like a pyramid constructed of newspapers.

"Be it ever so humble, there's no place like home," Steve Cropper said.

The roof was still intact, but had only seconds left before it fell, the victim of simultaneous blasts of exploding gas rocking it at a dozen points. Soon smoke and splinters were everywhere, the antiseptically clean initial discharge having given way to a violent downdraft that sprayed the area of detonation with a superheated cloud heavy with debris. The smoke soon drifted away, however, pushed by a brisk breeze from the south that reduced the entire explosion to something no larger than the cloud of dust made by several bulldozers.

The fire burned itself out as quickly as it had flamed to life, the building softening into a gray mound only a couple of feet high in less than a quarter-hour. Presently all that remained was a low ridge of smoldering ashes.

"You're a genius, Elwood," Steve said admiringly. "That's the best thing I've ever seen. Ain't had so much fun since I was a kid."

"Well, let's finish the job," Blue Lou said, trotting toward the Cat and attacking the pyre. Racing back and forth across the soft, smoky mass, he had soon reduced it to nothing more than a huge gray circle surrounded by mud.

"Get some shovels and start hauling some dirt over here," Lou called out.

For another half-hour the boys dug up neighboring lawns in order to cover the ash heap that had once been Bulmer's proud Mediterranean model home. As the earth was deposited on the scorched area, Lou tamped it down until the disguise was perfect.

"That's that," he said, being sure then to drive the bulldozer to a spot far removed from the scene.

"Boys," Jake said, "you do good work."

As they stood enjoying the final moments of the experience, a low whistle gradually increased in volume and intensity, the sound heralding the appearance of a slow-moving object in the sky heading in their direction. Shimmering in the early-morning sunlight, its great silver body seeming to move despite rather than because of the trio of outsized engines, it gradually passed over them at an altitude so low that Jake could make out faces at the windows.

"There she goes," Blue Lou said. "Right on schedule. The eight o'clock plane for L.A. She'll be in Tinsel City a couple hours before noon, their time..."

"Yeah," Jake said. "I guess you could call that the Heartbreak Special."

"If we're lucky," Tom said cautiously.

chapter eight

The idea had occurred to Dietrich Albrecht as he lay nursing his sore back and battered forehead, and now, having carried it to fruition, he began to experience genuine hope. Once again he had proved to himself, his most important critic, that he was light-years ahead of other political-military geniuses. Setting a trap at the Jovial Club using his own men was a somewhat obvious step; reporting the activities of the Blues Brothers to the Chicago Police was also obvious, although quite necessary; going to the musicians' union, on the other hand, was a stroke of genius. Most ordinary schemers would have assumed that Jake and Elwood were in good standing with this organization and not bothered to explore it as a likely vehicle for revenge. Not so Dietrich Albrecht. He was, if nothing else, thorough.

Now he smiled smugly as he saw the fire burning in the eyes of the man who called himself Louie the treasurer. "Anyway, sir," he concluded, "I thought you ought to know about this activity they have planned tonight. Being a strong union advocate myself, I know how much depends on all good union men sticking together and weeding out the bad apples."

"Yeah," Louie said, not looking at Albrecht.

Instead, his eyes were riveted on the crude but effective flyers advertising the Blues Brothers' appearance that very evening at the Jovial Club. First they had failed to pay their dues, then nearly destroyed his bulletin board, stealing several dozen information cards in the process, and now this. Louie felt he definitely looked like an asshole.

"What the fuck makes them think they can just walk in some club and start playing?" he hissed. "Their memberships ain't up to date and even if they was, I just might not let 'em play on general principle."

His hand reached for the telephone.

"Pardon me," Albrecht said. "But if I may make a suggestion, if you alert the proprietor of that establishment now, they may be able to deny everything, whereas if you caught them *in flagrante*, so to speak, it would be an open-and-shut case."

"Yeah, maybe you got something there..."

"In any event, I happen to know that both brothers are wanted by law-enforcement officials, one for parole violation and the other for several hundred traffic violations. It would seem in the interest of justice to set a trap for them."

"Well, up to a point," Louie said. "According to the by-laws, I gotta warn 'em that they can't play. First, you know. It ain't like the law where you gotta catch somebody after he's done the crime. If I know they got no business in that club, it's my duty to tell 'em ahead of time."

"But surely you can wait until the last possible moment. The police will be most grateful. The worst thing that could happen now would be for them to receive some sort of premature warning."

"No, I won't do that," Louie said. "What I'll do is take a couple of the boys and meet you at the club at, say, six-thirty."

Albrecht beamed. "That will be fine. Everything should be set by that time."

None of the Blues Brothers band members had visited Calumet City for three years, so they were surprised and delighted at the physical change that had transformed the Jovial Club from a semi-rustic bar with occasional live entertainment into one of the best clubs in the entire state. Previously the place had been one of many beer joints isolated from Calumet City's main drag, a huge building made of logs, clapboard and fieldstone that was faintly reminiscent of private hunting lodges of the 1930s. While in a state of disrepair, as it was during the 1960s and early 70s, the Jovial Club building appeared damp and forbidding; now, spruced up and completely renovated, it seemed a sumptuous throwback to Prohibition days. Inside as well as out, it showed the loving touch of someone who knew how to make money. Even the obligatory deer heads and other stuffed items were arranged with a flair that amazed the more taste-conscious of the musicians.

"We're in the wrong place," said Al Rubin, as the group moved through the cavernous lobby. "I just know it."

"Not a chance," Jake shot back. "When I arrange a gig, it's in a class spot."

A classy-looking woman of about thirty, dressed in collarless shirt, tweed jacket and French blue jeans, came out of an office door next to the registration desk just as the band arrived.

"You're the bug men?" she asked.

"No, ma'am," Jake replied. "Some of us are just kinda short."

"Oh. You're not from—"

"No, ma'am," Jake said. "We're the Blues Brothers. The band for this evening."

The woman looked puzzled. "There's a new group supposed to be here tonight," she said, "but it's not the Blues Boys—"

"Blues Brothers."

"Yes, I'm sorry. It's Waldo and the Wall-Walkers." She pointed to a poster just off the lobby. "See? Surely there's a mistake. That group is supposed to be here any minute.

As a matter of fact, they're overdue."

"Yes, ma'am," Jake said, noticing that she had a fair couple of jugs tucked away beneath the shirt, the open top button of which revealed a soft slope of cleavage. "That's why we're here. You see, Waldo and the Wall-Walkers won't make it tonight. They were supposed to give you a call, except that Waldo's kind of a coward about breaking engagements, so maybe you won't hear anything, ever."

"I don't understand," the woman said.

"Last night," Jake continued, trying to sound as sympathetic as possible, "the Wall-Walkers were offered a job for a little more money, so they called us and asked if we'd fill in for tonight and maybe the weekend, or even the rest of their engagement if you like us."

The woman's jaw dropped. Good teeth, Jake thought.

"Well, I wasn't too happy about doing it for them," Jake pressed on quickly, "but Waldo insisted, said it was a chance for them to pick up some loot, you know. When I asked what I should tell the people here, he said, 'Oh, give 'em some bullshit'... Pardon me, ma'am..."

"Go right ahead."

"Well, he said to give you some song and dance about being called to Hollywood, because that's one excuse everybody falls for and forgives you for."

"Hmmmp," the woman snorted. Good flaring nostrils, Jake thought.

"I'm sorry," Jake said. "Personally, I don't think that's a good way to do business, but I owe Waldo a favor. He saved my little sister from drowning when she was a baby. Now we're even, I guess."

"It's a *rotten* way to do business," she murmured. "Now we have a full house and I'm stuck—" She paused, smiled. "I'm sorry. It's just that I've never heard of the Blues Brothers."

"Ma'am, you're in for a treat. Hey, boys! Start setting up in the main lounge."

He trotted back a couple of paces and pointed the way. The

woman came from behind the desk, clearly apprehensive at the turn of events but indecisive as to how to deal with it.

"Take down that crappy poster," Jake ordered. Then, turning to the woman, he smiled and said, "Once you hear us, you'll never want to have another band in here, least of all Waldo and his Weak-Kneed Wall-Walkers."

"Listen," she replied. "After what they did, if your group's even half-competent, they'll have to use dynamite to get in this place."

"In that case, ma'am," Jake said, "we've got it made."

As the band raced around looking for outlets and began to set up the gear, the woman relaxed a bit. "By the way," she said, "you don't have to keep calling me 'ma'am.' My name is Lee Crisp and I'm one of the owners."

"Jake Blues here."

"Pleased to meet you. I'm sorry for thinking you were the exterminators."

"That's all right. I've been called worse. But not by anybody prettier."

She laughed lightly. Jake's mouth opened just as Tom blew a loud blast on his trombone.

"We're ready!" Steve yelled.

"Pardon me," Jake smiled.

He trotted over to the bandstand, went into his countdown and sent the boys roaring through three of their best numbers. By the time they were finished, the lounge was well populated with kitchen employees, chambermaids from the adjoining motel, bartenders, and a generous assortment of young people, including an extraordinarily high percentage of high-breasted chicks. At the conclusion of "Who's Making Love," Jake brought them to a powerful crescendo and waited for the applause.

It came. A moment later, Lee Crisp was at Jake's side, her blue eyes wide with excitement. "That was terrific," she said. "I mean, really good. Everything's going to be just fine." She took his arm and led him back toward the main lobby. "But we've got to do it up right, you know. I'll tell you what. One of those women in the contest tonight is a hell of an artist . . . Joyce, I believe her name is . . ."

"You're having a contest?" Jake asked.

"Yes. Before you go on. It's for Miss Wet T-Shirt. We have it once a year. It's a big favorite."

Her eyes caught sight of one young woman and she moved quickly after her. She returned presently with the prominent-pectoraled person and introduced her. "I'd like you to draw us a poster for the lobby tonight," she said, "using Mr. Jake Blues here as your subject."

"And my brother Elwood," Jake said.

"Of course."

The girl nodded, not too enthusiastically, however, lest she weaken her chances that evening. "Sure, I can do that," she smiled. "Where will the band be this afternoon?"

"In the L-Wing rooms," Lee replied. "Only the best."

"Hey, you're a beautiful human being," Jake said. "I just hope nothing happens to spoil it."

"Like what?" Lee asked.

"Well, like if the Wall-Walkers call and play on your sympathy or maybe try to lean on you—"

"Lean on me?" Lee snorted. "I'd like to see them try. No sir, as far as I'm concerned, they're more than two hours overdue and I just hired a new band."

Jake tried to restrain his urge to smile. "But suppose they show up?" he asked timorously, a fair imitation of Lou Costello twisting his tie nervously. "They could try to use force or—"

"Forget it," Lee said. "I'll alert the men at the door and we'll have a couple dozen really big fellows standing by."

Jake smiled wickedly. "Golly, you think of everything."

"I try," she said, wondering what he looked like without the dark glasses.

The letters on the frosted glass door read:

ILLINOIS STATE POLICE
OFFICE OF INTELLIGENCE
RICHARD T. LAPIERRE
COMMANDER

Inside the office, a top-level conference was taking place, the participants being Commander LaPierre himself, a large white man with a flat-topped brush cut, and Burton Mercer and Wade Fiscus. Fiscus' hands were wrapped in heavy bandages and Mercer had several small pieces of tape on his forehead and lower jaw.

"You realize that I'll have to have the chief sign an executive order to call up that many men and cars," LaPierre said, putting down his copy of *Police Chief* magazine, which he had been idly studying.

"Yessir," Mercer replied. "We feel it's of sufficient importance to ask; otherwise, we wouldn't have made the request."

"There are at least six child molesters working on consecutive strings in the Skokie area, a gang of muggers in Des Plaines, the mysterious shopping center rapist in Elmhurst, and the crossbow killer still at large in Evergreen Park," LaPierre said. "The public knows of these enemies and has demanded action, the TV stations have demanded that we step up the number of patrols, and yet you feel confident that we should commit more than two dozen men and no less than eight vehicles, including one armored car, so that we can arrest a pair of jazz musicians in Calumet City?"

The others may have blinked slightly at the commander's counterattack, but Wade Fiscus was as solid as a rock. "Yessir," he said in a high and decisive voice. "Absolutely. For one thing, the one known as Elwood is a known traffic-ticket scofflaw. He must be brought to justice and shown as an example to the public. Disregard for paying traffic tickets may not seem like much, but it leads to disrespect for other laws, so that before one knows it, the double-parker has become a shoplifter and then a burglar and then an international assassin. Crime, like disease, must be curbed at its very inception."

"Sergeant Fiscus has a point," Mercer added. "We have reason to believe that the Blues Brothers had something to do with that big vandalism case in Champaign-Urbana that just came in this morning."

"What was that? I don't remember. Maybe you'd better run it down for me."

"Somebody stole a hundred-thousand-dollar house in a development tract south of Rantoul."

"Stole, Mercer?"

"Yessir. It was there last week when aerial photos were taken of the plot. But this morning when a couple stopped by to visit their home, there was nothing on the lot. So more aerial photographs were taken and the house is missing."

"You have reason to believe these two musicians were involved in this case?"

"Yessir. They're also tied in with a certain Donald Dunn, who apparently hijacked a van from the Ray-Dex alarm system company nearly a week ago."

"It's as I said," Wade Fiscus interjected. "One small crime leads to another and then to larger ones and then to the stealing of homes. It's inevitable. For these reasons, sir, we'd like to see this office authorize a priority-pursuit program," Fiscus said.

"We can't take this upon ourselves unless we really have a perfect trap laid," LaPierre agonized. "If we fail, the public will laugh at us again. We can't afford any more bad press. If we make such a commitment of time and money, I want to be sure the Blues Brothers are dangerous criminals and I want to be sure they don't get away."

"We guarantee that your trust in us will be repaid, sir," Mercer said solemnly.

"Shit," LaPierre muttered.

"I really don't know what came over me," Lee said, leaning back against Jake's ample chest and stomach, which rose and fell rhythmically to the tune he was humming. "Usually I don't get carried away, but there was something about you. I sensed a hunger, a need, a kind of undercurrent of desire that I knew only I could satisfy."

"Yeah," Jake said.

"Most men are so super-sophisticated and cool," she continued, stroking his leg. "They try to pretend it's such a common thing that they're not even excited any more. Their macho image requires that they keep the woman occupied for six or seven hours, because that's supposed to mean they're strong. But with you, Jake, it was over in two minutes. Two minutes."

"Yeah," he said. "I was trying to make it last as long as possible. You see, I had three years of prison to make up for."

"Oh, it must have been terrible."

They lay together in the four-poster bed, far removed from the rest of the guests, for perhaps another five minutes. Then Jake stirred, started to get up.

"Oh, please don't go yet," Lee said. "There's one thing I'd like you to do for me."

"What's that?"

"Take off your glasses."

Jake shook his head. "Sorry," he said. "There's some things I don't do for anybody. Besides, I don't have time. I have to get back to our room so's that artist can finish painting my picture."

"One eye?" Lee pleaded. "Can't I even see one?"

Residents living close by the Jovial Club were used to large Friday-night crowds, but on this particular evening it was as if Elvis Presley were the opening act. It was Miss Wet T-Shirt Night, of course, and they knew that helped. But somehow the number of cars seemed the largest they had ever seen.

The influx began well before dark, when a half-dozen plain Chevy Novas entered as a group but fanned out to different parts of the lot. Next, at least twenty vehicles, all manufactured in Germany, performed the same sort of maneuver. In between the two convoys came dozens of other cars, singly, each containing a young couple or quartet of well-dressed persons out on the town. At one point a schoolbus arrived, filled predominantly with black people. By dusk, there was hardly room on the lot for a Honda.

Inside the Jovial Club, there was an atmosphere of expectation, almost as if an expensive new show were about to open, the success or failure of which could affect many lives. Customers circulated noisily about the bar, but their eyes invariably returned to the bandstand of the main lounge, hoping to catch the first glimpse of the fabled group that was still talked about in some musical quarters, despite a silence of more than two years.

Jake, meanwhile, was introduced to a variety of guests, some of whom were merely curious, while others hoped to use the Blues Brothers to further some pet project or deal. One of the well-wishers was a dapper man with an upturned mustache named Michael Glabner, who entered with Rob Woods, another of the Jovial Club owners.

"Hey, Jake," Rob said. "I'd like you to meet a friend of mine. Jake Blues, this is Mike Glabner, President of Clarion Records."

"Hiya," Jake said.

"I came here to take in Waldo and the Wall-Walkers," Glabner said. "Too bad they couldn't make it. But I guess I'll stick around to catch your act."

"Don't do us any favors," Jake retorted.

"No trouble at all," Glabner replied, smiling. "Matter of fact, I know your work, saw your act at the Falls End Hotel two-three years ago, before . . . before your problem."

"Well, maybe we can make a record for you," Jake suggested offhandedly.

"A blues record?"

"What else?"

"I don't think so, man. I mean, I love the blues but it's old-hat now. No label can back a blues band. It doesn't sell."

"We've changed our show a lot since you saw it," Jake lied, hating himself for bothering to take the trouble with such a wimp. But the urge to get something going was irresistible.

"Well, I'll see it tonight." The huge Glabner smiled beneath his handlebar moustache. "Good luck."

"Yeah. Thanks."

The man left.

"Asshole," Jake muttered.

Next on the visitors' agenda was a striking red-haired black woman dressed in a lavender jumpsuit with a Star of David armband on each sleeve. Displaying a fine set of large, even teeth, she smiled graciously as she explained that her newspaper, the *Illinois Jewish Times,* was interested in a piece about his comeback following the dark years in prison. Still, there was something disturbingly familiar about her. Yet Jake agreed to talk. The woman expressed a certain reluctance to interview him unless they could remove themselves from the rest of the band, who were just a few feet away in the next room.

"You see," she explained, "there are some rather searching questions I'd like to ask, and I feel that privacy would be beneficial."

"Sure, I guess so," Jake replied. Still feeling good about his afternoon tussle with Lee Crisp, he wondered if it would be possible to screw this good-looking black. A quick look at his watch, however, indicated that it would be nearly impossible to fit her into the time slot available, even if she were willing to fit him into her. "Why not start with the easy questions first?" he said.

"They'll take care of themselves," the woman replied, flashing her teeth. "I'd prefer to start with the difficult ones."

"Maybe we'd better save the interview for after the show, okay?" Jake said. "We're coming up to the Miss Wet T-Shirt contest in about ten minutes, and I see that my boss is waiting for me."

He looked toward the door and smiled at Lee Crisp, who had just come in.

"I'd like to speak with you...and Elwood, too, I guess," she said, her tone sounding secretive.

Jake nodded. "Sure."

"I'll stop by later," the black woman said.

When she was gone, Jake called to Elwood and indicated that Lee wanted to speak with them. When he arrived, Lee said, "I think you boys may be in trouble, so I have a warning or two."

"Go ahead," Jake replied.

"A guy named Maury called."

"From the booking agency?"

She nodded. "He said the police questioned him about you and Elwood."

"How did he know where we were?" Jake asked, looking quizzically at his brother.

"Are you kidding?" Elwood said before he could stop himself. "With all those flyers?"

"What flyers?" Lee asked.

"Oh," Jake ad-libbed. "It's like this. When we found out we were taking over for Waldo, we quick printed up some notices for people in our old neighborhood. Nothing official, you know. Just some backyard printing press stuff."

"I don't get it," Lee murmured. "But it's not important. The fact is—"

"Wait a minute," Jake interrupted. "Did Maury tell the cops where we were?"

"That's what I was getting at. He didn't find out where you were from some flyers. He found out from the police. *They* told *him* where the Blues Brothers Band could be found."

"Goddamn," Jake hissed. "Now how the hell did they find it out? They hardly ever slow down to fifteen miles an hour in our old neighborhood. And even if they did, why would they bother to notice some flyer? It just ain't fair!"

"Anyway," Lee said, "this guy Maury called to warn you that a whole bunch of cops are on their way up here tonight."

"Thanks."

"That's not all. Your band is non-union, isn't it?"

"Some of us are, some of us aren't," Elwood stalled, not recalling which, if any, of the boys were up to date on their dues.

"Maury also received a call from someone from the local union. He said they were heavy types. Apparently somebody named Louie the treasurer found out you were playing here with expired cards. They said they'd be back tonight to stop the show."

"Goddamn."

"Looks like our mission for God is going to hell," Elwood muttered, kicking at the floor with the toe of his shoe.

"And that's not all," Lee continued after a respectful moment of silence.

"There's more?" Jake asked, aghast.

"I have a friend—well, just an occasional date—who's in the Illinois Nazi Party," she went on. "Generally he goes along with what they do, but apparently he drew the line when he heard they were coming up here tonight to drag you two out and lynch you. So he gave me a warning to get you out if I could."

"Well, we have to make an appearance, sing at least a couple songs, or we'll disappoint the people from our neighborhood who gave—"

"Who gave us their fine support," Elwood interrupted, jamming his foot down on Jake's toe.

"Personally," Lee said, "I'd just as soon see you bug out. As much as I'd enjoy seeing you give the folks a good show, I'd hate the idea of any violence."

"It's nothing," Jake reassured her nonchalantly, spreading his palms. "Just the union and the cops and the Nazis and maybe Waldo and the Wall-Walkers for good measure. That's it? Shit, you ain't said nothing about the Canine Corps or the Marines or the Daughters of the American Revolution. The way I figure it, it's a cakewalk. Short numbers."

"You don't think there'll be a fight?"

"Nah. First and most important thing is, they'll all probably wait until the show's over and most of the crowd's gone. Then they'll try and nab us. But suppose we get out before then?"

Lee smiled. "It could work, at that," she said. "And just to make sure, don't just take off out some door. They may have cops or Nazis or whatever watching. Come to my office and I'll find some way to smuggle you out, okay?"

"You're a peach," Jake said, kissing her cheek.

"A piece of wholesome white bread," Elwood said, kissing the other.

"Now let's go knock 'em dead," Jake shouted.

The band could feel the end. They had fought the law and won; they had brought Soul back to the midwest but it felt strange to see a dream die.

Matt "Guitar" Murphy flexed one monstrous bicep and smiled sadly. "Jesus we ain't goin' out like *Love Story*. We got nothing to be sorry about. Man, we're the goddamn Magnificent Ten and we're gonna blow these motherfuckers down to Decatur."

The Blues Brothers cheered as one. Jake shook his head, holding up his hands for quiet.

"This may be the last Blues Brothers show for a while,

but while there's a breath of bullshit left in my body or any white bread left in Elwood, we'll be back."

Some members swore they saw a tear glint behind those black shades.

Jake screamed over the crowd noise. "Now let's go out *smokin'*!"

Slapping his hands together like a high school football coach, he led them onto the bandstand. The master of ceremonies, Joe Santis, was just winding up the contest.

"... And finally, contestant number ten in the Jovial Club's annual Wet T-Shirt contest, from Kenosha, Miss Sandy Ann Greene..." he announced.

The audience applauded. Jake and the boys waited at the edge of the bandstand while Lee Crisp pranced onto the stage a moment later with an envelope. Taking it, Joe opened it, withdrew the card, paused dramatically, then said, "The winner... Miss Suzanne Clark from Sturgeon Bay, Wisconsin..."

He gestured toward his left, where one of the girls, blushing wildly, raced onto the stage and accepted the award.

When the audience settled down, Joe took the microphone once again, held up his hands for silence, and said, "Good evening, ladies and gentlemen. We hope you enjoyed the annual Wet T-Shirt Award here at the Jovial Club. You know, we have this set-to every year because we like to keep abreast of what's going on up front—"

Jake felt a hand on his arm. He turned and looked into the ratlike eyes of Louie the treasurer, who was flanked by two hefty bruisers.

"Jake Blues," he said. "We're from A.F. of M., Milwaukee Local 252. Your show is cancelled."

"Anyway, ladies and gentlemen, now that you've seen our little bit of local titty-lation, the management is proud to present, direct from Chicago, the Blues Band of Joliet Jake and Elwood Blues, the Blues Brothers..."

He gestured to the empty bandstand behind him. Elwood, meanwhile, moved quickly to the dressing room and withdrew a couple of large aerosol cans from his battered suitcase, then trotted back out just in time to see the pair of hoods grab Jake by his lapels. The master of ceremonies, having correctly assumed that something was amiss, had returned to his T-shirt patter, but was obviously scraping the bottom of the barrel.

"Take your mitts off me," Jake ordered.

"This is a union house," Louie the treasurer said. "It must be cleared of non-union personnel within ten minutes."

"I mean, these girls you just saw are intelligent," the master of ceremonies continued, looking hopefully backwards over his shoulder. "They're not just a bunch of boobs, you know."

Elwood handed an aerosol can to Matt, held up one himself. The label on each read: "NITROUS OXIDE/COMPRESSED ETHER." Attached to the spray top was a mouth mask. Quietly the rest of the band moved to a position close behind the union men, distributing themselves so that one man was in place to grab each arm while a third administered the knockout gas.

"I paid my dues," Jake stalled. "I mailed them yesterday, for Christ's sake!" Jake stalled.

"Bullshit!" Louie the treasurer hissed.

"Yessir," continued the master of ceremonies. "Liquor and breast-worship are the same in that I've always said a little nip'll do you a lot of good."

The audience groaned.

"Jump 'em!" Jake shouted.

Matt and Elwood sprang into action, placing the masks over the two bruisers' faces while the other members wrestled them to the ground. Jake, at the same time, landed a solid punch to Louie the treasurer's midriff. Amid considerable thrashing and cursing, the tranquilizers finally took hold, the band dragging the subdued union men out of the area toward the dressing rooms.

"As you probably heard," the MC continued bravely, "we've just had a little altercation offstage. You see, one of the customers was so enamored with our young ladies that he just tried to cop a feel. But all he succeeded in doing was feeling a cop."

Jake and the others raced back and indicated that they were ready to go on. With a sigh of relief, the master of ceremonies repeated the introduction. The audience applauded warmly.

While the introduction was taking place, Elwood had a sudden flash of inspiration. "Jake," he said, "can you carry the first set by yourself?"

"Yeah, guess so. Why?"

"I just had an idea. I'd like to grab those girls before they get away and have them doctor some of the cars in the lot."

"What do you mean?"

"I mean I got some cans of stuff that'll make it a cinch for us to get away without being followed. And this is an ideal time to do it. If we wait till intermission, people will be on the lot. But if we do it now, I can send them out and nobody'll see."

"Okay, man. Do it."

"—The Blues Brothers Band!" the M.C. repeated.

The boys ran onstage. Elwood turned and trotted back toward the dressing room.

"Gimme a little 'Shotgun Blues,'" Jake said to the band just before the applause died away. Then, when the music started, he grabbed the mike and began his voice-over. "Thank you, thank you, and good evening," he said. "You know, ladies and gentlemen, I make my home in Chicago, U.S.A., but I have traveled throughout the North American continent from Nome to New Orleans, from Gainesville to Eugene, and of course I have crossed the border into Canada, and I want to talk a little bit about that tonight. You see, for a while I took a job in Detroit, where every day I glued trunk rubbers into the 1970 Cadillac Eldorado. And people, it was there on the line that I learned how to do the 'General Motors Moan.' You see, the plant executive used to come into the shop and walk down the whole line, and as they would pass each station, everybody used to commence with the 'G.M. Moan' . . . 'Oooooaaaah' . . . I know you know what I'm talking about . . ."

"Are we covered?" Walter asked Dietrich Albrecht, who sat with his hands folded at a rear table.

"Absolutely. We have a man or two at each and every door. There's no way they can get away."

". . . Anyway," Jake continued, "I'd go up to Canada to taste some of that seven-percent Canadian beer and it was in the city of Windsor that I met the most beautiful woman I have ever had. Her name was Kay and she hugged me, loved me, squeezed me and pleased me. But, you know, she had an old man and he was the biggest, meanest Canadian Mountie alive. Him and me, we had some trouble, and consequently I can never go back to Canada again . . ."

"Are we covered?" Wade Fiscus asked Burton Mercer, who sat with his hands folded at a rear table not far removed from Dietrich Albrecht.

"Absolutely. We have a man or two at each and every door. There's no way they can get away."

"That reminds me," Fiscus said. "Only the fat one's onstage. Where's the scofflaw?"

"Take it easy," Mercer whispered. "If he doesn't come back in ten minutes, we'll go looking for him."

". . . But I could still cherish that woman, Kay," Jake went on. "And I would sincerely love to get a message up to her. So if any of you people get up to that Windsor town and you happen to meet a very special lady named Kay, and there's only one, I wish you'd pass this message on to her from me . . . Yes, people . . ."

The band broke from its quiet accompaniment into the full melody as Jake sang the song, "If You See Kay."

Back in the dressing room, surrounded by ten luscious young ladies, Elwood heard Jake launch into the song and knew he'd better hurry since he had a lot of explaining to do.

"Ladies," he said. "I have a mission for you. I have no one else to turn to. If you choose to accept, you must face the responsibilities of your actions alone."

"Sounds terrible," one of the more outspoken young ladies said. "Whatever it is, what will we get out of it?"

"The thrill of seeing the law embarrassed, of seeing the Illinois Nazi Party in shambles. You see, we're in very serious trouble."

The girls conferred, thought about it. Then, one of them, who had obviously been selected spokeswoman for the group, said, "We'll probably go along with what you want, unless it requires us to ball creepy characters who sweat a lot and look like shit."

"Nothing like that," Elwood said. "All we want you to do is perform a little sabotage."

"Oh!" one of them yelped. "Like 'Mission Impossible.'"

The rest voiced general assent.

"If any of you want out," Elwood cautioned, "say so now. Only the man upstairs knows how this will turn out."

"We'll help you," they said, almost in unison.

Grabbing his briefcase and opening it, Elwood pulled out a large aerosol can.

"This is a can of air-grade metal epoxy," he explained. "It's a strong glue used in aircraft construction. It dries slow. Now I'd like you to go to the parking lot and spray this in the doors of every vehicle except our Bluesmobile and the van that has Ray-Dex Alarms written on the side. Any questions about which is the Bluesmobile?"

"Oh no," the spokeswoman said. "That's the weirdest-looking shitbox Plymouth I've ever seen."

"Okay," Elwood continued. "Now, if you can get the car doors open, you can also spray some of this on the brakes and gas pedals."

The girls nodded, took a can apiece of the epoxy.

"Now I also have some cans of compressed isopropyl butane," Elwood said, withdrawing several canisters with different-colored labels.

"What's that do?"

"Manufacturers add it to shaving cream to make it come out hot. Go to the back tires of some of the police cars or any with swastikas on the windshield, insert the canister in the air valve and wait until you feel resistance."

"It won't blow up, will it?"

"No," Elwood assured the girl. "But as soon as the tires start rolling, they'll heat up and that gas will expand and blow the tires."

"That's dangerous," the leader said.

"It's still not too late to back out," Elwood said sternly.

"No," the girl replied. "Just thought I'd mention it. Any other weapons, sir?"

"These are cans of overcompressed propane. Any heat at all will blow them. Place them in or near exhaust pipes and radiators. Who thinks they can get some car hoods open?"

Five or six raised their hands.

"Good." Elwood tossed the propane canisters to those who indicated their ability along this line.

"Wow, you know, this really *is* sabotage," the young lady who won the contest said, holding the can of propane between her high and erect pectoral appendages.

"That's right," Elwood said. "And if you don't stop that, your lungs'll be all over three states."

Wade Fiscus felt better as soon as he saw Elwood Blues, who joined the band after the first series of songs. Now it was near the end of the evening and he was edgy, having sat too long worrying about what might go wrong.

"Can't we make the pinch now?" he asked Mercer.

"It won't be long," Mercer replied. "You heard what they just said. After this two-minute break, they'll do one more piece and that's it. We'll wait for the crowd to thin out and then move. We don't want a riot on our hands, you know."

"Yes, I know, but—"

"Stop worrying, Fiscus. We've got a perimeter of men drawn around this building that's airtight. Your scofflaw is going to jail and my parole-violator is headed back to dear old Stateville."

"I hope you're right."

"There's a trapdoor near the rear of the stage," Lee Crisp said, taking Jake's hand. "It leads to the wine cellar and a small door at the back of the place that looks like ordinary planking. If you're careful, you'll be able to make it to your car without being seen."

She grabbed Jake's arm, shaking her head in exaggerated anger. "You sonofabitch. You and your goddamn mission from God." There were warm tears in her eyes and there was dampness in her cleavage.

"Jake, you may be the biggest hustler in Illinois or you may be the fuckin' Savior. But take this before I change my mind."

Lee thrust a brown paper bag into Jake's chubby hand. "What is it?" Jake asked.

Lee was already running back to the stage. Through her sobbing she screamed, "Lunch money, you asshole."

In the half-light, Jake peered into it. There was at least five thousand dollars in small bills stuffed into the bag.

"Well, fuck me blind," Jake muttered.

"Jake!" Elwood screamed, breaking his brother's reverie. "Let's get the hell outa here!"

The two men scurried down the darkened subterranean tunnel. Suddenly what little light there had been disappeared. Standing in the shadow was the enormous record mogul, Michael Glabner.

"What is this, the scenic route?" Elwood spat.

Glabner reached for Jake, who assumed his standard sumo wrestler's defense pose.

"You guys are monsters. You're fantastic. I wanna sign you to Clarion Records," Glabner spieled.

"You mean keep the band together?" Jake asked. "You're bullshittin'."

"I don't bullshit," Glabner answered. "Here's ten thousand dollars. It's your advance."

Jake shook his head. "Give fourteen hundred to Ray at Ray's Music exchange in Calumet City and spread some among the band . . . also make sure Lee Crisp gets what's owed her. Listen, pal, we'll call you at the office. We're in sort of a hurry."

As they crept through the musty basement, largely feeling their way toward the sliver of light ahead, they heard the solid, familiar sounds of the Blues Brothers Band reverberating toward them. It was a comforting serenade to their flight. A minute later, pushing open the rickety door, they looked out onto the rear of the parking lot. Not a cop was in sight—until they looked in the direction of the main building, where they could see small knots of men clustered about each exit.

"We'll take it very slow and easy," Elwood whispered.

Walking with extreme caution, it took them nearly five minutes to circle around to the Bluesmobile. When they reached it, not a soul was visible.

Click.

It was very metallic and heavy, like someone opening the bolt of a door. Or someone cocking a rifle or machine gun.

Elwood and Jake froze. Then they saw her, the striking black woman with the Star of David insignia on her arms, nearly invisible in the darkness of the parking lot. She was less than ten feet away, and in her hand, pointed directly at them, was an AR15, a deadly rapid-fire weapon capable of dispatching both Blues Brothers in less than a second.

"Who is she?" Elwood asked.

"I guess she really does want an interview," Jake muttered.

"Well, Jake, you won't get away this time," the black woman said.

"Wait a minute," Jake pleaded. "That voice. It's different. You're not what's-her-name from the *Jewish Times*. You're—"

"Yes. You contemptible pig."

"Why? Why do you say that? I'm a little overweight, but—"

She silenced him with a wave of the weapon. "You know perfectly well why I say it," she snapped, her voice brimming with hatred. "I remained celibate for you. I stood at the back of the cathedral, waiting, in celibacy, for you, with three hundred friends and relatives in attendance. In my home, my mother and my grandmother labored for six days beading my wedding veil with imitation pearls. My uncle hired the best caterer—Rumanians yet—in the state. To obtain the seven limousines for the wedding party, my father used up his favors with Mad Pete Trullo. So, for me, for my mother, for my grandmother, my uncle, my father, and the common good, I must now kill you and your brother."

"Jake, I have the feeling there's something you didn't tell me about," Elwood said.

Jake nodded wistfully. "You remember back two years ago when we were talking about the robbery and you said let's do it tomorrow and I said no, it's got to be today because there's something I have to do tomorrow but I forget what it is?"

Elwood nodded.

"Well, the thing I forgot to do was marry her."

"Really?" Elwood said. "I don't remember any black girls in your life. Not that it makes two shits—"

The mystery lady opened fire, ripping up the damp planking all around Jake and Elwood. They both dove (Jake with surprising agility) to the ground.

"I hope she's on our side," Elwood whispered.

The lady straddled the tunnel, silhouetted ominously, the AR15 automatic rifle slung all too casually in her hands.

"Let me handle this," Jake hissed. And then, in a completely sweet, cooing tone, "What a wonderful, wonderful surprise to see you, sweetheart . . . and right here in Calumet."

The mystery woman, shadows exaggerating her evil grimace, spat, "Shut up, you pig."

Jake, better than Clint in *A Fistful of Dollars* or the Duke in *The Alamo*, marched up to the lady until the automatic's muzzle made a dent in his greasy white shirt. The two enemies/lovers eyed each other. Jake searched desperately for a chink in her hatred. This was the showdown. *Mano a mano*. The big man considered her stony face for a moment, then fell to his knees, screaming.

"Oh, please. Please. Pretty please, don't kill us. I didn't mean to leave you! It . . . it wasn't my fault! Oh, please don't kill us . . ."

Her grimace hardened (if that were at all possible) into a sneer.

"You slimy, groveling scumbag. You can't talk your way out of this. You left me. Now kiss your fat ass goodbye."

Elwood lay on the ground and shuddered; he realized his brother held their lives in his pudgy hands. Had Jake finally met his match? Elwood shut his eyes and prayed to Sister Mary Stigmata.

But Jake hadn't slid this far on looks alone. Up against it, he pulled out every whimpering stop.

"Me?" he whined. "I didn't, honest. I ran out of gas. I had a flat tire. I lost my tux at the cleaners. Someone stole my car. There was an earthquake, a flood . . . Remember that horrible pestilence? It really wasn't my fault. I swear."

Elwood sneaked a peek at the armed Ice Princess. "We're dead men," he thought. Suddenly Jake was struck by that lightning bolt of ingenuity, that ruthless instinct that had never before deserted him, not in Joliet or St. Helen's: Jake took off his shades!

Confronted with the biggest, brownest, most soulful eyes since Bambi lost his mother in the forest fire, the mystery lady softened. Just a slight resignation.

Jake was on her like a bad cold, sweeping her into a tongue-smothered, Clark Gable movie-star kiss.

"Oh, Jake . . . my Jake," the defenseless woman moaned.

Jake, in a flash, flipped on his Ray-Bans again, dropped the mystery woman on her ass and he and Elwood tore for the parking lot.

The brothers flew into the Bluesmobile and Elwood fired it up. The machine rumbled reassuringly. Elwood, his exhaustion turning to steel, gripped the wheel.

"It's two hundred and forty miles to Chicago. We got a full tank of gas, half a pack of cigarettes, it's dark and we're wearing sunglasses."

Jake clenched his jaws and, without a second's hesitation, spit out his answer.

"Hit it."

Once again, it was the Brothers against the world. One last high-speed screaming run at the twentieth century. With only a shitbox Plymouth, a few great cassettes and God on their side.

The mystery woman opened fire on the car in full-throated fury. Elwood burned rubber (nudging a few parked cop cars) and headed for the slab and sweet home Chicago.

Inside the club, a quick burst from her AR15 provided a

deadly back-beat to the funky "B-Movie Boxcar Blues" that the band layed down. And Burton Mercer's highly tuned cop's ears and agile civil servant's mind told him the awful truth.

"The fuckers got away," he shrieked in an unlikely falsetto. Cops and Nazis swarmed for the exits in a jumble of uniforms. Out in the parking lot, tires and exhaust pipes exploded in a hurricane of rubber and shrapnel. Sparks flew as axles met asphalt; driverless cop cars bounced around like Dodgem cars. Lee Crisp watched from the club's picture window. The entire parking lot was a sea of burning wreckage.

"What a guy," she murmured, smiling widely.

An ultramodern office bathed in poisonous fluorescent light clicks into sterile action. This is the Illinois Bureau of Investigation, Office of Intelligence, Tactical Division. Down a long row of radio control boards and futuristic tracking devices, operators and officers speak simultaneously. The officer tracking the computer readout issues a mechanical directive: "Request assistance in pursuit of black 1974 Plymouth Fury heading south on interstate 101. Dispatch cars number 12, 21, 17 . . ."

A Nazi blackshirt listened attentively to the broadcast on his CB.

The officer continued, ". . . 19, 54, 27, 33, 14, 29, 32, 20 and 23. Immediate assistance required. Occupants of the vehicle, one Joliet Jake Blues, one Elwood Blues, considered extremely dangerous. Use of unnecessary violence in the apprehension of the Blues Brothers has been approved."

The blackshirt leapt up, spilling the CB into a garbled heap. *"Gruppenführer!"* he screamed.

Elwood was locked into the machine, all 440 cubes synchronized with his legendary robot reflexes. The Bluesmobile might be a dinosaur, replaced by sleeker, newer equipment—just like the two losers at its wheel—but right now it was kicking ass. It flew over embankments, Jake grabbing the dash for support, blew past traffic at 120 mph, its machine-gun, Detroit engine rapid-firing. Every cop in the state was after them. There was pride on the line—these two assholes were making *them* look like assholes.

Suddenly there was a wall of wailing, flashing cop cars behind them. Jake looked over at his brother.

"Well . . . ?"

Elwood unhesitatingly threw the car into a ninety-degree turn, right across all four lanes of the expressway. The cops tried to duplicate this move and ended up in the largest collision in Illinois history.

"What a fuckin' piece of business you are," Jake said admiringly, patting Elwood on the shoulder.

The silent one smiled and negotiated the intense traffic that was heading right for them—they were doing a hundred, the wrong way down a one-way street.

THE BLUES BROTHERS

The Nazi Pinto lurked in the alley, waiting. Squawking over the CB were the hysterics of the various police forces.

"Stupid, pathetic incompetents," Albrecht chortled. "They'll be coming past us in seconds. Is everything in readiness?" The sound of rifles and guns being loaded filled the tiny car.

Suddenly, the Bluesmobile, like a black-and-white dust storm, rocketed by.

"For the *Führer!*" the blackshirt screamed. The souped-up Pinto burned rubber after them.

The bouncing of the Bluesmobile at this speed made it difficult for Jake to light his cigarette. Irritated, he looked in the rearview mirror.

"Jesus, mother of mouse ears," he choked.

The Pinto, bristling with Nazis, all firing at them, was a few car-lengths behind.

"Where the fuck did they come from?" Jake wondered.

Elwood smiled, the closest expression to evil his face knew.

"Watch me now," he sang.

The Bluesmobile crashed through the sign reading DANGER CONSTRUCTION; the Pinto followed all too closely.

The blackshirt had finally snapped. He shrieked, "They cannot hope to escape us. We'll prove just who is destined to lead the Aryan people to victory."

The Bluesmobile streaked up a steel ramp with the Nazis close behind. Elwood jammed on the brakes and spun the steering wheel in one motion. The Plymouth literally backflipped up and over the Nazi station wagon, and roared off in the opposite direction.

The Nazis soared up and off the unfinished ramp. The only sound was the rushing air as the Pinto dropped a thousand feet onto downtown Chicago. *Deutschland Über Alles.*

The Bluesmobile thundered toward the Cook County Building, Jake and Elwood like statues inside. Suddenly oil began spurting from under the hood, blacking out the windshield. Elwood stuck his head out the window and screamed, "Goddamn con rods! We've thrown a rod, maybe two . . . I don't know if we'll make it."

Jake checked the rearview; every form of city, state and federal heat was gaining on them.

"Bull shit!" he screamed. "We'll make it." He leaned out the other window as the car chattered painfully, and wiped the windshield with his coat. This was war.

They pulled up to the imposing neo-classical mausoleum known as the Cook County Building and jumped from the bleeding car. It shuddered, steam hissing sadly from one of its many wounds, and died. Elwood took his hat off and put it over his heart. Jake grabbed him and they flew up the steps and into the building.

Once inside the lobby, the brothers hurled Coke machines, wooden benches, candy machines—anything around—to block the door. Already they heard cars pulling up outside. Elwood ran over to the building's directory.

"Cook County Assessor's Office—1201," he read. Just as machine-gun bullets fired through their makeshift barricade the brothers made it into the elevator. They whistled along with the Muzak "Norwegian Wood," watching the floors drift slowly by.

Outside, choppers landed Marines on the building's roof. Troop trucks pulled up and heavily armed commando units in full battle dress leaped out. SWAT teams grappled up the sides of the marble building on rappelling lines.

The doors to the twelfth floor opened and Jake and Elwood burst out. A sign on the door of 1201 read BACK IN 5 MINUTES—OUT TO LUNCH. Jake straightened his oil-stained tie and tucked in his shirt.

In the plaza below, tanks rumbled into position. A tornado of orders shouted through bullhorns filled the air.

The door to 1201 opened slowly and a meek, bespectacled clerk, still munching a sandwich, moved behind the counter.

He recoiled as the two sinister-looking, oily men in suits and shades blew into his office. Jake reached across the counter and pulled the squirming clerk toward him.

"This is where you pay taxes, right?" Jake said through clenched jaws.

The terrified clerk nodded, maybe even tried to speak, but only bits of baloney and bread dribbled out.

Jake grinned. "Okay, pal, this money is for St. Helen of the Blessed Shroud. That's an orphanage in Calumet City, Illinois."

He pulled out the greasy five grand. Together, the brothers slapped it on the counter. At that instant, cuffs were slapped on them. The entire room had filled with uniformed cops and soldiers—their rifles with fixed bayonets.

Jake looked over at his brother. Elwood. A better-than-average harp player and surely the greatest driver who ever lived. And suddenly the big man began to laugh. No one, not Sister Mary Stigmata or Elwood or the band—not even Artesia Papageorge—had ever heard Jake Blues laugh. But Jake knew, really *knew*, they had done it. Together, the Blues Brothers had beat the fuckin' heat. They *were* winners and anybody who thought different could just look at big Jake Papageorge Blues.

The cops moved closer, hundreds of 'em crammed into the tiny, anonymous assessor's office. Jake raised his free hand and for some reason they hesitated. "Ladies and gentlemen," he boomed, "please welcome the band of Joliet Jake and Elwood Blues . . . the Blues Brothers!" And somewhere Otis's "Can't Turn You Loose" was ripping up the joint.

DOLLY PARTON
A PHOTO-BIO
OTIS JAMES

DOLLY PARTON: A PHOTO-BIO is a fascinating, photo-filled chronicle of the woman who has single-handedly turned Americans on to the delights of country music. This full-length biography, an intimate and revealing portrait of Dolly, includes a musical commentary and discography.

☐ 05157-8 DOLLY PARTON $1.95

Available at your local bookstore or return this form to:
JOVE BOOK MAILING SERVICE 1050 Wall Street West
Lyndhurst, N.J. 07071

Please send me the title indicated above. I am enclosing $_____ (price indicated plus 50¢ for postage and handling—if more than four books are ordered only $1.50 is necessary). Send check or money order—no cash or C.O.D.'s please.

NAME_____

ADDRESS_____

CITY_____STATE/ZIP_____

Allow three weeks for delivery.

the BEE GEES

A DAZZLING PHOTO-BIO

Kim Stevens

The story behind the Bee Gees is as exciting as the three brothers themselves. In this spectacular photo-bio, you'll learn the inside story—from their early beginnings playing matinees in Manchester, England, to their wildfire spread of disco fever from coast to coast.

☐ 05158-6   THE BEE GEES $1.95

Available at your local bookstore or return this form to:
JOVE BOOK MAILING SERVICE 1050 Wall Street West
Lyndhurst, N.J. 07071

Please send me the title indicated above. I am enclosing
$_____ (price indicated plus 50¢ for postage and handling—if more than four books are ordered only $1.50 is necessary). Send check or money order—no cash or C.O.D.'s please.

NAME_____

ADDRESS_____

CITY_____STATE/ZIP_____

Allow three weeks for delivery.

You loved 'em on "Saturday Night Live."
You bought their records by the score.
They're making their movie debut in Universal's
spectacular summer hit, The Blues Brothers.
Now, find out who THE BLUES BROTHERS
really are in...

BLUES BROTHERS—PRIVATE

by Judith Jacklin and Tino Insana

Now, *you* can get the lowdown on The Blues Brothers. These are the records (report cards, loan applications, prison records, etc.) from the personnel file of dear Sister Mary Stigmata, the loving nun who raised them. These files (hidden from prying eyes in a cracker box and only recently unearthed by sweet Sister Mary) tell the whole story of the brothers'—and the band's—rise to notoriety. Get the inside "dish"—in BLUES BROTHERS—PRIVATE.

Available at your local bookstore or return this form to:
**PERIGEE BOOKS Attn: Sales Dept. (BB)
200 Madison Avenue New York, N.Y. 10016**

Please send me _____ copies of BLUES BROTHERS—PRIVATE @ $7.95 per copy. I am enclosing $_____ (price plus $1.50 for postage and handling. Please add 50¢ per book for each additional copy ordered.) Send check or money order—no cash or C.O.D's please.

Name _____
Address _____
City _____ State _____ Zip _____

Allow three weeks for delivery.